THE PRESIDENT'S MOTHER

★ ★ ★

THE PRESIDENT'S MOTHER

★ ★ ★

GLORIA WHELAN

Servant Publications
Ann Arbor, Michigan

Vine Books is an imprint of Servant Publications especially designed to serve evangelical Christians.

This is a work of fiction. Apart from obvious references to public figures, places, and historical events, all characters and incidents in this novel are the product of the author's imagination. Any similarities to people living or dead are purely coincidental.

Published by Servant Publications
P.O. Box 8617
Ann Arbor, Michigan 48107

Cover design: Diane Bareis
Cover photograph: Bettmann

96 97 98 99 00 10 9 8 7 6 5 4 3 2 1

Printed in the United States of America
ISBN 0-89283-942-2

LIBRARY OF CONGRESS CATALOGING-IN-PUBLICATION DATA

Whelan, Gloria.
    The president's mother / Gloria Whelan.
        p.   cm.
    ISBN 0-89283-942-2
    1. Presidents—United States—Family relationships—Fiction.   2. Mothers and sons—United States—Fiction.   I. Title.
PS3573.H442P74   1996
813'.54—dc20   96-11047
                                                                              CIP

For Marjorie and Mike

PROLOGUE
NOVEMBER 23, 1965

In her black dress and veil, Maida Lange was little more than a shadow in the darkening room. The cover of darkness felt soothing, and even the slight effort of lighting a lamp was beyond her.

Her husband, Peter, sat across from her. At thirty he was only a few years older than Maida, but in his gray suit, neatly trimmed mustache, and wire-framed glasses, he appeared middle-aged. His stiff posture was self-imposed. For as long as she had known him, discipline had been his god. Once, Peter had told her that life was an edifice of cards. If you exercised the greatest of care, you might build a lofty tower with your cards, but the least unguarded movement would bring it tumbling down. Now the tower lay in ruins.

After years of disbelieving in happiness, Maida had allowed herself to lower her defenses. She had nearly forgotten the past, and her life had seemed hopeful. Then suddenly their son, Robert, had died two months after his first birthday, confirming for her all the sad experiences of her life. At the funeral service the minister had said one must not despair. "Despair," he said, "shows a lack of trust in God." Still she despaired. All her prayers were angry ones.

Their older son, a child of two and a half, ran into the silent room holding out a picture he had drawn. Maida saw him hesitate, frightened by their stiff misery.

"Come here, Robert," his father said.

Maida's voice trembled. "Don't call him that, Peter." In her confusion and anger she lapsed back into her native German. *"Das ist nicht sein Name!"*

"Speak English, Maida. We have been in America for nearly two years. And please take off that veil. It frightens the poor child. Such veils are not worn to funerals in this country."

Turning to the boy, Peter said, "I am going to give you a gift of a new name, Johann. You are going to have your brother's name. You are Robert now. That is a nice American name. Then when you go to school, the children will not tease you as they would if you were called by your old name. We will never use the name 'Johann' again. From now on you will be Robert."

Puzzled, the small boy looked uncertainly at his father.

"Come here, Robert," Peter ordered.

The boy, obedient by nature, approached his father but kept a wary distance between them.

Maida noticed that Peter was looking at the boy in the same affectionate way he had often looked at his younger brother. The child must have sensed it too, for he gratefully crept a little closer and was rewarded when his father lifted him up onto his lap.

"You must be our hope now, Robert," said Peter. "It is given to some of us to do great things. It is only a matter of setting goals. It is not possible for me, but one day you shall have the prize." Peter patted the boy on the head and lifted him back onto the floor. "Now, go to your room. Later tonight Papa will play the geography game with you. If you can name ten states there will be a nice reward."

"Papa," the child said. "Can I have Robert's teddy bear?"

Maida gasped, and Peter grew quiet. After a moment he said, "Yes, Robert. You shall have the teddy bear. You have been thinking of that all day, have you not?"

The child nodded his head waiting for an answer.

"That is a goal, Robert, a small one. You wanted some-thing, and when the time came you asked for it." Peter seemed almost pleased. The boy threw his arms around his father, then scrambled down and ran out of the room.

"Peter, what can you be thinking?" Maida choked. "It is

horrible that he should have been waiting like a vulture for his dead brother's toy."

"Always, Maida, you are too dramatic. You exaggerate. He is only a little boy who wished to have a teddy bear. Control yourself. If you are not careful, you will bring on one of your asthma attacks."

"You will ruin the boy with your great plans," she said in a bitter, accusing voice. She felt her chest tighten as she tried to breathe, and she quickly reached for her inhaler. "It is not normal to bring up a child in such a way. I am almost glad the baby is gone. Had he lived, you would have destroyed him."

She knew her words stung. She knew he accused himself, a physician, of failing to recognize the seriousness of the baby's sudden illness. The child had been fussy with a fever for a few days, then the vomiting had started. But there had been flu going around, and Peter had a doctor's suspicion of other doctors and hospitals. He thought he knew best how to treat his own child.

When they noticed the stiffness in the child's neck, they rushed him to George Washington University Hospital, where Peter had his practice in the nation's capital. There was no one with whom they could leave their older son, so they took him along. Maida sat in the front of the car holding the sick baby. The two-year-old sat in the backseat, sucking noisily on his thumb. Peter had spoken sharply to the boy, reducing him to tears for the rest of the trip.

At the hospital the baby's chest was x-rayed. Peter ordered a battery of tests and told Maida to leave the room. She refused and remained to watch as they did a spinal tap, trembling for the vulnerability of her son's small, soft body as the long needle probed delicately for the spinal fluid. The doctor's first attempt was unsuccessful, and Peter cursed under his breath. The needle was withdrawn and reinserted. When the results came back, to their horror, a diagnosis of viral encephalitis was made. A day later the child died. And then Peter did the thing Maida could not forgive.

The nurse had come with a form. She was young and evidently had little experience with grieving parents. In her attempt to be professional, all the nurse could manage was a kind of timid deference. She apologized for having to ask questions "at a time like this."

"The baby's name is Robert?" she asked.

"No, no," Peter said. "Johann."

The nurse looked at him puzzled. "When he was admitted the mother gave the name Robert." She looked at Maida.

Before Maida could confirm the nurse's words, Peter said, "My wife was upset and confused. Robert is the name of our other son."

Maida, torn between her own despair and her attempt to control herself for the sake of the older boy, watched the nurse scratch out Robert's name and substitute Johann's. The tears dried on her face while she stared with hatred at her husband.

During the two days that followed, Maida said nothing of what she felt as she went through the motions of a wake and funeral. A few acquaintances at the hospital where Peter practiced stopped by to give their condolences, but none of them had known the Langes well enough to remember the children's names. They referred to the dead child simply as "the baby." Dutifully, Maida accepted the casseroles and cakes they brought and fed them to Peter and the boy. But she herself ate nothing, apart from a little tea and some applesauce that felt pleasantly cool as she swallowed it. She had become giddy from her self-imposed fast but she had something to say to Peter. Now, after the funeral and with the child out of the room, she turned to her husband.

"Peter, you are..." She searched vainly for the right English word to describe his madness, then reverted to her familiar mother tongue. Her mind whirled as her outrage found a voice. "... *verrückt von deiner Besessenheit.*" Crazy with your obsession!

For one dreadful unguarded moment, his eyes blazed with anger. It was so unlike Peter that Maida drew back, afraid that he might reach out and strike her. But he regained his composure as quickly as he had lost it.

She tried to control her shaky voice. "You want to use our child to fulfill your own delusions of grandeur. You must let him alone. Think, Peter. Our relatives in Germany will surely remember it was Johann who was born in Germany."

"They will also think that it is Johann who died. I will write them that it was."

"You will be writing a lie."

"Maida, the child must be seen to have been born here," he insisted.

"But he is sixteen months older than Robert."

"Twenty years from now that will mean nothing."

"But when he goes to school...."

"We will start off teaching him at home. I will inform the school that he is sickly. After a year, with what we will teach him, he will be admitted to his correct grade or higher. By then he will seem merely large for his age."

She was horrified at how calculated his reasons were. "How can you think of all of these things when your son has just died? It is a sign of your *Besessenheit*."

Peter removed his glasses and wiped his eyes. "Maida, I am as sad as you are. All of this last year since our son was born I have said to myself, 'We are like the holy family. Humble people who have come to a distant place and had a child who will grow into a great leader.'"

"Our son was not a Christ. He was only a baby, and now he is gone from us. How do you know it is not God punishing you for your blasphemy—?" She stopped, afraid of her anger.

"That is a cruel thing to say, Maida. We are in a new country now, and here everything is possible. Remember, you were as anxious to come to America as I was."

She knew his words were true. Her memories of her childhood in Germany during the war were horrible nightmares. She once had a grandfather like Peter. Her grandfather had been a decent man who had done evil things because he believed he had a mission.

Peter pleaded with her, "In Germany it would have been twenty years before I had an appointment at a university. At least here I have already been asked to give lectures to the medical students. Think of it, Maida. In this country everything is possible. Why should it not be possible for our son as well? Plato, himself, says one may be allowed to lie for the public good."

"You make fun of my religion," she accused, "but you have your Plato as a god."

"It is not unusual to train children to become proficient in something," he insisted. "Look at the training of a gymnast or a concert violinist. It begins at the earliest age. Why should we not train a child to attain to the most powerful position this country offers? You and I know how important it is to live in a country governed by a good man, we who grew up in a country nearly destroyed by its evil leader.

"If in time Robert does not wish it, we will forget all about it. But suppose he does? Are we to deny him a chance simply because he was not born in this country?"

"Peter, you are asking that we all live a lie. How can something good come from deceit?"

"Maida, it is only a little thing. I promise not to push the boy. You, yourself, will see to his education his first year. You were a brilliant student. Who could better prepare him than you, his mother? Here the schools are not so rigorous. Together we will give him a better start than he would get in a classroom."

Maida was shocked to see tears in Peter's eyes. It was the first time in all these terrible hours that he had allowed her a glimpse of what he was feeling. With a rush of contrition she remembered that Peter, too, had lost a son.

Peter hid his face in his hands. Tenderly she reached out and touched his arm. In the twenty-three years she had lived, she had seen so much evil, evil she could do nothing about.

She would give in to Peter. Weighed down by her own misery, she did not have the strength to oppose him. In her weakness she pitied him. His gods were reason and power, cold comfort at a time like this, while her God had suffered as she was suffering. Even in her despair He never ceased speaking to her, like an insistent bird calling or a gentle wind rustling the leaves.

Maida told herself, not quite believing it, that Peter's obsession would pass in time, and he would come to see how foolish his notion had been. But as she listened to the November rain chilling into sleet against their windows, she could not shut out a frightening thought. Suppose Peter's wild dream came true? What kind of leader might emerge from such a child—a child who had been bullied and twisted by someone he loved into a shape he never wanted to assume?

I
MARCH 10, 2002

The knife sliced through the air and Sheila Covell screamed, collapsing onto the floor. As the crimson, sticky ooze seeped over her silk blouse, the cameraman zoomed in for a tight shot. She lay as still as she could, forcing herself not to breathe. The take dragged on forever. While she struggled to hold her breath, Sheila wondered if this really were her last scene. The end of her job would be a kind of death for her. With the fade-out she took a deep breath, opened her eyes and smiled up at Lanny, the director, who stretched out his hand to help her up.

"Pitiable, Sheila darling, a real tearjerker. And dignity in spite of that goop leaking all over you! You're such a pro I can't believe this is your last day." Lanny lowered his voice, "Look at what I'm left with—Dan and a mob of teenyboppers who haven't a thing to offer but heads full of big, white, twinkling teeth. Did you notice how Allen stumbled over all his lines today? If the words on his cue cards have more than one syllable, you can see his mouth sounding them out."

Sheila smiled and thought about her time with Lanny. He had always been good to her. She knew it amused him to play the maternal role of den mother to the entire cast. He never seemed to stop fussing over their health—prescribing obscure vitamins and exotic herbs. He took great pleasure in celebrating romantic couplings, and when a bitter divorce did occur, he managed to remain friends with both parties.

The cast of "Day into Night" crowded around and embraced Sheila, crying or pretending to cry. One of the disadvantages of all of one's friends being actors was their pleasure in melodramatics and their honed skill at deception. Sally, who played one of her daughters in the soap, said, "It's going to be desolate without you."

Sheila shuddered as she looked around the set. There was something atavistic in this gathering around her, as though the cast were playing out an ancient ritual associated with her death. The heavy makeup, false eyelashes, wigs, and bright lights lent a counterfeit air to the whole scene. For a moment she was overwhelmed with disgust for her profession, for its spurious duplicity. Over the last eight years she had seen reality meld into role-playing, so that every action and every reaction became suspect. It appeared that life only went on when an audience was present. Sheila knew that, apart from Lanny and Dan, the cast weren't really sorry to see her go. "I am old and therefore expendable. With my character written out of the soap, they hope there will be more lines for the rest of them."

Sheila wanted to slip away to the solitude of her apartment, but she had one more ritual to endure. Whenever a member left the soap, the whole cast would gather at the Russian Tea Room to say their farewells. There amongst the red banquettes that swallowed you like a gaping mouth, over blinis and caviar and champagne, they would retell all the highlights of the program for years back. "Let me change, Lanny, and I'll be right with you." She tried to keep her voice upbeat but a shrillness crept into it. She was frightened. She was fifty-nine, not an age when women's roles were abundant. At least, she told herself, she no longer had to worry about supporting Ava, her younger sister, who depended on Sheila for everything. Ava, who had stayed a child all of her life.

It was only when closed the dressing room door of her behind her that she managed to get control of herself. The room, which for years had been the center of her life, remained unchanged. In the unpardoning mirror, with its frame of ruthless light bulbs, she had watched her face smocking into wrinkles, her jowls fill out, the skin under her chin loosen. Then an unexpected windfall, a guest shot on

"Aspen," had produced enough money to coax the second-best plastic surgeon in New York to give her a second lease on life. After the frightening image of black and blue turned slowly to a hideous yellow, the mirror had generously given her back a younger face.

But today, in her apprehension, every one of her fifty-nine years showed. Even her high cheekbones, the joy of cameramen, seemed to have softened so that her face lost its focus. Dourly, she remembered that Bette Davis and Joan Crawford had spent their last years playing horror roles. She would rather starve than stoop to that. When Ava was alive she had not been able to put money aside, so now there was nothing to fall back on but her pension fund with Equity.

A publicity shot stared down at her from the wall as she creamed away her makeup. She remembered the night when she received her Soap Opera Digest Award for "Best Villainess of the Year." The hairdo on the faded photo looked quaintly outdated, a collector's piece. It wouldn't take long to pack her things. Actually there wouldn't be much to take along: her electric teapot and an ample supply of Formosa oolong tea she replenished each month at Balducci's. She saw no point in keeping the empty magnum of Moët Chandon she and Dan had shared with the cast the first day they had started on the soap. She had been only fifty-one. In those days there had been time to flit from one dead-end relationship to another. There was even a brief period when she and Dan, who acted opposite her in the soap, had tried to comfort each other after unhappy entanglements. But in the last year Dan had married again, and since Ava's death two years before, Sheila had been alone.

In the soap she and Dan were cast as the parents of a Kennedy-like family, following the ups and downs of a passel of political gluttons. Still, no matter how outrageous the plots concocted for them, they never seemed to approach the bizarre events of the real world. Of course, Sheila did not care much about the real world. She couldn't remember the last time she had read the front page of *The New York Times*. Her slight curiosity with the real world was satisfied with a mere five minutes of CNN's "Headline News."

Taking care of her sister and her work consumed her life, leaving Sheila no time to develop friendships. Each day started when the cast limousine picked her up at five forty-five. It traveled down Fifth and across the Park, then along the reservoir where sometimes you could see the geese and ducks paddling. Once, Sheila had spotted a great blue heron sweeping down from nowhere, so mysterious an aberration in the city that it had made Sheila lighthearted all day. On the West Side they stopped to pick up Dan in his retro apartment, then sped down Broadway, where in the early morning the deserted street appeared even more depressing than it did when it was crowded with the dissolute denizens who roamed it at night. They stopped in Chelsea and TriBecA for more cast members, and with everyone too sleepy for more than a dilatory conversation, they crossed the Brooklyn Bridge to the studio. Day after day, the monotony of the routine never wavered, except when a sudden story change kept them on the set until ten or eleven at night. Often it was a never-ending cycle of drudgery. It had never been what she wanted to do, only what she'd had to do.

When her parents had died within months of each other, Sheila escaped to New York, leaving her seventeen-year-old sister, Ava, behind with an aunt who didn't want her. As sweet and loving as she was, Ava had the mind and simple needs of a six-year-old. Nineteen-year-old Sheila had come to New York from Detroit with a thousand dollars, her inheritance. At the time it had seemed to her a huge amount. Now she wondered what her parents would say if they knew she had once spent that much money for a dress.

She had loved dressing up ever since her childhood, when she would go to her mother's closet and then totter around in her mother's clothes and high heels. When she turned twelve, she made a feeble attempt at making her own clothes, stubbornly insisting on wearing them in spite of puckered seams, twisted sleeves, and dipping hemlines. Even now she winced as she remembered her first prom dress. Its low neckline was trimmed with feathers that later had come undone and wafted over the dance floor. Her clothes had always been disguises, artful illusions that, like a magician, hid what actually was there.

Sheila was never happier than when she threw her energies into being someone else. Nothing about her real self held much interest for her, and her emptiness attracted few friends. People said she was strikingly attractive and fun to be with, but when she departed a room, she left nothing behind. Like the cleverest magician, she made herself disappear.

She had been there for the golden age of Broadway: Arthur Miller, Rodgers & Hammerstein, Tennessee Williams, Eugene O'Neill. She had played many walk-ons but never seemed able to land a good part. She had been too large a woman for ingenue roles and too attractive for character parts.

When the opportunity for a television role came along, Sheila quickly deserted the theater for a weekly paycheck. As soon as she was settled in a small apartment on Tenth with a landlady who was willing to help her, she sent for Ava. Sheila depended on guest shots until she landed the part of a madam on a western that ran for years. When the western closed down, "Night into Day" had come along. Now, at fifty-nine, she expected little else. Her agent, Lois Markman, had talked encouragingly of guest shots, but Sheila knew that if she wasn't working regularly she wouldn't be on anyone's mind. And without a regular job there was no way she could continue to live in New York, the most expensive of all America's cities.

There was a brief knock on the door and, without waiting for her response, Dan walked in. Though he was a year older than Sheila, he looked ten years younger, thanks to several episodes of plastic surgery, a personal trainer, and a wealthy wife who treated him like an expensive investment. Older women inundated Dan with requests for his picture. Sheila wasn't so fortunate. Older men passed her by, wanting pictures of the younger women in the cast.

Sheila saw that Dan had taken out his contact lenses, which bothered him. Only his familiarity with the layout of the room kept him from stumbling into something. "Not a good day," he smiled sympathetically, looking in her general direction.

"I don't know why they did it to me," Sheila said, glad that she did not have to feign cheerfulness with Dan. "Nothing in the plot these last months hinted at it. If you ask me, it was completely arbitrary. The story line screams for a mother."

Two weeks earlier, when Lanny had walked into her dressing room with a hangdog look, Sheila had prepared herself for bad news: a cutback in her role, maybe even a short hiatus. She never imagined that her part had been written out. Lanny had been apologetic. "Sheila, sweetheart, it doesn't make any sense." Trying to cheer her up, he added, "I think you should look on it as a career opportunity. Let's face it, your talent is being wasted here. Let me look around. I heard about a pilot they're considering about shenanigans in a retirement home...." He stopped himself when he saw the look on her face.

Dan settled in a chair and helped himself from a tin box of Scotch shortbread on her dresser. "I hate to be the bearer of bad news," he said, "but the rumor is they're writing in an episode where I marry again."

"That means they *wanted* to get rid of me. Why? Look, Dan, tell me the truth. Have I been slipping? I mean, I've been doing this role for so long I don't think about it anymore. I've stopped seeing myself, sometimes I don't even hear myself when I read lines." She thought back to when she had started out, how she used to sit and avidly watch every episode on TV, studying her performance. But after a few years she found she couldn't bear the inanities she had to utter, and she hated to be reminded of how she had sold out.

Dan squinted at the blur in the mirror as Sheila removed her makeup. "You're the only one of us in this mess that understands what a camera is for. Listen, I don't know whether I should even mention this, but I heard that it was someone higher up who wanted you out."

Sheila stared into the mirror at Dan, who was looking uncomfortably back at her. She swung around, anxious for flesh and blood instead of reflection and image. "How much higher up?"

"All the way."

"That's crazy. Why would a man like Everett Kingston have anything to do with a soap? He's had his hands full for years with a cable network. And now with all the demands of the major network he's added to his empire, what possible interest could he have with my job?"

"It doesn't make any sense," Dan agreed. "You'd think he'd be too busy running back and forth to the White House so he knows what kind of spin to put on the news. The truth is the guy is strange. No one can decide whether Kingston bought the network and then courted the president, or, what's more likely, the president secretly encouraged Kingston to buy the network so the White House would have a news program they could count on." He regarded the Armani suit Sheila was wearing with approval and put an arm around her. "You look terrific."

"You're only saying that because you can't see a thing." Sheila knew Dan would miss her, but she also knew he would not make much of an effort to keep in touch. In this business people drifted apart. Seeing her on the way down would only remind him that his own days were numbered.

She didn't know how she would find the courage to walk out of the dressing room and close the door behind her forever. Even if she could manage that, she didn't know how she could endure two hours of the cheerful wake that awaited her as the cast bid their farewells. She grasped Dan's arm firmly and said, "Let's go feed the sharks."

By drinking a little too much champagne, a foolish idea since it always made her ill later, Sheila managed to get through the cast party. The minute she saw an opening to escape she made her apologies and began to edge out of the crowded Russian Tea Room. She turned down a half-hearted dinner invitation from Lanny at the door.

She was reluctant to take the Madison bus home and then have to face the walk down to First with the cold March wind whipping at her heels. Instead, she splurged and hailed a taxi in front of the building. As she rode in silence back to her apartment, Sheila cautioned herself that it would have to be her last extravagance.

When the cab pulled up on 86th near York, she paid the fare and hurried into the building. Her apartment was in a well-kept twenties building, redolent of the arts-and-crafts style of architecture. The garrulous doorman, Archie, bestowed his palmy blessing on all who lived there. His uniformed presence guaranteed Sheila that someone would say something nice to her at least twice a day. Her apartment had a living room with a stepped-up dining area, a pocket-sized kitchen, and two bedrooms, one of which she used to store her large and stylish wardrobe.

She loved clothes and simply couldn't part with any of them. She still had every dress she had bought since coming to New York. A couple of times a year the studio had a sale of clothing worn on "Day into Night." The cast got first choice, and could buy the things they had worn on the soap at a sizable mark-down.

When Sheila had an afternoon to herself, she often visited the textile galleries of the Met or the Cooper Hewitt, luxuriating in crushed velvets and laces and silk chiffons, joyfully losing herself in more elegant times. The cunningly finished garments with their rows of tucks, French seams, and embroidery and beading were examples of masterful workmanship. "Masterful workmanship." The two descriptive masculine words applied to the product of dexterous and nimble feminine hands always made her smile. What had they thought of, she wondered, those turn-of-the-century modistes as they labored hour after hour over their creations. Suppose, she imagined, instead of a museum of their work, there was a museum of their thoughts, all gracefully displayed in glass cases with suitable notations: a carefully crafted early 1900 daydream of a French count rescuing a poor seamstress, or perhaps a fantasy of a couturier strangled in his *atelier* after refusing his seamstresses' requests for better lighting.

When the old elevator reached the floor of her apartment, Sheila waited as Archie hastened to open the door, making some remark about March coming in like a lion. He swung the elevator gate back for her as he informed her of his brother's prostate surgery. Thanking him she fumbled through her purse for her keys. While she was still unlocking the door, she could hear the phone ringing. She hurried into the apartment and, kicking off her shoes, grabbed for the receiver.

"Is this Sheila Covell?" The voice was unfamiliar. This was puzzling, as her number wasn't listed. In the days when she was in the phone book, she used to get an incessant stream of calls from viewers of "Night into Day," telling her how to handle her unruly, wicked, and raunchy soap children. In response to her tentative acknowledgment the man continued. "I wonder if I could come by and talk with you about a job, one I think you would be interested in."

"Have you talked with my agent?"

"Lois Markman? No. This is something I think we had better talk about alone."

"I'm afraid you'll have to go through Lois." In Sheila's work one had to be cautious, for it attracted every kind of crazy.

"This could mean a great deal of money as well as a challenging role, possibly the most challenging of your career," the voice persisted.

"Why can't you talk with my agent?" said Sheila, curious in spite of herself.

"If I tell you why, would you promise not to say anything about this call until I see you and explain?"

Against her better judgment she agreed, equally intrigued and skeptical.

"It has to do with national security."

"What!?" Her hopes deflated instantly. After the last hours at the Tea Room, she was in no mood for a practical joke. Just as she was about to slam down the receiver, the voice went on.

"I don't want this to get any further. Could I come by now? I can assure you I have proper identification." Without waiting for her assent he hurriedly added, "I'll be there in five minutes. I'm just down the street. Don't make any calls. Your line is being monitored."

* * *

Sheila Covell's line was not being monitored, but Ted Coulter was sure she would not know that. He hoped the lie would ensure a measure of anonymity until he made his offer. As he walked toward the building where the actress lived, the cold wind blowing grit into his eyes, he wondered just how much he was compromising himself and the president. Even though he would use a fictitious name until he was sure of her, Coulter worried about the risk he was taking. After all, as Special Advisor to the President of the United States he was in the public eye. She might recognize him. But he had no choice. He was the only one Robert Lange trusted, the only one the president could depend on to do what was necessary. Coulter knew that if the woman didn't accept his offer, the danger of her having seen him was a serious risk. Yet having arranged for her to lose her job, Coulter was quite sure she could be handled with enough money and a modest amount of intimidation.

She would take the job, though. Of that he was almost certain. She had no savings, and he had learned from an IRS contact what her income was. He had managed to get a copy of her credit card records as well. They clearly showed she spent far too much on extravagant clothes. And there was the financial strain of years of caring for her developmentally disabled sister.

Finding her in so short a time had been pure luck. Her resemblance to Maida Lange was uncanny. She could easily pass for her twin. She had the same features, the same high cheekbones and the same hooded eyes. Her figure, much like Maida Lange's, was well-built and elegant, such as one saw in a Sargent or a Whistler portrait, one with more amplitude than was currently fashionable.

To Coulter's surprise, he had discovered another advantage. Sheila Covell didn't seem to have many friends. Even with all the risks, Bobby—for that was how he always thought of the president—had agreed it was the best they could do.

When Bobby had called him recently and confided to him Maida Lange's threats, Coulter had at first felt astonishment and then an overwhelming sense of importance. Ted Coulter began to regard himself as the most powerful man in America, a man even more powerful than the president, for now the president's secret was in his hands. Not that he would ever use his knowledge as leverage for power, Coulter told himself. Not against a man who had been a close friend since law school, a man he admired, even idolized. What Coulter admired most about Robert Lange was the man's ability to get what he wanted no matter how unsurmountable the odds. In Congress they joked that Robert Lange was a man whose grasp exceeded his reach.

Coulter wished he could tell his parents how he had been entrusted with information that would shake the world if it were known. It bothered him that his parents considered his advisory position to the president to be at best that of a cup-bearer, and at worst that of a political flunkey. Their appraisal tormented him; for all of his adulthood he had tried to make up to them for what he had done as a young boy. Their refusal to forgive him only made him strive all the harder. Years before when he realized how far Robert Lange would go in the political arena, Coulter had ingratiated himself with Lange and never looked back.

Coulter worried whenever he allowed himself to consider the recent shift in his relationship with Bobby. That the president would entrust his very future into a friend's hands like this was an ominous harbinger of what could lie ahead. The one thing the president never tolerated in himself was any sign of weakness; his recent disclosure and dependence on Coulter could very easily jeopardize their friendship. That thought was too painful to dwell on, for Robert Lange's friendship was the most important thing in Ted Coulter's life.

Coulter checked the address in his notebook before entering Sheila's apartment building. The doorman hardly looked at him. "She called down, sir. She's expecting you."

When Coulter knocked on her door, Sheila Covell addressed him through the small slit. "Put your identification in the mail drop."

Coulter approved of her caution. It had been a simple matter to convince Randall Godden at the FBI to fix him up with something official. Godden had appeared satisfied with Coulter's offhand, "Just playing a little practical joke on a friend."

"It's not the real thing," Godden had warned him. "I couldn't do that. But you'd have to be smarter than ninety-nine percent of the citizenry to spot it."

II

Sheila watched the laminated card flutter from the mail drop to the floor. She bent down to pick it up, aware that her hand was shaking. Ever since she had found out that her days on the soap were numbered, she had sensed an uncharacteristic recklessness stirring in her. The impulsiveness had begun a year ago with her sister's sudden death.

She had made her usual weekly journey to the New Jersey group home where Ava lived with six other people. Though physically and chronologically adults like Ava, their emotional and intellectual development had stopped at varying levels. The home was an attractive ranch house with a large fenced yard where the residents could enjoy picnics or spend time working in the garden. The inside of the house resembled a college dormitory with furniture pushed haphazardly about, posters on the bedroom walls, magazines strewn about in untidy piles, and the constant odor of food being prepared.

Mrs. Sykes, who ran the group home with the barest of order and a surplus of affection, had called Sheila and mentioned that Ava was not eating. "And she hasn't any get-up-and-go." When Sheila pulled up in front of the home that day, her sister had not been at her usual place by the window waiting for her, eager to greet her with the usual excited hugs and kisses. Instead, Mrs. Sykes was explaining, "So I made an appointment to take Ava in for a checkup today. I wanted to wait until you were here. You know how she gets with strangers." Appointments for Ava's haircuts and dental and physical checkups were scheduled for Sheila's day off.

"Hepatitis B," the doctor had said grimly. "She could have picked it up from someone in the home; it only takes a cough or a sneeze. It's an unusually virulent form. I'm afraid she'll have to be hospitalized immediately." In two weeks Ava was dead. Shortly after Ava's funeral Dan had said, "I don't know how you managed with her all these years."

It had never occurred to Sheila to ask that question. She was only doing what she had to do, and what she wanted. Ava was the one tie she had to a life away from acting. For Sheila, Ava, even in her simple way, was the real world. She knew Ava loved her unequivocally. No one else ever had. A few months after Ava's death, Sheila caught herself taking risks she never would have dared take in the days when she knew her sister depended on her. At first they were small, innocuous risks: dashing into the street for a taxi, ignoring traffic lights and oncoming crosstown traffic, an occasional ad-libbing of lines. One night she ventured further and let a man pick her up in the lounge of the Carlyle. She went with him to a couple of Soho night spots and then got into an argument with him when he insisted on going home with her. It was as if, while Ava was alive, it was Ava who watched over Sheila, not the other way around.

Now Sheila was about to allow a stranger into her apartment.

The card looked official, complete with an embossed seal and the picture of an unprepossessing face. The name was Edward Brown. For a moment she stood there holding it in her hand. Then, impulsively, she opened the door to see before her the face pictured on the card.

"Come in, Mr. Brown." She stood aside, noticing his eyes dart around the room as he cautiously stepped inside. When she handed back his identification, he took it with pudgy fingers and slipped it into a Gucci wallet. He was a short, plump man with a round face, apple cheeks, and small glittering eyes. "A child's face," she thought, until she noticed the cynical smile. Somehow, Sheila had the feeling that for the first time in her life she was about to audition for a position commensurate with her talent.

"May I sit down?" His question was polite, but the crisp

timbre of his voice suggested he was more accustomed to giving orders than to making requests. For some reason that air of authority reassured her and she nodded. Sheila, no longer feeling at home in her own apartment, remained standing, uncomfortable with the way the man was staring at her.

Ted Coulter slowly eased himself into an armchair so cushioned with down it seemed to devour him. He couldn't take his eyes off of Sheila. Seeing her in person was even more startling to him. The resemblance was striking, and to think he had discovered her himself! Ellenda, the woman who cleaned for the Coulters, was an afficionado of the soaps. She would turn on the TV in the room she was cleaning, and then turn it off as she moved to the next room. Coulter had been home with the flu one day, pacing the house like a caged animal, when Ellenda had said to him, "I just love your house. You got a TV in nearly every room."

"I have to keep track of what the media is accusing us."

He had been about to tell Ellenda to get back to her work when she had said, "I just love her. She's *sooo* evil." He looked at the set and saw Robert's mother, the same tall, large-boned figure with a regal carriage. She had the deep-set, hooded eyes, the prominent cheekbones, and the full mouth. She was a woman who in earlier times might have sat at court as a queen or fought on a battlefield as a warrior. Only it wasn't Lange's mother. It was Sheila Covell, an actress.

Coulter hadn't thought to mention the amazing similarity to Lange until the day Bobby had confided in him. The audacity of the idea had been his own, but Lange had heard him out and had been cautiously enthusiastic. There had been only one problem. If Sheila Covell had a good-paying job, why would she even consider another one, one filled with risks?

Coulter made a few discreet inquiries and then went to see Everett Kingston. There was a lucrative station Kingston wanted to pick up in Texas, a station that would easily bring in millions of dollars in profits. It hadn't been up for sale, but it wasn't too hard to search the files and find an obscure non-compliance of which the owner was guilty. Seeing that his license might be pulled, the man agreed to take Kingston's generous offer. Kingston was more than glad to repay the favor. Coulter had not suggested he fire Sheila outright; instead, he had cleverly mentioned the name of an actress he felt would be great on "Day into Night." "She's a terrific actress. I see her as the stepmother of that brood." Kingston had been left with the impression that Ted Coulter, who appeared to have the sex appeal of an ice cube, was a sly rake who was having a clandestine affair with some actress to whom he had probably promised a job.

Coulter fought the cushions that engulfed him and managed to maneuver to the edge of his chair. "I'd feel a lot more comfortable if you would sit down," he told Sheila. He watched admiringly as she settled down on a straight chair and arranged her skirt gracefully. With the movement a little cloud of expensive perfume wafted his way. Coulter guessed the woman was always "on stage." He took a deep breath. "What I am going to tell you is something no one else but the President of the United States, and I the head of the FBI are aware of." He had told only one lie. Her eyes widened. "You must give me your word never to tell to anyone—*anyone*—what you are about to hear." He waited.

Sensing the enormity of what was coming, nervously she said, "You have my word."

"Perhaps you are aware that the president has a mother?" She stared at him. He had meant to be dramatic and saw that he had merely been banal. Who wouldn't have a mother? "What I mean is that perhaps you have read something about her. Of course pictures of her are very rare."

Sheila shook her head. "I don't really keep up with the news."

"Well, I'm not surprised you don't know much about her. She lives in a small house in Alexandria, Virginia, and keeps a very low profile. I don't think she's been photographed more than once or twice since her son became president.

"Tragically, Mrs. Lange appears to have developed a debili-tating mental illness. The doctors think it is some sort of early senility, but there are paranoid delusions connected with the illness. She says things about the president that would be very embarrassing if leaked to the press. Of course none of the things are true, but you know how the media can be."

"I don't see what this has to do with me."

"I'm sure it must be puzzling, but please let me finish. It will be necessary to hospitalize the president's mother. In-definitely. The doctors are afraid it's a progressive thing. How-ever, if her illness became known, particularly the nature of her delusions, the media would go after her. They may even give the delusions credence. You know how people are. Gullible. Eager to believe the worst about anyone. With the president shepherding along his new Compassionate Care Bill, it's imperative that nothing like that happen.

"The minute they learned she was hospitalized, the media would find a way to get to her, or her nurse, or her doctor, or some attendant. The tabloids would have a field day. She has to be given care, of course, but it has to be very discreet. There is an excellent private facility we have in mind staffed with the best doctors."

He could tell the actress was dazed by the flow of informa-tion. It was apparent she wanted to say something, but she seemed unable to find a point of entry into the conversation.

Coulter inched further to the edge of his chair. "We want you to take the place of the president's mother." He watched her carefully, trying to read any reaction.

"For a day or two?" she asked guardedly.

"No. Indefinitely. You wouldn't have to do anything but slip into her life, which is very pleasant, very nonpressured. She has a nice little house and garden in Alexandria." He could see the simple lifestyle did not attract her. Hurriedly he added, "You would be paid handsomely."

"But why have you chosen me?"

Coulter took out a small picture and handed it to her. It was a photo of the president standing outside of his mother's home, his arm around his mother, who looked acutely uncomfortable. Coulter had taken the photo himself on a visit with Lange to her home.

Sheila let out a little gasp. "She looks exactly like me. It's uncanny. Only her hair is gray. Would I have to..."

"Yes, I'm afraid so." He looked regretfully at her brown-gold hair. Colored of course, he decided, but still very nice. "There's something else. She has a slight German accent. Could you manage that?" He noticed the slightest beginning of a smile on her face. He felt relief, guessing she was caught up in the idea, even excited by the strange offer.

"Yes, of course. I'll go to the Library of the Performing Arts at Lincoln Center. They have tapes on file of every kind of foreign accent. It would help, though, if I had a sentence or two of hers on tape."

"I'm sure we can arrange that. We'll get you a full history of her background. You can study it. I suppose it won't be too different from preparing for any part. She doesn't drive. She doesn't go out to speak of, except for a little grocery shopping and a weekly trip to the library and church. You would carry on those routines to avoid suspicion. Oh, one other thing. Her clothes are not fashionable. I don't mean she's dowdy or anything like that. Her taste is excellent but she doesn't have a *lot* of clothes."

A twinge of alarm showed on Sheila's face. "So you know I'm fond of clothes. You must have investigated me before offering me the job. You mentioned the FBI. I suppose you would have to know all about me before you could allow me to assume the role of the president's mother?" Angrily she asked, "Is that why I lost my job?"

Coulter looked away. She was more perceptive than he had given her credit for. He would have to be careful.

Coldly she asked, "What if I don't want the job? It's a free country. I can do as I please."

"Yes, of course," Coulter said. "Still, I'd be less than candid if I didn't remind you of how difficult it is to find work—you'll pardon me—at your age. Even very famous actresses find that more and more difficult."

She was quiet for a moment. "What about my apartment and all of my things?"

"We would pay the rent on your apartment, and your things could stay right here. We'd rent it under another name until you want it back."

"Why is that?"

"Your friends will want to know where you are. We can't have them dropping by and finding no one here. They would become suspicious. I suggest you tell people you're going out to the coast to investigate employment in a sitcom or another soap opera. As for your agent, I believe it's not unusual to change agents. You could tell her you're getting someone on the West Coast. Perhaps I am wrong, but I have gathered that you don't have a great many close friends. I'm sure in your busy career there wasn't too much time for those kinds of relationships."

Sheila bristled at his intrusiveness but it was true. Most of her life she had to assume other identities, live her life as someone else.

"And of course we know about your sister who died a year ago. I'm sure that was a financial burden. May I ask why you took it on?" Ted was curious. He found the devotion to the sister unusual in someone in so narcissistic a profession. He had learned she had financed the care herself rather than relying upon the state. It appeared Sheila Covell was independent. It was the one aspect of her about which he was most uncertain, even wary. He wanted it cleared up.

"When my parents died an aunt took her in, but it was too much for her. Eventually, she had to put Ava in an institution. Ava had some physical problems as well, and the people in the institution refused to give her the care she needed. At the time I was in New York, and I wasn't making enough money to support her. I thought about moving back home, but even there I would've had to work, and she couldn't be left alone all day. As soon as I landed a job in TV and began to earn regular money, I brought Ava to New York, got her proper medical care, and hired someone to stay with her in my apartment. As hard as I tried, it didn't work. She hated being cooped up in the city, and she was too much for the woman who worked for me. I finally found a group home in the country that would take her. It was expensive but she loved it. She had friends there and I used to see her on weekends. But I suppose you already know all of that. What you probably don't know is how much I loved my sister, how much I looked forward to those weekend trips and the excitement and pleasure on my sister's face as she ran to meet me. Ava was my childhood, my hold on the past."

For a man as self-serving as Ted Coulter, he was genuinely moved. The woman was obviously sincere. And she was someone who would make sacrifices if she felt it her responsibility. "I admire that kind of loyalty," he said. "I hope you have that kind of loyalty to your country, because I can assure you your country needs you."

Coulter had also sensed in her explanation a loneliness he had not suspected. That suited him very well, for he had been worried that the simple lifestyle of Maida Lange would prove too isolated for Sheila Covell. Now he saw it was not that different from the one she was used to. Reassured, he said, "I think it's time we got down to particulars. Since you will be doing highly secret government work you will be well compensated." He named the figure they would be paying her.

For the first time Sheila smiled at Coulter.

He smiled back, relieved at his success. He was convinced it was the enormous amount of money that had done it, and that gave him a sense of power and security. And there were plenty of discretionary funds still left from the campaign.

Ted Coulter felt sure enough of the actress to say, "Something you should know. The name Edward Brown is an alias. I didn't know whether you would take the job. I'm really Ted Coulter, the Special Advisor to the President." He saw from the expression on her face that she was at once impressed and somewhat confused.

"What I do needn't concern you. I mention it only to let you know how close to the president I am and how important absolute secrecy is. You will be dealing *only* with me. There will be a number at which you can contact me if a question should arise. Be aware that one injudicious word on your part could put the whole country at risk, and, in these dangerous times, perhaps even the world."

*　*　*

Sheila went to the window and watched Archie hail a taxi for Ted Coulter. She thought him an unprepossessing man to be uttering such intimidating words. More than anything else it was what convinced her of his authenticity.

Coulter was wrong in thinking it was the money that attracted her. She was pleased about the money, pleased that there would be no more worries over what would become of her. What really piqued her excitement were the words "secret government work." Lately, at the end of a day, and especially after she knew she had lost her job with no prospects for another, Sheila had found herself dreading the thought of living with herself, with the woman she had avoided for all these years. That unnerved her more than the economic uncertainty, frightening as that was.

Even when she was a small child, fantasy had played an important part in her troubled home. It helped her to escape the terrible fights between her parents brought on by her father's incessant drinking. He was a charming man sober, but a cruel and vicious transformation occurred when he was drunk. As a child, Sheila felt as if she were watching some evil magician's trick take place. Many nights she had escaped by shutting herself away in her bedroom when the sound of her parents' outbursts trespassed the thin walls of the house.

Alone, Sheila would take out her little store of makeup from the ten-cent store. With an old dress of her mother's from better days and a gaudy shawl, she would transform herself into someone else while the storm raged between her parents. Miraculously, for a few hours she would *be* someone else, and manage to forget her parents' frightening fighting.

Every Saturday her mother gave Sheila two precious quarters. Sheila looked forward to those days. She would take her sister by the hand and dash off to the movies. They'd pass the afternoon enjoying cartoons and serials and a double feature. She had seen Hepburn in "The Philadelphia Story" and Joan Fontaine in "Suspicion" and Vivian Leigh in "Gone With the Wind." But the film that had made a tremendous impact on her life was the very first one she saw. She couldn't have been more than three or four, but she never forgot Katherine Hepburn in "Morning Glory." Even at that tender age she had understood that the movie was about an actress.

The moment she was old enough she escaped from her home altogether. By the time Ava died, Sheila had become so absorbed by her role-playing that her own identity had completely disappeared. It was disconcerting, like staring at a mirror and seeing an empty shell. And nothing terrified her half so much as the prospect of having to live with that absent person for the rest of her days.

Now Ted Coulter was offering to rescue her. His startling plan would give her another disguise, someone else to hide behind. Only this time she would be doing something useful, "secret government work." And it was lucrative! She smiled to herself, thinking, "It will probably be the first useful thing I've ever done. Even if there is no one there to applaud, I'll make it the best performance of my career."

III

Vice President T. Russell Ranta stood on the White House lawn waiting for the helicopter rotor to switch off. A Marine attendant stood at attention in dress uniform nearby waiting to take his post by the helicopter steps as soon as the president emerged. Ranta (the T. was for Toivo after Ranta's Finnish grandfather) regretted not taking the time to put on his topcoat. Washington spring was either summer or winter. Today the frigid wind, combined with the helicopter wash, pressed its way into his very bones. It was on this kind of day that the Finns up on the Minnesota Iron Range where he had grown up would be making their annual dash into the lake. He had a vision of them naked, chopping a hole into the ice, and plunging into the water. Then they would run to the sauna in Finn Hall, which stood next to the icebound lake.

Watching Robert Lange emerge from the helicopter, the vice president decided all the media pictures of presidents descending from the heavens played into the image of Olympian omnipotence. Ranta was having a hard time making the transition from the sweltering heat of the Caribbean to the chilly, gray March day. "I'm getting soft," he accused himself. After all, he had grown up on the Iron Range where he had walked to school on winter days that fell to forty below.

He had been gone nearly a month on a state visit to Britain and France, and then Moscow to meet with Obronsky, who, along with the military, had organized the latest Russian coup. Obronsky had assured Ranta he had no design on the Baltics, which Ranta didn't believe for a moment. From Moscow the president had sent him to the Caribbean. He had stayed on, ordered to make a tour of the neighboring islands. On one of these islands he held a secret meeting with a Cuban agent who confirmed what intelligence reports had caused the Oval Office to suspect. Aid was once again flowing into Cuba from Russia. The man filled Ranta in on the construction that was going on, which tallied with the information they were receiving from their satellite pictures. Russia would give its scarce resources to another country for one reason only. They hoped the military buildup so close to home would goad the United States into giving them what they wanted: a free hand in the Baltics. All of that would have to be reported to Robert Lange without delay.

Ranta knew the president had kept him out of Washington on purpose. The Compassionate Care Bill was inching its way through the Congress, and Robert Lange didn't want Ranta around to lobby against it as he surely would have done in spite of the fact that the president was supporting it. Costs for the national health care plan put into effect by the last administration had become astronomical, seriously affecting the budget.

The Bill was a misnomer, for it was anything but compassionate. In fact, it would precipitate drastic cutbacks in care to the elderly, the mentally impaired, and those battling AIDS. At first the country had resisted the cutbacks, but when their own health care benefits were threatened and the administration had launched an all-out campaign to support the Bill, the opposition quickly died. The president would know why he was there waiting for him on the White House lawn. And he would not be pleased.

Robert Lange was returning from Walter Reed Hospital after the removal of an impacted wisdom tooth. It was a poor time for a confrontation, but what Ranta had to say couldn't wait. As the chopper's blades spun their last lazy revolution, Ranta strolled across the White House lawn to greet the president.

Even with the puffiness on the side of his face where his wisdom tooth had been extracted, Ranta had to admit Robert

Lange was a handsome man: the tall, slim figure kept in perfect shape with a daily five-mile run; the prominent cheekbones that suggested character; the frank blue eyes; the shock of blond hair that fell beguilingly over his forehead. All together they made the president appear a perfect photo op: Our Young Leader. That was the polished image the public saw, a Nordic Jimmy Stewart who affected a kind of shy boyishness, as though no one could be more surprised than Lange that he was the President of the United States.

Still, appearances were deceiving. It was not Lange's boyish good looks that had won his seat in the Oval Office. Although the vice president regarded himself as a man who could outmaneuver anyone, Ranta had learned a thing or two from the thirty-nine-year-old president. In the years since they had first met, Ranta had come to regard Lange as a cross between a rattlesnake and a robot: dangerously focused and relentlessly driven. Lange would go to any length to achieve his goal. And he had a knack for orchestrating it all without ever ruffling his spit-polished exterior.

Even the hitchhiking stunt during the campaign as he traveled from town to town had worked because he had been careful to keep the Secret Service cars that followed and preceded him out of camera range. Even more effective had been the shot of him taken on the eve of the election standing alone at the Lincoln Memorial at midnight, his dark figure silhouetted against the illuminated Lincoln. He had tried—unsuccessfully, of course—to grab the camera from the photographer, saying it was an incursion on a private moment, when all along it had been Lange's staff that had made arrangements for the photographer to be tipped off in the first place. Ranta had long since decided that President Lange had not so much been elected as he had been cast.

Robert Lange hurried down the steps of the helicopter so obviously upset at the sight of Ranta's big frame and enigmatic grin that he nearly forgot to snap a salute to the Marine standing at attention. The vice president knew he was a thorn in Lange's flesh. He also knew the president would have preferred to look on him as an old buffoon, a back-slapper, a fossil from the days of smoke-filled rooms, full of doubtful tales of the range in northern Minnesota where he had grown up. Though he gave the appearance of treating everything as a joke, among those who mattered Ranta had the reputation of being a shrewd politician and, more important, a man of his word. He was a man of conviction, not easily bent to the will of another, which was the spark of contention between him and Lange. His favorite method of bringing two opposing sides together was to sit them down around a table and lock the door. No food, no bathroom breaks for as long as it took to settle the matter.

Only once had Washington insiders seen Ranta let down his guard. Three years ago, when the vice president's wife of thirty-five years had died, he had fallen apart. He secluded himself in a Washington hotel room for a week and refused to see anyone but the bell boy, who delivered an ample supply of bourbon. In the past he had not been a man given to drinking. In his line of business one needed a clear head, but the loss of his wife had left him bereft, pushing him over the edge.

Locked in his room, the world a blur, Ranta's depression swallowed him like a black abyss. His wife's death had shaken his faith to the core. In his despair he fought with God, who had remained silent in the face of his desperate prayers, a God who appeared either powerless or disinterested. His agony deepened, and he might have drunk himself to death trying to cope with his pain except for the hotel's habit of pushing *The Washington Post* under its guests' doors each morning. He had kicked it aside, but Robert Lange's photo in the convention issue stared up at him. He glanced at the article on presidential contenders and then read it more carefully. It appeared the Lord did not mean for Ranta to drink himself to death. There was still something for him to do. He would not turn over the country to Lange unless he was there to keep an eye on him. He showered, shaved, changed into clean clothes, and escaped the airless room.

He headed straight for Capitol Hill and collared the head of the party, insisting the man throw his full support to Ranta for the vice presidency. All Ranta's years of traveling around the country giving speeches in the hometowns of any congressman who asked him had paid off. He got what he wanted.

When Ranta informed Robert Lange that he intended to run on the ticket with him, Ranta saw through Lange's condescending smile. Lange soon discovered that T. Russell Ranta was not an old party hack who was easy to manipulate. Lange found the man had backbone. Ranta watched him like a hawk. Soon Lange learned what most of Washington already knew: Ranta only appeared to be a fool in order to disarm his opponents.

As the president walked briskly toward him from the helicopter, Ranta said, "Your face looks like you were in a fistfight. Wait'll the hornets see this." *Hornets* was what he called the White House Press corps. "The morning shows are going to be full of dentists and videos of wisdom tooth extractions. I was hoping they'd give you some kind of anesthetic that would put you out so I could go on TV and reassure everyone I was in charge. Wouldn't you know I'd have the luck to be lady-in-waiting to a guy who isn't forty yet?"

"You're looking a little under the weather yourself." The president's voice was terse.

Ranta knew that was true. He wrapped his arms around his big frame to keep from shivering. His chest felt as if it were in a vise. Probably pleurisy, he told himself.

Robert winced. "The Novocain's beginning to wear off. I'm not exactly anxious to hear about some new crisis, but I know you wouldn't be here unless you had a good reason."

The president waved to the coterie of press corps that assembled on the lawn to see his return. The full complement was there, always hoping for the worst because it would make for a better front-page story. He shook off the barrage of questions, pointed to his swollen cheek, and gave them the thumbs up sign. In a few minutes they would all crowd into the press room for a short briefing on how the extraction went.

Ranta began telling a story about a plumber on the Minnesota Iron Range who used to do extractions for half the price the local dentist charged.

Impatiently Lange cut into the story, "What'd you find in the Caribbean?"

"Mr. President." With pleasure, Ranta saw Lange tense at the amount of withering contempt Ranta could crowd into those two words. "Mr. President, forget the Caribbean. We have a little *contretemps* on our hands to deal with right here." Ranta enjoyed tossing a French word into his conversation from time to time, knowing it was so complete a contradiction of his yahoo posturing that it always irritated Lange. Lange had once asked Ranta if the rumor that he was something of a Shakespearean scholar was true. The vice president had merely laughed.

Ranta could sense the man was in no mood for levity. "What's the problem?" said Lange, wanting to get to the point.

Ranta grinned. The lad was focused. You had to give him that. "The papers are full of the triage section of the Compassionate Care Bill, Mr. President. Looks like you want to get rid of a whole bunch of citizens: crazies, dim bulbs, sick gays, and old codgers like me."

"Ranta, you can't talk like that. You can't use those names even with me. You could be destroyed for that."

Ranta's affable, joking manner evaporated. "You little pompous fool," he snarled, "I knew that would get a rise out of you. You're worried about me *calling names*. You're planning to *kill* those people. I've been telling you for months the committee that put that legislation together is out of control. You promised you'd rein them in. Instead, I get back and find their outrageous plan spread all over the papers."

They were nearing the entrance, too far for the press corps to see their faces. Robert stopped. "Who do you think you're talking to? We're not killing anyone. We have to cut back on services. You of all people know that. If we start our campaign next year with the national debt skyrocketing to the moon, the other party will swoop down on us like vultures. From the reports you've been sending back from Moscow, it's apparent I need to bolster congressional support for more defense money. Where do you think that is going to come from if we don't cut back on health care? Walter Jensen told me exactly what the Committee decided, and I told him he'd have our full support. And that's the way it's going to be! After the election we might be able to phase out some of those cuts."

Ranta sighed. He had underrated Robert Lange's determination on the issue. He was torn between laying it all out for Lange right there and escaping the biting cold. In his rush to arrive at the White House Ranta had skipped breakfast, making up for it with too many cups of stale coffee. He was feeling light-headed now, and the pain continued to gnaw at his chest. He would leave the explanations for later and get to the bottom line. "Lange, I'm not talking about '*cuts*.' I'm talking about *lives*. I'm not going along with this, and you may as well know up front I'll do whatever it takes to stop it." He turned on his heel and without waiting for the president to precede him—an unforgivable breach of respect not lost on the Secret Service agents—hurried inside the West Wing.

In the Oval Office Lange threw his coat to his secretary, Andrea. "Get me some aspirin, Andy, will you? And get my wife on the phone."

Andrea, who debated throwing the coat back at him, folded it neatly over her arm and left the office without saying a word. She loved her job, but Robert Lange was a machine to work for. It didn't cheer her to know that part of the reason she had the job was because his wife Paige had given her approval. The day of the interview, the president's wife had singled out Andrea from some strikingly attractive women. She had looked at Andrea's skinny figure, her mousey hair, her too large nose and thin mouth and said, "That one."

The light on his phone winked and Robert picked up the receiver. "Hi, Paige." Before saying anything else, he waited anxiously to hear how she sounded today. He knew it shouldn't affect him, but when she was irritable it cast a shadow across his day.

Paige had met Robert Lange at a Washington dinner party when he was an active member in the House of Representatives. Because their courtship progressed so rapidly, tabloid stories suggested some overwhelming attraction had drawn Robert Lange to Paige. The truth was that Lange had been looking. He was twenty-eight and unmarried. Without a wife he was finding himself the odd man out at all the Washington parties, where most of the guests who matched his achievements were both older and married. Lange thought Paige arresting, with her drift of red hair and large hooded green eyes, but what had intrigued him most was the confident way she had come up to him to inquire if he had any influence at the National Museum of Women in the Arts where an exhibition of contemporary art was planned. "She can't bear not to be included," he thought and suspected there wasn't much she wouldn't do to achieve her ends. He was amused at her tenacity, feeling at last he had met his match, or at least someone he could spar with equally. When a few influential words from him got her into the exhibition she was wildly grateful, eager to "pay back" the favor. Lange decided it would be a beneficial relationship, an expedient union in which they would use each other. Paige's ambition had been great, but what he would one day offer her matched it.

"Bobby, did it hurt?" Paige's voice was sympathetic and relaxed. She didn't wait for the answer. "Something absolutely wonderful. Gianni said he'll give me a show in his gallery. I'll have to share it with another artist but that's a real breakthrough." Paige Lange was an artist. She had been painting with no success for years. People said she worked hard but lacked an original style. She was eclectic; one week she was

Morris Lewis and the next week she was Motherwell.

Lange surmised Gianni was only including Paige in the show because she would attract the right people to the gallery, which would help pay for the announcements and the opening. All he said was, "Great news, Paige. I'll be over there to hear all about it as soon as I can break away." Lange often congratulated himself on his choice of wife. Paige, with her East Wing studio, her gala parties at the White House for artists and musicians and actors, her appearances at opening nights and benefit entertainments, created a nonstop hype of excitement and involvement in the White House; best of all it distracted people from real issues. In fact, the media gave more attention to the star-studded benefit for AIDS cosponsored by Paige than it did to the High-Rise, Low-Risk AIDS Sanctuaries that the Compassionate Health Bill was advocating to remove people with AIDS from the community.

* * *

It was noon when Ted Coulter walked into the Oval Office. "What did they do? Take it out with a pliers?" Coulter meant to be sympathetic, but he saw the jaunty ring in his voice annoyed the president, who sat there with his hand on his swollen cheek.

Lange ignored his question. "We've got more important things to discuss. Ranta is threatening to stir up trouble about the Compassionate Health Care Bill. First Mother and now Ranta. This thing is starting to get away from us." He sunk into his chair and pushed a thick dossier toward Coulter. "The figures are here. The Bill isn't going to do a thing the Netherlands or Sweden or Britain aren't doing now or will be doing soon. Well, maybe our limitations on care are a little more stringent, but we've got the inner cities. I know I can sell the program. It's either that or more taxes, and we've gone that route so many times people are squeezed dry. They're fed up with the mention of the word 'taxes.'"

Coulter winced under the president's assaying glance. He had always considered himself Lange's best friend. Since their days together at the University of Virginia's law school, Ted Coulter had resigned himself to two important facts about their friendship: Lange always found a way to get what he wanted, and Robert Lange was Ted's ticket to being a major player in the world of power. Coulter had never challenged Lange's dominance, but now, in asking Coulter to do his dirty work for him, Lange had unwittingly put himself in Coulter's hands.

Only one other time had Coulter seen Robert Lange appear vulnerable—fifteen years ago. They were seniors together at the University of Virginia Law School. Lange's father had died early in May, and a week later Bobby had unexpectedly dropped out of school and seemingly disappeared. Ted went to see Bobby's mother, Maida Lange. "Please, Ted, let him be," she had urged. "Escaping the life he's been living these last years is the best thing that could happen to him. Believe me, Ted, Robert is running for his life."

Ted was appalled at her words. "He's a brilliant student, Mrs. Lange. He's destined for great things."

Maida had given him a long glance that made Coulter feel a fool. "You don't mean great things, you mean *power*. I'd be a poor mother if I wanted that for my son. Listen to me, Ted, I know you mean well, but Robert has just learned something that he has to come to terms with. Please, I beg you give him some time. If you bring him back now you will only destroy him." Looking at her anguished face, listening to the distraught words, Coulter had decided that Maida Lange had become unbalanced by her husband's death.

Against her wishes Coulter began to track Lange. It turned out to be quite easy. Nelson Everly, the second classmate he canvassed, looked surprised. "What's all the mystery? Lange wanted to get away for a while. I think he was a little shaken by his father's death. That sort of shocked me. I mean Lange's such a cool character. I gave him the keys to my folks' fishing shack. It's near the George Washington National Forest." Watching

Coulter scribble directions, Everly scowled. "I think the idea was that he wanted to have a little time to himself, Coulter."

Coulter had paid no attention to the remark. An hour later he was on I-81 traveling south through a blizzard of white dogwood blooms which he hardly noticed.

The cabin, nothing more than one large room with bunk beds, a fireplace, and rudimentary cooking facilities, sat all alone at the end of a dirt two-track. Coulter found Lange sitting on a log deck cantilevered over a small stream.

Lange stood up and shot a furious look at Coulter. "I don't recall asking you to join me."

"I'm sorry, Bobby." Coulter did not like to think of how many of his conversations with Lange over the years had consisted of apologies. "I'm here because I don't want you to do something you'll later regret. You've got to come back to school."

"No, Ted. That's just it. I don't have to go back to school. I'm free for the first time in my life to do exactly as I wish." After a moment he gave Coulter a wry smile. "I have to admit, though, I'm finding solitude a little intimidating. Actually, it scares me to death."

"What have you been doing?"

"That's the interesting part. I haven't been doing anything. No… that's not entirely accurate. I've been watching the river. Would you believe that it seems to know what it's doing? It keeps flowing along peacefully hour after hour and I don't have to do a thing. Someone else seems to be in charge. Not only the stream, Ted. Ducks and mink and otter swim by. Who tells those creatures what to do, Ted? There seems to be a world out there full of small miracles. This morning I watched a heron drop down on the river and spear frogs with its cruel beak. It was how I used to imagine my mother's God swooping down on the world to punish sinners. But here the shadow of those great wings seemed to shelter me. I don't intend to leave this place."

Coulter was appalled. "You have to. Finals are coming up. You've got to graduate."

"No, Ted, I don't. I don't have to do anything I don't want to do. My father's gone now. I'm through living someone else's life for them, fulfilling someone else's dreams. I'm going to start living my own life. I was nothing more to my father than a puppet to manipulate. All these years I've had no life of my own. As for going back with you, Ted, what do you have to offer me? More of the same. You want to take my father's place."

"I just don't want you to throw away your life. I've covered for you at the university, but they're starting to ask some questions. It's not like you're just one of a thousand others there. You happen to be their outstanding law student just like you were their outstanding undergraduate."

"With their precious honor code, I wonder what they would say if they really knew what I was like."

"What do you mean? You don't have to cheat on tests. You could pass anything they throw at you."

"I'll leave the cheating to you, Ted," said Lange, his voice edged with sarcasm.

Coulter winced. Bobby had never referred to Coulter's being expelled from the Virginia Military Institute. He didn't understand why he was doing it now. The depth of Lange's anger slowly began to dawn on Coulter, but before he could find some way to leave his friend alone, which was so clearly what he wanted, Lange strode into the cabin and began throwing things into his duffle bag.

"I'll go back with you, Ted, but we're tied to each other now; you'll have to accept some of the responsibility." Although Coulter would later understand Lange meant his charge as a warning, at the time Coulter was flattered at the prospect.

All the way back to the university Robert Lange sat beside Coulter, silent and remote. He spoke only once. "You don't care about what's good for me, Coulter. You want me to succeed because that's the only way you'll ever achieve anything. That's all anyone but my mother has wanted for me: *their* success. I'm like those hippos you see wallowing around in Africa with the birds perched on their backs. First my father and now you. Faustian, that's what my life is. But is it you or my father who's the devil?"

* * *

Now fifteen years later, as the president looked across his desk at him, Coulter saw the old resentment welling up. "You know, Ted, if you hadn't dragged me back from the river years ago, none of this would be happening. I wouldn't be planning the kidnapping of my own mother." As his mouth began to tremble, Lange covered his face with his hands. A moment later he had regained control. "Have you made all of the arrangements?" he asked.

Coulter knew immediately what Lange meant. He'd started to answer when Andrea returned with two aspirins on a little tray and a glass of water. Both men remained silent. Understanding she wasn't wanted, she placed the tray on the large desk and left. As soon as the door was shut behind her, Coulter said, "No problem. Sheila Covell's going to be perfect for the job. She jumped at it. We'll just keep her out of the way. No one will think twice about that; the media has come to accept your mother's reclusiveness."

"What about Mother? I've been over this a thousand times trying to think of some other way."

Coulter saw sweat break out on Lange's forehead. He was breathing hard, as though he had been running a marathon. Coulter made his voice reassuring. "The nursing home is small and private, perfect for what we want. I've made the matter of confidentiality very plain to the couple who own it. One word to the authorities about their past and they're history. I'm going out this afternoon to check on the arrangements."

"I'll go and pay Mother a visit tonight. I know she's not going to change her mind, but I can't let her go without talking with her one more time. The whole thing probably seems barbaric to you, doesn't it?" Lange gave Coulter a piercing look.

"Look, Bobby, we've been over all of this. You've worked so hard and now you're finally in a position to do so much good that you can't let it all go down the drain because of a neurotic old woman—I'm sorry to have to use those words about your mother—and a senile politician like Ranta. Let me handle your mother problem. I'll leave Ranta to you."

"What can you put out about my visit to Mother tonight?"

"Well, we've always said she wasn't too well because of her asthma condition. I'll intimate it was a little worse and you were very concerned. Don't worry about it! Everyone loves a good son." Immediately Coulter saw his mistake and flushed.

"That's all right, Ted." For the first time since all those years ago when he had brought him back from the river, Coulter heard something close to dislike in Lange's voice. "I don't care for what I'm doing any more than you do."

Hurriedly Coulter said, "There's another thing. Sheila Covell needs a tape of your mother's voice. Could you record something tonight? Just a sentence would do the trick. She wants to work on the accent."

Suddenly, the shrill sound of sirens startled both of them and they immediately forgot their differences. "What can that be?" Robert jumped up from his desk.

"I'll go and see." Coulter was on his feet.

Before he could get out of the room the door flew open and Andrea pushed her way in. She was crying. "It's the vice president. He's had some sort of attack." As she reached in her pocket for a tissue, she missed the glance of relief Lange and Coulter exchanged.

IV

Paige Lange's quick movements, her pelt of clipped red hair, her small sharp features, and her darting green eyes had once caused a columnist to describe her as feral. Lange thought his wife had the frenzied energy of a captive animal suddenly released from its cage. As she sat across the luncheon table from him chattering away about the upcoming exhibition at Gianni's, Lange smiled. He was amused to see she managed to use the time to open her mail, take a phone call, and sample the vichyssoise and omelet *fines herbs*, food easily swallowed and planned for him. From time to time she stopped what she was doing to commiserate with him, her voice droning on like a mother humoring a fretful child. It was only when Robert mentioned he felt like lying down for an hour that Paige gave him her full attention.

"In the seven years we've been married, I can't remember your ever resting in the daytime." Her smooth forehead wrinkled. "Actually, I've been wanting to ask you if something is wrong. I mean, I know there's always some crisis, but these last weeks you've seemed—I don't know, preoccupied. You don't talk. You don't sleep. You barely even eat."

He smiled. "You want me to give up my day job?"

"Well, at least I can tuck you in." She followed him into their bedroom and turned down the bed for him herself, covering him with her own pink cashmere throw. After she lowered the shades, she walked over and kissed him on the forehead, reminding him that he had promised to make an appearance at the opening of her exhibition. "Gianni says it's the one way we can be sure of coverage by the media." She tiptoed out of the room.

Lange lay on the bed. The throbbing pain hadn't let up. The aspirin wasn't taking care of it. The dentist had been about to prescribe something stronger when he stopped himself, saying with great self-importance, "Mr. President, I could give you a medication like Demoral if you have no need to be alert this afternoon."

Lange had thought the man a self-important fool, but even so he refused the painkiller. A president was not allowed to have weaknesses; he existed for the country, not for himself.

The comforting warmth of the protective soft cover soon lulled him into a reverie, and he remembered a time in his childhood when he had experienced a similar feeling.

It was second or third grade, he thought. Measles, perhaps, or chicken pox. It had been a memorable occasion because it was one of the few times he recalled his mother actually making a fuss over him. By that time Lange had come almost completely under his father's firm control. Peter Lange had given up his practice, teaching instead at the school of medicine so he could spend more time with his son. Lange suspected, however, that his father's real motivation was to be home as much as possible to keep him from his mother's influence. He had often been the battleground for his mother and father's disagreements. They had grappled for his soul, and in the end his father had won. After all, it was his father's years of unfaltering drive and ambition that had paved the way for this extraordinary prize for him.

Yet during that time, he had felt abandoned by his mother. Though she kept house, gardened, and cooked for the family, Lange felt she wasn't really there. She had slowly withdrawn. Although once she had startled him by whispering that she would never stop praying for him, Lange knew his father had triumphed.

Only an occasional childhood illness seemed to breach the emotional gulf between himself and his mother. With his father away at the university, his mother could dare to fuss over him. She would busy herself cooking his favorite lemon pudding, bake cookies for him, and let him help her with her intricate and mysterious hybridizing of flowers. "You can pick the colors you would like the iris to be, Robert," she said as they walked among the vivid flowers in her small greenhouse.

He recalled choosing a pale yellow. "Can it have a green throat?" He remembered her explanation of how that miracle might be accomplished.

At night as he lay ill, she would read German fairy tales to him from a book of which his father disapproved. "There is enough in the real world to engage a child's interest without resorting to fantasy," his father had scolded.

When several days passed his father said, "Robert, it is time now for you to go back to school."

"But I still don't feel well." He was gloriously happy with his mother's attention and not anxious to return to his father's strict academic regime.

"Then I must examine you." After a brusque examination, his father declared him well. "Tonight we will resume your lessons and tomorrow you will return to school."

Once again his mother became a shadow moving about the house filling her time with domestic duties.

After Peter Lange's death, Coulter had dragged Robert back to his old life, and his mother became even more distant. She watched silently as he followed the path his father had set for him. He worked in the state prosecutor's office making a name for himself as someone who was relentless in his pursuit of criminals. He became a staff member to the House Committee on Drugs. There were two terms in the House and then the surprise victory in the senatorial race. And always, his mother stood aside watching him, her disapproval of his deception a constant reminder that on his rise to the presidency the lie would always be there, waiting to destroy him one day.

Sometimes as he stood gazing out from the Oval Office, he thought the danger was part of the attraction. He never knew from day to day whether or not he would be exposed for the imposter he was. Yet the prize had been irresistible and the whole thrust of his life had culminated in becoming the president. Now his mother was threatening to snatch it away.

A month ago she had called him and in a determined voice announced her intention of coming to the White House. This in itself was surprising. In the past she had refused any and all invitations. He had offered to send a limousine, but she had refused. Instead, since she didn't drive, she insisted on arriving in a taxi, which caused, for a moment, a flurry among the Secret Service agents.

"I didn't want to create a fuss," she said apologetically. "I simply wanted to see you for a few minutes." She looked about her. "It is just what I imagined."

Lange didn't know what she had imagined. He escorted her to the family quarters, where Paige gave her an impersonal kiss and then, much to his relief, immediately excused herself to attend the opening of a show at the National Gallery.

It took him several moments to get used to seeing his mother there in his living room. Attempting the part of the host, he offered her something to drink but she raised her hand to stop him. "Robert, you know I have never interfered with your position here. How should I know what to tell the President of the United States to do? But now I have been reading of this Compassionate Care Bill. I have come to ask if you mean to support it as the press says you do. I cannot believe that of you."

After all these years he could still hear the faint German accent. Living so much to herself she had never lost it. And when she said "Robert," he could see her longing to call him "Johann."

Her sudden interest in politics was a complete mystery to him. He could have been no more surprised had his mother come to ask what the deficit would be two years hence or the status of the new space station. All he could manage was a puzzled, "Why do you ask?"

"I ask because it is my fervent hope that you will not support such a terrible thing. Robert, I don't blame you for what has happened. It is myself I blame. I told you that after your father died. All those years he was too strong for both of us. Now I can't keep quiet. I must know. A society, Robert, must be judged on how it watches over its weakest citizens."

Her intensity stopped him from some dismissive answer. Instead he said, "Mother, I have to support the Bill. Because of national security I can't go into all the reasons. Surely you can understand that you cannot build a great country if all of your resources are squandered on the impaired and the ineffectual." Robert told himself it was unnatural for a mother to put some obscure pretensions of morality ahead of her son's future. "You will just have to trust me," he said, trying to keep the condescension he felt out of his voice.

"I do not trust you, Robert. I love you but I do not trust you. I must tell you that I will stop you."

Robert felt a sudden twinge of alarm. He wondered if his mother had lost her mind. Defensively he said, "You can't stop me. I'm the President of the United States." At once he saw how pompous he sounded. He laughed nervously.

"Yes, Robert, I have the means to stop you. I have evidence that will prove to the whole world that you have no right to hold this office. You have not forgotten your Constitution? Let me remind you of what I told you after your father's death. No person except a natural-born citizen shall be eligible to the office of president..."

His whole body was seized by a cold chill which turned into a burning fury. His knuckles went white as he clutched the arms of his chair to keep himself from leaping up and striking her. He saw her calmly watching him. And she was not afraid.

"I have very little left to live for, Robert. You can do what you wish with me, but if I choose to tell the truth you cannot silence me. This is not a whim. This is not between you and me. It is between me and my God. In spite of your position and all your power, Robert, God is on my side."

* * *

In the month that had passed since her visit, Robert Lange had tried to convince himself that his mother had been wrong. The plan that Coulter was carrying out was risky, but to be publicly exposed as a fraud was unthinkable. He would not allow his mother to dictate his actions and ruin everything he had worked so hard to attain.

As he lay ensconced in the darkened room Lange worried that someone on the White House staff might have slipped and let the media know he was not in the Oval Office carrying out his daily responsibilities. In some press room a reporter would be busy writing a story that would be headlined: "President Felled by Tooth Extraction." Ridicule was their favorite weapon. Any weakness would be instantly flashed all over the world. In Russia, Obronsky would look more hungrily at the Baltics; in Japan, they would demand a greater trade edge; in the Middle East, borders would shift. After portraying him as weak, the media would hurry to blame him for the ensuing consequences. They had the advantage of morning, afternoon, and evening shows, specials and talk shows. There was no mistake in the people they chose to interview; the experts were *their* experts. So far they had been kind to him, but all they cared about was making headline news. Robert knew if his mother carried out her threat, the press would have the Washington scoop of the century.

Once before Robert had run away but Coulter had insisted on bringing him back. "I can run away again," he thought. "Say I'm ill. Resign." He knew the media would ferret out his secret. There would be Senate hearings. Ted Coulter had pointed out he might face criminal charges and even be put in jail. His own legal knowledge confirmed that.

Lately he did not like to think about Ted. He had noticed the new confident swagger in Ted's walk, the frequency of his visits to the Oval Office, the way he often called him "Bobby" now instead of Mr. President. In confiding his dilemma to

Coulter, Robert had delivered himself. Yet he, himself, could not carry out the plan, and the only person he could rely on to accomplish it was a man who was not trustworthy. Robert Lange knew Coulter was following his instructions because Coulter would do anything for him, but Lange also knew what that kind of political loyalty would demand: he must be as faithful to Coulter as Coulter was to him. He knew himself well enough to know that was not possible.

He was becoming increasingly irritated with his pain and his self-imposed invalidism. It was too hot under the wool cover. His clothes were damp and wrinkled. He needed to shower and to rinse away the taste of blood from his mouth. He would see his mother again and explain why the Compassionate Care Bill was absolutely necessary. She had hinted that there was another reason, something else that was motivating her. He was afraid of discovering what that reason was.

V

The drive through Alexandria and into the Virginia countryside was pleasant this time of year. Ted Coulter was not a man particularly fond of nature, the enjoyment of which required being alone in remote places, but the warm spring breeze through the open window of his car was soothing and the comfortable sedan protected him from the hostile outdoors. He thought about continuing on to Fauquier County after he had completed his business. Fauquier County was where he had grown up and where his parents still lived. Their house was one of those pseudo-colonial mansions embellished with tall pillars and a sweeping circular driveway. Behind the house was a stable, for his mother still enjoyed riding with the local hunt. Both of his parents were Anglophiles. The house was full of British magazines: *Country Life*, *Harpers & Queen*, *Horse and Hound*. Every spring his parents made their annual trek to England for the Grand National. He had never forgotten his mother practicing her curtsy when she learned they would be there on the day Her Majesty attended.

He was glad he would not have to explain his visit to his parents. The truth was he wasn't up to their scrutiny. He was nervous about his mission, apprehensive about how deeply he was entangling himself with this hazardous scheme. His mother particularly would notice his uneasiness. She had a way of asking questions about his life that reduced him to a defensive incoherence.

None of his accomplishments had ever quite satisfied his parents. He had enrolled in the Virginia Military Institute because his family had been educated there since the Confederacy. His father served on the prestigious Board of Visitors of the Institute. He remembered his first visit at the Institute with the intimidating ridge of mountains in the background and the formidable mass of barracks where he would have to live as a cadet. His father had been anxious to show him around and explain everything: the New Market Monument where the Confederate soldiers lay, the parade ground, the Opening Hops.

Of the four new cadets in his room, he was the only one, with his short stature and pudgy figure, that looked ridiculous in his uniform. That first year he and all the new cadets were labeled "rat." Every morning they had to assemble in a "rat line," walking at rigid attention on a prescribed route inside the barracks. There were double-times up and down barracks stairs and school songs and yells to memorize. If he had been able to find someone in his class who hated it as much as he did, he might have survived, but the others seemed to thrive on the protocol and military-style discipline.

His first year, struggling with analytic geometry and German, he became depressed. He had never had a knack for languages or math. Desperate to pass the exam he had gone to a test with German verb forms inked on his hand. He thought his fellow cadets would be loyal to one another instead of the school. That was when he learned the unforgiving power of the Code of Honor. When he was reported and called before the Honor Court he did not know which he dreaded the most: acquittal, which meant he would have to stay on, or the alternative, a dishonorable dismissal. When the commandant read his dismissal, Ted was almost relieved but his father had been devastated. He was outraged that his son had marred the family's name. He could still hear his father's pronouncement on the day of the Honor Court's verdict: "I'm resigning my position on the Board of Visitors of the Institute, Ted. I will never set foot in VMI again." In all these years his father had never forgiven Ted.

Coulter had transferred to the University of Virginia, where he had finally found himself. He became a star in the Jefferson Literary and Debating Society. After graduation he stayed on to pursue law school, where he did fairly well. However, his academic achievements never quite lived up to his parents' expectations. He joined a Richmond law firm, but his parents were quick to point out that it was neither the most prestigious nor the oldest law firm in Richmond. He married an affable, attractive woman, but her parents belonged to no exclusive club, so Ted's own parents insisted the wedding reception be held at their club. Ted Coulter was Advisor to the President of the United States but he was not the president. It was a no-win situation with his parents—and always would be.

Despite his parents' disappointment, Ted Coulter was satisfied with his life. In law school Robert Lange had always been the golden boy, the one who was destined for great things. Everyone knew it. Yet Lange had picked him as his best friend and now Robert Lange, President of the United States, had entrusted his career, his entire future to him. Why should he want anything else? It was true Bobby had asked him to do something questionable, but he had asked it for a legitimate reason, for the good of the country. Hadn't he painfully learned at VMI that one's duty was to one's country? If he was unwilling to help the president through this personal crisis, he was sure there would be havoc throughout the land, a debacle a hundred times worse than Watergate.

Twenty minutes outside of Alexandria, Coulter turned off onto a two-lane road. The road followed a serpentine path to Singleton, which appeared to have the usual small-town combination of diminishing grace and ugly modernity. The storefronts were embellished with unsightly siding in garish colors. Where there had probably been a feed store and perhaps a general store there was now a tacky supermarket and a video shop. A diner advertised with the single commandment: "Eat." The old post office must have been torn down, for the present one was an architectural atrocity. It was built of cinder blocks and looked more like a bunker than a place of convenience. All along the main street, large old homes with vestiges of a former glory were quietly decaying; several were now apartments or rooming houses.

The house Coulter was looking for was one block east of the main street. The graceful old homes on Arnold Avenue were in somewhat better condition. There was a bed-and-breakfast sign hanging on the porch of one. A nursery school had a yard full of play equipment. Farther down the block was a shabby place with a Victorian cupola and yards of carpenter's lace. A sign in the front yard read: Bunge Nursing Home.

As Coulter rang the bell he saw the familiar pudgy faces peeking out from the soiled lace curtains, but it was a minute or two before the bell was answered. "They think they can up the ante if they don't look too eager." But he wouldn't forget those faces peering greedily from the window.

When Tom Bunge and his wife Liz finally greeted him they were friendly enough. "It's nice to see you again, Mr. Coulter." Their heartiness, and the strength of their grasp as each in turn wrung his hand, was suffocating. They were in their early fifties, but they had the round faces, bright eyes, and spritely manner of children. Children blown up into grotesque balloon creatures. Coulter was overcome by their size. It was hard to separate their bulk, but between them, he thought, they must have weighed five or six hundred pounds.

Ted tried not to look at the home's ugly interior, which Tom had told him on his earlier visit was the result of Liz's decorating skills. Clearly Liz had been busy. Frenzied was more like it. The living room was frosted with a variety of starched white doilies and aswirl with ribbons and ruffles. It was the Victorian age gone mad. An elderly woman in a wheel chair propelled herself into the room. "When's lunch? We ain't had lunch." She stared at Coulter. "Who're you?"

Liz reached for a pink glass candy jar and dumped its contents into the woman's lap. "Suck on those, Flora. Lunch'll be ready in a few minutes." She turned the wheelchair around and hastily pushed the woman away, leaving behind an unpleasant miasma of urine.

"We're anxious to show you how we followed your instructions," Tom said.

Suddenly Coulter felt an overwhelming desire to escape. He wanted to flee the house and its occupants. He was still young but someday he would be old. Grimly he agreed, "I'll look at the apartment you've fixed up for my mother. Nothing more will be necessary."

"Follow me, it's off the kitchen stairway. Private like you wanted. It's not connected with the rest of the house, and like we told you all our guests are either bedridden or in wheelchairs like Flora. They couldn't get to your mom."

Following them through the kitchen Coulter noticed a large pot of vegetable soup simmering on the stove. It smelled rather good and he felt a little better. At least Maida would have decent food. The narrow stairway that must once have been the servants' stairs led to a small bedroom, a pocket-sized sitting room with a television, and a bathroom. The door into the suite had a newly installed lock. All the rooms had been freshly papered and the woodwork painted white. The lampshades in the sitting room were festooned with bows. Pictures of kittens in beguiling poses hung on the walls. The bedroom with its ruffled curtains and spread looked more like a room for an eleven-year-old than a woman of fifty-nine, but at least it was clean. In marked contrast to the fresh paint and ruffles were the wrought-iron grills on the windows. Although he had ordered the grills, Coulter winced at the sight of them. They brought home what he was about to do.

After a cursory examination, Coulter felt satisfied with the arrangements and nodded approvingly, then said, "Please, let's sit down for a moment." He settled on the edge of the bed while Liz sat in a rocking chair. Tom brought a chair in from the sitting room, carrying it aloft in one massive hand.

Coulter turned to Liz, who never seemed to stop grinning. "You're sure you can give injections without any trouble? Mother has rather serious asthma and I expect moving her here may upset her and bring on an attack. It's possible she'll need a shot of adrenaline."

Liz put a hand on Coulter's knee and leaned toward him. "I think you're the best son in the world, the way you're so worried over everything. Of course I can give shots. I'm a registered LPN. You want to see my certificate?" she said, a coy smile turning the corners of her mouth.

It took all of Coulter's self-control not to rescue his knee from its captor. "That won't be necessary. I would like to tell you something of the nature of Mother's illness. As you can imagine, it's painful for me to have to go into it. But since you'll be the ones dealing with it, I think you should know. Especially since the symptoms are somewhat unsettling."

"There isn't much we haven't seen," Tom said, shrugging off Coulter's concern. Liz nodded her agreement, emphasizing their expertise along these lines by a friendly squeeze of Coulter's knee.

"I know you've heard of grandiose delusions." Their blank faces indicated that they had not. "You know, thinking you're Napoleon." Now they were with him. "Mother has a very strange delusion. She thinks she is the mother of the President of the United States."

Liz and Tom evidently thought this hilarious but caught themselves in the middle of their laughter. Tom's attempt to work his expression into something approaching seriousness was not lost on Coulter.

"I'm sorry, we shouldn't laugh. I'm sure her condition merits special care."

"Yes. That's why I've finally decided, given my position in the government, that I have to do something. She's read all about the president's childhood, so she's very convincing. The upsetting thing is that she is also very angry at the president. She blames him for everything. I'm sure she'll blame him for putting her here. In fact, she's written him some threatening letters and I'm terribly afraid of what she might do. That's why security is so important. If she attempted to harm the president I'd never forgive myself. The Secret Service followed up on those letters and as much as told me that if she weren't in a protective setting she might end up in jail. You can see why I would go to any length to avoid that."

At the mention of the Secret Service, Tom and Liz exchanged nervous glances. Their sympathetic expressions slid into worried frowns. Liz quickly withdrew her hand from Coulter's knee. "I don't know," Tom said guardedly. "You didn't mention the Secret Service when you called. Would they be coming around here?"

"Absolutely not," Coulter said. "They wouldn't even know where she was. Just that she was safe. Now, I'll be honest with you. Before entrusting my mother's care to someone else, I'm sure you understood it was necessary that I do a little investigating. I happened to run across some trouble you were in. I believe it was in Ohio. Something about strongly encouraging your patients to give you their Social Security checks to cash. I know how misunderstandings of that sort arise, and of course I would never mention it to the authorities here in Virginia. I don't know what it would do to your license. It will just be our secret."

The ruffles and swags on the curtains appeared to droop. Tom and Liz were silent. At last Tom said, "That sounds like a threat." His eyes were slits in his great round face, and his mouth twisted down into a sulk so that he looked like a moldering jack-o'-lantern.

"Absolutely not," Coulter said smoothly, pleased that he had gained the upper hand so quickly. "Don't misunderstand me. I merely want an adequate place for my mother, and I'm sure you want to run a profitable business. Now that we understand each other, I'm entirely satisfied and we needn't mention any of this again." Reaching into his coat pocket, Coulter pulled out an envelope. "I've brought payment for my mother's first month of care. I prefer to deal in cash. I don't suppose you mind?"

Liz's hand was back on Coulter's knee. She gave it a gentle squeeze. "We don't mind at all," she said as her husband quickly reached for the envelope.

Coulter drove down Pennsylvania Avenue on his way to his stylish home in Georgetown. He had no pressing reason to stop at the White House. Before leaving that afternoon he had cleared his desk, and Lange was hunkered down with Senator Jensen, who would be guiding Robert's Compassionate Care Bill through the Senate. When Lange decided it was time, Coulter would return to the Bunges' home on a much more difficult and dangerous journey.

He turned onto N Street. This evening he and Elly were taking the children to the D.C. Armory to see the Ringling Brothers' Circus. For the first time that day he felt himself begin to relax. When he pulled up in front of the house, lights were on in every room. He would have to have a talk with the children about conserving electricity. Still, the blaze of light in the darkening March evening made the house appear welcoming and festive, like a ship about to embark on a pleasure cruise. It was a haven from the mounting tension of the whole affair with Maida Lange. Coulter found he was actually looking forward with childish excitement to a night out with his family at the circus. Parking would be a nuisance at the Armory, and for a moment Coulter considered ordering a limousine from the White House pool but dismissed the temptation as unethical.

VI

O utside the meeting room in the Capitol the cameras were busy recording a fight that had broken out between two covens of elderly protesters, members of the American Association of Retired Persons (AARP) and members of the Patriotic Elderly Americans for Sacrifice (PEAS). It was disconcerting to see men and women who should be bouncing grandchildren on their knees slamming one another with canes and outsized pocketbooks. One woman who looked ninety brought her sharp knee well into the groin of an intervening guard. A distinguished white-haired gentleman in a blue blazer and gray flannel slacks lowered his head and butted an African American woman who was holding a sign that read: Compassionate CARE IS NO CARE.

The Compassionate Care Bill was a bipartisan effort supported by a reluctant majority in the congress. The Health Care Bill passed in a previous administration had spun out of control. Billions were once again being channeled into defense as a result of a series of mounting world crises: the rise of the fundamentalists in the Middle East, the incursions of North Korea into the south with the threat of a nuclear attack, and, most troublesome, the coup of Communist revisionists in the Commonwealth of Independent States who were lusting after the Baltics and Ukraine and consequently had taken to calling itself the Soviet Union again. As the baby boomers aged, entitlements were burgeoning. The alarming fact was that not only had the deficit soared, but the country was running out of money for Social Security checks.

President Lange had called a committee of congressional leaders together to address the issues. To show his good faith, rather than have them come to the Oval Office, he had come to Capitol Hill, where he held a series of meetings in the elaborately embellished President's Room. The committee, hailed by the press as The Slashers, had revised The National Health Care Plan, reducing benefits. But it was the Compassionate Health Care Bill with its controversial Triage classification that was inciting the most furor. There was the Exclusion Section which mandated a cutback in health services available to those age sixty-five and older. The country appeared to be accepting the White House spin calling for older citizens to sacrifice for their children and grandchildren. It was becoming fashionable for older people to announce proudly that they were refusing heart by-pass surgery or hip replacements. Organ transplants for older patients had been unacceptable ever since PEAS coined the phrase: "Have a Heart, Refuse a Part."

Under close government scrutiny hospitals were drastically scaling back the care given to the elderly. In spite of the opposition of physicians, Euthanasia Houses were springing up across the country.

Massachusetts was serving as a prototype for the AIDS Segregation Component of the Bill. At first there had been considerable opposition from gay-rights advocates. However, all but the most vocal of the activists had been satisfied by the attractive apartments—many of which had been furnished by the country's leading decorators—the lure of the best health and nursing care available, and the promise that drug addicts with AIDS would be housed at a separate facility several miles away.

Unlike the proposed federal program, the Massachusetts model had begun as a voluntary program, although any AIDS patient who would not agree to participate in the program was cut off from state or federally financed health care. A silent agreement existed within the committee that the federal program would not be able to replicate the quality of housing or the health care of the Massachusetts model, which was even now being cut back.

The Child Licensing Section, whereby all fetuses must undergo gene examination, had become the most controversial aspect of the entire program. The legislation had instigated mandatory abortion for all fetuses genetically predisposed certain conditions, including but not limited to schizophrenia, Alzheimers, Huntington chorea, mental retardation, Tay-Sachs, muscular dystrophy, and Down's Syndrome. A child inadvertently brought to term suffering from any of those diseases was automatically dropped from any benefits in the health care system. It was rumored that as soon as the gene technology was sufficiently developed, the list would be expanded to include multiple sclerosis, diabetes, and any cancer that would eventually require expensive surgery.

Six senators bracketed by guards hurried into the meeting room, waving away the gauntlet of reporters. The chairman, Walter Jensen from North Dakota, appeared worried over the fisticuffs between AARP and PEAS. He had all but promised the president the hearing on Bill S. 80321 would go smoothly. But ever since the vice president had told NBC the Bill "had compassion only for the healthy," the Bill, formally titled the Compassionate Care Bill, was now being touted by the media as the No Care Bill.

Jensen did not like controversy. When his name came up it was often in association with a story once told by a former chairman of Jensen's committee about the great compromiser, Senator Russell Long. There was a town in Louisiana that was searching for a geography teacher. Half the school board thought the world was flat and half thought it was round. To be a successful applicant a two-thirds vote of the board was needed.

There were three applicants for the job. The first one went in to be interviewed and when he came out, the other two asked, "Have you got the job?"

"No," he said.

"Why?" they asked him.

"Because I teach the world is round."

The second applicant went in and came out. He was asked if he got the job. "No," he said, "I told them I teach the world is flat."

The third applicant went in and came out and they asked, "Did you get the job?"

"Yes," he said. "I did."

"What was your answer?" they asked.

I told them, "I can teach it flat, or I can teach it round."

Walter Jensen's innate ability to compromise was not so much a gift as it was a ploy to assure his reelection and thus reassure his second wife. An easterner, she had told him after her first visit to North Dakota that if she had to live in the middle of nowhere she would divorce him. "Where are the trees?" she asked. "Where are the houses? There's nothing to hide behind."

The president had made himself clear to Jensen. "I'm counting on you, Jensen. The House is greased. All you have to do is get it through the Senate. We should have enough votes for a simple majority. It's imperative we get health care costs back down to fourteen percent of the GNP. With the national debt pushing six trillion, we're going to have to make choices. And the only way to sell it to those geezers is to convince them that by refusing health care they'll be giving something back to their country. To help make the point I've arranged for a meeting with PEAS this afternoon in the Rose Garden with media coverage."

Jensen glanced back over his shoulder at the melee of elderly combatants, which appeared to be escalating, and wondered how a few black eyes would look on the evening news.

Accompanying Jensen were five other senators, four of whom he was fairly certain he had in his pocket. Senator Earl Trager from Illinois had come to politics from corporate law. For Trager the bottom line was profitability for business. He held the all-time record for PAC money. Businesses were alarmed over their rising health care costs. Clearly the

Compassionate Care Bill would be in their interests. Trager knew that, and used it to his advantage.

Monica Mott was in her first term and flattered to even be on the committee. She had come to the Senate straight from Hollywood. She was an actress whose movie career had been on the wane. During an interview she made a flippant remark that politicians "are nothing but actors with terrible scripts and bad directors." An irate senator challenged her to run herself if she felt that way. She did and won by a landslide. After her election she caused quite a stir by hiring almost her entire staff from the homeless plucked from the streets near the Capitol. "They're giving me input," she said, "and I'm giving them jobs."

Senator Howard Draper had been returned to office repeatedly from Connecticut by a loyal constituency. He knew how to haggle and swap to get his voters what they wanted. The minute increases in military expenditures had been announced, Draper saw his window of opportunity and was on the phone with the president. The following day the Pentagon announced the reopening of a large Connecticut naval base. He had a vote for sale, the president had pork to offer, it was as simple as that.

Senator Kenneth Grant had started out as a county prosecutor in Virginia and worked his way up to Assistant to the Attorney General before coming to the Senate. If you could find it in a law book Grant would buy it. Grant's friends said he had never seen a law he didn't like. How the laws were arrived at, and what went into their making, meant nothing to him. "That's no more important," he said, "than the brushes and paint that go into a masterpiece."

Two days before the hearing, the president had called Grant to tell him that he had received confidential information that a Supreme Court Justice was dying of cancer. "We've got to put someone on the court that appreciates the law," the president had said. "I don't suppose you would consider…" The president gained another friend, and the political power-brokering of the Oval Office had won another vote for the Compassionate Care Bill.

The only senator of whom the chairman was unsure was Lillian Harris, an African American from Detroit. She was a scrappy older woman who reminded those who met her of their fifth-grade teacher who never let them get away with a thing. She had come to Congress after helping the governor of Michigan revolutionize a floundering welfare system. The evening news had shown a fast-paced clip of her storming into a house at eight A.M. to physically drag a man out of bed and drive him to work, and another shot of her scrubbing down a kitchen and preparing a nourishing dinner for a welfare mother and her children. Once, she was seen with a twelve-year-old turned over her knee while she administered a spanking for his skipping school.

* * *

HEARING
before the
COMMITTEE ON
LABOR AND HUMAN RESOURCES
UNITED STATES SENATE
on
S. 80321

Printed for the use of the Committee on
Labor and Human Resources

The committee met, pursuant to notice, at 9:32 AM in room SD-430, Dirksen Senate Office Building, Senator Walter Jensen (chairman of the committee) presiding.

Present: Senators Jensen, Mott, Trager, Harris, Draper, Grant.

OPENING STATEMENT OF SENATOR JENSEN THE CHAIRMAN. The Committee will come to order.

Our hearing today will focus on the triage section of S. 80321, the Compassionate Care Bill. This is the fourth and the final hearing held by our committee on the Bill. I believe this hearing will provide us with a realistic estimate of the true costs and benefits of the Bill.

Senator MOTT. Mr. Chairman.

CHAIRMAN. The Senator from California.

Senator MOTT. I would like us to be totally aware of how with just a little bit of sacrifice on the part of everyone, we'll save enough money to do a lot of really good things for those people truly in need. Spending a lot of money to make older people more healthy or to bring into this world babies who have something wrong with them leaves less and less in resources for the poor and homeless. In fact, from firsthand experience with my own staff, I happen to know that many of the homeless are mentally ill, so if they had undergone a gene check years ago they wouldn't be a financial burden today.

Senator TRAGER. Mr. Chairman.

CHAIRMAN. The Senator from Illinois.

Senator TRAGER. I feel a responsibility to speak up for the hundreds of thousands of business men and women out there who work hard to make this country what it is. Saddling them with escalating health care costs for every man, woman, and child is driving them into bankruptcy. Let us look at the facts. People over the age of seventy-five are the fastest growing group in America. Most of the visits to doctors are made by the elderly. Older people consume twice as much medication as all other age groups combined. They fill 40 percent of the nation's hospital beds. Eighty percent of all heart attacks and 60 percent of all cancer deaths strike Americans sixty-five or older. I am pleased to see that some older Americans are unselfish enough to forgo medical treatment, but I'm afraid that, unless we make it compulsory, it will not have a measurable impact on health care costs. If businesses could take some of the money that goes into financing the health care of their former employees now on pensions and invest it in new expansion, the unemployment index would drop to zero.

Senator DRAPER. Mr. Chairman.

CHAIRMAN. The Senator from Ohio.

Senator DRAPER. I want to concur with my esteemed colleagues and add a little point of my own. We ought to look at this Bill for what it is—a compassionate bill. How many of us have been saddened to see those dying of AIDS, or children with severe handicaps, or the elderly in ill health lingering on. It is out of our sadness and compassion for these people that we wish to end their misery and suffering. As you know, I sponsored the Euthanasia House Safe Haven Bill which has enabled us to set up Safe Havens all across the country for those who wish a quick and dignified death. Painless, of course. In this and every other opportunity to show compassion, I have been at the forefront of progress. I applaud the president and the Congress for having the courage to face the issue head on and to propose the Compassionate Care Bill.

Senator GRANT. Mr. Chairman.

CHAIRMAN. The Senator from Virginia.

Senator GRANT. I understand we are going to hear from a gentleman from the ACLU this morning opposing the Child Licensing and the AIDS Sections. I just want to say that I bow to no one in my respect for the law. The protection of the law, ladies and gentlemen, has been my life. I find nothing to suggest the Compassionate Care Bill is not constitutional. I wish to remind you we have now performed fifty million legal abortions in this country, and the majority of those fetuses, most likely, were normal and medically sound. Where then is the legal argument against ending the life of fetuses who do *not* meet our standards or who, after Gene Investigation, prove they will eventually become a liability to society?

As for AIDS Segregation, we can see how effective that has proven in Massachusetts. Since the High-Rise, Low-Risk AIDS Sanctuaries have been enforced, new HIV cases are almost nil. Speaking to the legal basis of this Bill, let me remind you that similar cases have recently gone before the

Supreme Court and have had successful outcomes. The court, quite correctly, mind you, has put the welfare of the general public above the demands of special interest groups.

Senator HARRIS. Mr. Chairman.

CHAIRMAN. The senator from Michigan, although I must remind the senator that time is moving on and we have an obligation to hear our witnesses.

Senator HARRIS. Mr. Chairman, I don't recall you cautioning the other senators about a shortage of time. I trust our esteemed chairman is not singling me out.

CHAIRMAN. I assure the senator I am not. We will be pleased to hear whatever our esteemed colleague has to say.

Senator HARRIS. That's fine because I mean to take as much time as necessary. This legislation is known in the press as the No Care Bill. That is a euphemism for murder.

CHAIRMAN. I would like to admonish the spectators that applause will not be tolerated in this committee room. With all due respect, Senator Harris, I hope you will moderate your rhetoric.

Senator HARRIS. Senator, if you will not moderate this Bill, I will not moderate my rhetoric. Like many of you in this room, I attended Sunday school. Our minister taught us that there are sins of commission and sins of omission, and they are both sins. What this Bill proposes are sins of commission and sins of omission, and they are both sins.

Many families in America have a television, a VCR, and a computer in their home at a combined cost of a couple of thousand dollars. Sixty years ago who would have imagined any of these luxuries, let alone thought of spending that much money on them. Technology has given us medical miracles. Yes, they are expensive, and yes, we may have to squeeze our budget to get them, but what is wrong with spending money on health? Who, if they had to choose between more material things and good health and a longer life, would not choose the latter? We should not deny *anyone* that choice. As to the esteemed Senator Trager's announcement that "80 percent of all heart attacks and sixty percent of all cancer deaths strike Americans sixty-five or older," of course they do. That is how most older people die. What is his point? That older people shouldn't die, or that they ought to die from something else? And if something else, I'd like him to tell us exactly what he has in mind.

CHAIRMAN. If there are any further outbursts of applause on the part of the spectators, I will have the room cleared.

Senator HARRIS. As to the High-Rise, Low-Risk AIDS Sanctuaries in Massachusetts, you are all aware of the bill I have cosponsored to outlaw such discriminatory abominations. Likewise, the Child Licensing Section is completely unacceptable. You will note that buried in the verbiage of that section, one of the criteria for the licensing of a child before it can be born is the availability of a suitable home. I have heard that there is some debate as to whether single parent families will meet those criteria. Do you know how many African American babies would be denied licenses? This Bill will decimate the African American populace. I tell you, Mr. Chairman, this is not a bill. This is a license to kill!

CHAIRMAN. I would request the Sergeant at Arms remove the group in the last row who are exhibiting the kind of poor manners that we will not tolerate in this hearing room. Thank you.

Now after what I must regretfully call an immoderate and exaggerated presentation by my esteemed colleague, Senator Harris, I want to put this hearing in its proper frame of reference. Only last month our government made its final Savings and Loan bailout payment of sixty billion dollars. Next month a bill comes due of eighty billion on the shortfall in pension plans. Our national debt has soared. Paying the interest on that debt requires eighteen percent of the government's budget. While we now have health care for everyone, our costs since 1991 have nearly doubled. And for this year of 2002 we are projecting the costs will represent nearly thirty percent of the nation's Gross National Product.

I would like to take this opportunity to commend the president for the strong position he is taking in support of the Compassionate Care Bill. He has put the country's welfare first and so, I might add, have the Patriotic Elderly Americans for Sacrifice. To show our deep respect for this group, I am inviting them to be honored guests in our hearing room to take the place of the disorderly, and, if I may say so, the unpatriotic group we have ousted. Later today I understand they will meet with the president. Now I would like to call our first distinguished expert.

VII

Maida stood at the window watching for her son. He would not simply appear as any other son would do. There would be the usual carnival procession of media, police, and Secret Service agents. In these last days she had argued with God. She did not see how she could take from her son, whom she loved, the very thing that was life itself to him. Yet for his sake she knew she must. She thought back all those years to the evening of her son's funeral. Would God ever forgive her for not being strong enough then to oppose Peter? Her weakness had now led to this impossible confrontation. She had kept something from Robert. Telling him might make all the difference. If not, what would Robert do? She could not be sure, but of one thing she was certain. He would never forgive her for taking the presidency away from him.

The limousine drove along the cobblestone streets of Alexandria, along Cameron Street past Christ Church, where George Washington had worshiped; past Carlyle House and its gardens, where the crocuses were wilting and the tulips bravely pushing up; past the boyhood home of Robert E. Lee. Lange recalled those days when as a child he had walked these streets with his father while Peter Lange recounted the fascinating history of the places they passed.

Robert Lange tried not to think about his childhood. Life had become tolerable only when he was finally able to go away to school and begin the journey that had culminated in the fulfillment of his father's dream. At home he had been the battleground for his mother and father's constant disagreements. They had grappled for his soul—and his father had won. It was his father's drive and ambition that had catapulted him over every obstacle to gain this extraordinary prize.

And now, if his mother went public with her threat, everything he had fought for would be lost. All the sacrifices he had made, and all he had endured to reach the most envied position in the world would have been for nothing. Robert was furious that his mother would dare try to take the presidency away from him as though she were keeping him from some dangerous toy.

The motorcade pulled up in front of one of the red brick town houses. It was an odd way to visit one's mother, with a police escort, two cars full of Secret Service agents, an ambulance, and several vans crowded with media. The president knew his mother hated having the motorcade parked in front of her house. Robert would like to have arrived in something less noticeable, but the Detail Leader had been adamant. "Sir, if we think it necessary to airlift the limousine to California when you're there, it doesn't make much sense not to have you take it when you're only traveling fifteen miles from the White House." The Secret Service cars that bracketed the limousine emptied as the agents deployed around the house. The media vans got as close as the agents allowed and proceeded to set up cameras, hoping for a shot of mother and son. Reporters had often speculated why the president's mother was so reclusive.

Robert, enclosed in a phalanx of agents, walked up the path and knocked on the door. It was one of the few doors in the world where he would be kept waiting and where his welcome would be one of indifference. For the thousandth time he wished his father had lived to see him sworn in as president: what a different welcome his father would have for him if he were here.

Maida Lange opened the door and frowned at the agents who were unsuccessfully trying to melt into the shrubbery. She winced as one of the men's shoes crunched the fragile tip of an emerging hyacinth. "It's like a circus, Robert," she said, trying to keep a querulous note from her voice.

For a moment Robert Lange was overcome with regret and guilt for what he was about to do. That aging, irritable, still surprisingly handsome woman had once been his only refuge, his sanctuary. Countless times he had wanted to run to her arms for comfort when his father had pushed him to his limits and beyond. Impulsively Lange kissed his mother's cheek. She was nearly as tall as he and so coldly unresponsive that it was less a gesture of affection than a kind of salute from one determined warrior to another.

They walked through the living room. While his father had been alive, it had been somber and dignified, a fitting decor for the ambition he had set for his son. After her husband's death Maida had filled the rooms with odd, disparate things to which she had taken a fancy. It had become an inimitable collage all her own. It was, Robert thought, her way of getting rid of the last traces of his father.

Lange followed his mother into the small library with its neat rows of books that filled four walls of shelves. Old memories cast a shadow over his thoughts. It was in this room that all family matters had been settled, as though the wisdom of the books lent themselves to the decisions. His mother settled into a chair behind the desk, where a folder lay, as though awaiting attention. Seating himself at the wrong end of the desk, Lange felt his power drain away.

It was the impotence he had experienced again and again in his father's presence. Every evening after dinner—on Saturdays, even on Sunday, which had no significance for his father—Robert would be summoned into the library. He would find his father at his desk, wearing a cardigan sweater in the winter, a long-sleeved sport shirt buttoned to the top in the summer. Behind the wire-rimmed glasses, his father's eyes were amiable, his smile encouraging. "Well, Robert, today let us hear what you think of the Federalist Papers—Bismark, Machiavelli, the War of 1812, the Confederacy. Let us hear the difference between a democracy and a republic, between freedom and anarchy." Often his father spent hours exalting Plato's Republic. "'The perfect state,'" his father told him, "'is that which is ruled by the perfect man. That man is the philosopher statesman to whom it is given to know the absolute truth about ruling over a society. Such a man will from his early childhood be in all things first among all. Only then,' Plato says, 'will the cities have rest from their evils.'"

Peter Lange had read widely in Freud and Jung and Adler, but he was dismissive of them. "All that endless preoccupation with the self... those people are like pigs rooting around in the dirt," he told Robert. It was the psychologist J. B. Watson whom Peter Lange most admired. "The man says if he is given a healthy infant he can train him to become anything he wishes, 'doctor, lawyer, artist, merchant-chief, and yes even beggar-man and thief.' And why not President of the United States, Robert?" his father would add, with a gleam in his eye.

Peter Lange was insistent in his teaching, but he was not a cruel man. He would often stop and, looking tenderly at Robert, ask, "You are not fatigued? Let's see what Momma has in the cookie jar. Shall I have her make you some hot chocolate?" Often he would urge Robert, "Argue against me," but when Robert would try his father would easily win the argument. After a while Robert no longer challenged his father.

In good weather his father would drive him to Mount Vernon or Monticello where the environs of the country's fathers, Washington and Jefferson, were rich with incitement. "You will be even greater," his father told him, "for you will have prepared for this all of your life."

Robert's first year of schooling had been taught by Maida at the sunny kitchen table. His father had said, "You are not well, Robert. You must stay home for a year until you gain your strength back." Robert had not felt ill, but since his father was a doctor he believed him. After that first year his mother had tried to sit with Robert and his father in the library after school, but if she attempted to say something, his father would admonish her, "The beginning is the most important part of any work, Maida. Plato writes, 'Especially in the case of a young and tender thing; for that is the time at which the character is being formed and the desired impression is more readily taken.' It is best if you leave us and let us get on with our lessons."

At first Robert had resented having his mother sent away, but soon he became used to her absence. As soon as Robert and Peter began their daily session, she would go outside into her garden as though the very house were infected. To pass time, she had developed an interest in propagating irises, flowers which were named after the Greek goddess of the rainbow. By crossbreeding different varieties she devised whole palettes of rainbow colors. When her seedlings began to cover the kitchen counters and work their way into the rest of the house, his father had a garden shed with a small attached greenhouse built for her. He was obviously pleased to have her busy and out of the house.

There were times when Robert heard his mother and father arguing with each other. Often it was over religion. "Why must you destroy his faith?" Maida would plead.

"Your Christianity is full of humility and guilt," Peter accused. "How can you make a great leader of someone who is humble and guilty? A great leader must be a rational man, a man who looks to science for answers. I ask you if our men in the space station have seen a god or angels floating about? I won't have you filling the boy's head with your silly notions."

"Any leader who believes there is no one over him is a dangerous, lethal man," she had insisted. "He will be a Stalin or a Hitler. A man who believes in God will know how to doubt. Without having experienced doubt and uncertainty in his own belief, the people he rules will never be able to challenge him when he's wrong—or worse, cruel."

Robert had hated these arguments, for his mother, when upset, would wheeze and become short of breath. He was terrified that someday a severe asthma attack would kill her. Even now, all these years later, he saw from her rapid shallow breathing that she was still suffering from the asthma that had frightened him so as a child.

Once, he had innocently brought into the house a dog that had followed him home. He was unprepared for his mother's sudden reaction to the small animal. As she ran from the room, his father shouted to him to get the dog out of the house. He watched in fear as his mother struggled for each breath and was rushed to the hospital. Later, when they returned, his father explained to him that his mother was severely allergic to animal dander. Robert remembered how guilty he had felt as a little boy, believing he had nearly killed his mother.

She broke into his reverie. "What have you come to tell me, Robert?"

She was clutching her inhaler. He would not let himself feel guilty, telling himself that it was his mother's doing, that after all of these years she had no business trying to influence him. What did she know of governmental affairs? In supporting the Compassionate Care Bill, he had the best brains in the country on his side and most of the Congress. He felt as though she were punishing him, as though he were a child again. In all of his years of returning home, this was the first time that his mother had not hurried into the kitchen for cookies or coffee cake, some special treat she had ready for him. It appeared the only thing she had prepared for this visit was the menacing folder that lay waiting between them on the desk.

Robert looked at his mother. He tried to put on the beguiling smile he had turned on her when he was asking for a two-wheeler, but he had a feeling she would not be beguiled anymore.

"Mother, please reconsider. The country is in danger."

"It is the danger for the country that concerns me, Robert," she said.

"Mother, you just don't understand," Lange tried again. "It's our country's safety I'm most concerned about. The

Middle East is a virtual tinderbox ready to explode. There are incursions nearly every day into South Korea. Singapore and Japan are close to war. And, between you and me, there's a military junta in Russia that is threatening to send missile launchers into Cuba unless we give them more aid. We are going to have to spend billions to rearm and there is no money. We spent the peace dividend long ago. If we don't find that money somewhere, we are placing the economic stability of this country in real danger.

"The health system is killing us. People won't stand for more taxes. We have a debt of five trillion dollars. The Compassionate Care Bill is the only way to cut expenditures, and Congress means to pass it. And if I don't go along with it, they won't give me a penny for defense...."

Robert saw the determined look on his mother's face and decided to try a different approach. "Mother, you don't understand these things. They are beyond you. Why after all of these years are you involving yourself in politics—and why the Compassionate Care Bill?"

Maida sat up very straight. "Robert, it is very terrible to me that I cannot trust my son, but your father made of you a machine, and machines cannot be trusted. Believe me, I love you. I pray for you every day. I would give my life for you—and I may have to."

Robert winced, but she seemed not to notice.

"Robert, I have gone over the legislation a hundred times. If you pass this Bill, you will be sending people to their death: the elderly, the mentally ill, the handicapped, the people with AIDS. I cannot allow that. Once, you talked about rationing health care; now you speak of triage, of picking and choosing which human beings can live and which have to die. What will be next? You want to play God, but you don't have God's compassion and mercy.

"I am going to tell you something tonight your father made me keep from you." From the window of the library, Maida could see one of the Secret Service agents patrolling the yard. She leaned toward Lange, lowering her voice. "You believe my grandfather—your great-grandfather—was simply a little-known doctor outside of Berlin. You were told he died of a heart attack shortly after the war. Your father forbade me to speak of my grandfather's real history for fear the truth of his atrocities might become known. He knew full well the grandson of a murderer would never be elected president."

"Murderer! What are you saying?" Robert had meant to keep control of the evening, thinking he was prepared for anything. Her terrible words caught him off guard.

"When my father died I discovered locked away all of my grandfather's papers. My grandfather was the head of a mental hospital outside of Berlin. He was well-known in his field for his dedicated work on epilepsy and brain edema. He was not a zealot, but he and many other psychiatrists had evidently read a very popular book at the time.

"*The Release of the Destruction of Life Devoid of Value* was written by a psychiatrist, Alfred Hoche, and a jurist, Karl Binding. I held the book in my own hands. This book, written long before Hitler rose to power, helped to enact the despicable compulsory sterilization law of 1933, the year Hitler was appointed chancellor. By the middle of the thirties, my grandfather and many other respected psychiatrists had destroyed the lives of thousands of mentally ill patients—'useless eaters' they were called—in the name of 'eugenics' and 'euthanasia.' I saw records from my grandfather's hospital that told of a *Kinderhaus,* a place where mentally ill and retarded children were kept before they were murdered." Maida paused, struggling for breath, her hands clenched to prevent their trembling.

Appalled at what he was hearing and afraid of what was to come, Lange made a gesture to stop her, but she paid it no attention, hurrying on as though eager to get the tale over with.

"In 1941 at the psychiatric hospital in Hadamar, they celebrated the cremation of the ten thousandth mental patient. Psychiatrists, nurses, attendants, and secretaries all received a bottle of beer to celebrate the occasion. In Berlin there was even a special office, the Central Accounting Office, to keep meticulous records of the mental patients that were being eliminated. My father used to see my grandfather preparing detailed reports for that central office. Robert, by the end of the war 275,000 psychiatric patients had been systematically killed. And not by Nazi monsters, but by some of the best-known psychiatrists in the whole of Germany. That is what your Compassionate Care Bill will lead to, Robert. Hundreds of thousands will be done away with because it saves money for the state."

Lange's mind reeled as he thought of the political repercussions if this sordid history were to get out during the debate on the Compassionate Care Bill. He would be finished. At first he refused to believe such a monstrous story about his own flesh and blood. Then he remembered a picture of his great-grandmother that sat on his mother's dresser. Once, he had taken it out of the frame and examined it. One side of the photograph had been cut off. He had never thought to ask why. Now he knew.

"What happened to him?" Suddenly, he had a horrifying vision of the man rising up before them, his hands dripping with the blood of thousands of innocent victims. "What happened to your grandfather?" He could not bring himself to call the man "my great-grandfather."

Maida shook her head and then went on. "Deep inside he must have always known what he did was wrong. When the war finally came to an end and the truth became known, he began to see his wicked deeds through the eyes of the conquering nations. The world was appalled, and the Nuremberg Trials began. All the excuses fell away, and the horror of what he had done overwhelmed him. He committed suicide. He was not the only one. Many psychiatrists took their lives."

"Why doesn't anyone know about your grandfather?"

"Your father always insisted we refer to him only as a doctor with a modest practice in a small German town. No one has ever thought to investigate further. But I will tell everything that I have just told to you to the rest of the world, Robert—in addition to your real identity. The records are all here in this folder. I will wait no longer. I must have your promise tonight that you will oppose this legislation."

Robert's dignity was stripped away. He was no longer a world leader but a frightened child, numbed by what he had just heard. He found himself pleading, "Mother, you more than anyone should understand what I've gone through to get where I am. When other children were out playing, Dad made me sit here in this room memorizing the Constitution. When my friends were all dating, I had to stay home and read Plato. You remember when I brought a B home from college? Dad wouldn't speak to me for days. After all those years of suffering, I deserve this reward! My whole life was controlled by his ambition—and now you want to take it all away from me over some silly legislation."

"It is not silly legislation." Her voice flattened into a dangerous monotone. "It will do exactly what your great-grandfather did. He meant well. He thought he knew what was good for Germany, for the human race. He wanted a better world. Those people were costing Germany too much; there was no money for arms. Isn't that exactly what you told me tonight?"

"Robert," she said in a softer voice, "no one knows better than I what your father did to you. I hated him for it, and I would have left him long ago. But if I had, he would have kept you from me. I couldn't bear it. He would have taken me to court and proved me mentally unstable, an unfit mother. Rosa, who worked for us for so many years, worshiped him. She would have testified to my shutting myself up in my room. I did that at times when I couldn't control my worry over what your father was doing to you.

"I have told you about my grandfather. I had nightmares about him, and the pharmacist kept records of the tranquilizers your father generously prescribed for me to keep me from those nightmares that haunted me from the past and to prevent me from interfering with his plans for you. Your father would even have found a way to have me hospitalized in order to keep on with his scheme. He was a man with a *Besessenheit.*" The old German word for obsession came easily as though it had never left her mind.

Robert flushed at the irony. His mother was accusing his father of doing exactly the thing that he, himself, even now planned to perpetrate on her. He had thought himself rid of his father, and yet with horror he realized that even in death his father's influence was still there leading him, telling him what he must do.

Maida rose from the old walnut desk and walked over to Robert. Placing her hands on his shoulders, she rested her face against the softness of his hair. "Sometimes I think that if our second son had lived, you would have been spared to me. Johann, you must know I am doing this to save your soul. I won't let you commit such sins. That Bill is as bad as murder."

His body stiffened. The words "sin" and "soul" meant nothing to him but superstition, something his father had taught him to fight against. "Don't ever call me by that name," he said, his voice like ice.

Sensing his determination, she walked back to the desk, opened the folder, and handed it to him. "This is the release I will give to the papers tomorrow morning unless you promise me tonight that you will oppose your Compassionate Care Bill."

He read it slowly. It was all there and irrefutable. He was surprised at how thorough a job she had done. Somehow these last years he had let himself almost believe the whole thing was a dream, yet she had verified everything to the last detail. Not only would this finish his presidency; it would mean the end of everything. No one would touch him if this got out. He would probably go to jail. Staring at her, he told himself that what he was about to do to his mother was for the benefit of the country, but his father's keen training on rational thinking kept him from believing it. "Let me talk with the leaders at Congress and with the party chairman. I don't want to discuss my answer over the phone from the White House, but I promise to send Ted Coulter here tomorrow by four with an answer. Surely you can give me that much time?"

She nodded. "It may be that some miracle will happen and you will change your mind. I will pray that that is so. Unlike you, Robert, I believe in miracles."

He had not been able to turn on the tape. He could not have taped such a conversation. Now as he rose to leave he fumbled with the switch, as though reaching for his pen, and flicked the on button. "I wish you would hire someone to help you with the housekeeping," he said. He stared at the immaculate bookshelves. "How long does it take you to dust these?" He attempted a grin.

She smiled bitterly. "I should throw them all out. These are the books with which your father prepared you. As to help with the housework, what else is there for me to do?"

"You could have been part of my life." His voice sounded more wistful than he meant it to. It still bothered him that his mother had not even come to his inauguration.

"Your life is built on a lie, Robert. How could I ever be a part of that?"

Robert Lange left the library without looking back. As he seated himself in the limousine, he switched off the recorder. His words and his name would have to be edited out. It wasn't much for Sheila Covell to go on, only a sentence or two, but the anger in his mother's voice would certainly support the story of the disturbed woman with delusions about her son that Coulter had made up for the actress.

For a moment, he thought about simply telling the truth and resigning. Yet he was the leader of a great country, a country that needed him in these desperate times. He looked out of the window at the trail of media personnel. He grimaced at what they would make of his mother's story. They'd have no mercy with the fact that he had been born in Germany and thus was ineligible to be president, not to mention the nefarious deeds of his great-grandfather. Resignation was impossible. The resulting scandal would be devastating. Any woman who dared threaten him as his mother had must be mad and deserved to be locked up. He could almost hear his father's voice, "Isn't that why you were elected? To protect the country."

As the limousine crossed the bridge into the capital, Lange picked up his phone. Coulter answered on the first ring. "Go ahead with the plans," Lange said coldly. He felt as if his father were sitting beside him telling him as he always had, "You must keep your goal in mind, Robert. You must do whatever it takes to reach it."

VIII

Vice President Ranta picked up the phone by his hospital bed to find the president on the line.

"How are you doing, Ranta? I asked my office to check with the hospital there at Walter Reed to be sure you have everything you need."

Ranta gritted his teeth. "That's very kind of you, Mr. President."

"And I had a little talk with your doctor. He tells me you're getting along very well."

"Do I detect a note of disappointment in your voice, Mr. President?"

"Now, Ranta, why don't you just forget politics for a couple of weeks and concentrate on getting well. Sorry, I have to hang up now. I'm taping an interview on the Compassionate Care Bill. Just remember what I said. Forget about politics."

Ranta fumed. The president knew perfectly well with his allusion to the Bill he was waving a red flag in front of an angry bull. "The little fool thinks he can keep me here thrashing around in a hospital bed while he does his dirty work." Ranta knew rumors and leaks were already emanating from "sources in the White House" that Vice President T. Russell Ranta had suffered a severe stroke, was about to undergo bypass surgery, was near death. He was sure every one of the rumors had been planted in order to diminish his power. Ranta knew how the game was played. What politician would bother to support a man who might not be around the next day when you needed a favor returned?

The doctors had declared the angioplasty a complete success and detached the monitors, promising Ranta he would be out in a few days and back to his office. He meant to leave in ten minutes, as soon as the nurse came in with his medication. Shortly after that there'd be a change of duty, and the incoming shift of nurses would be occupied for fifteen minutes or so reviewing patient charts. Even now, standing at the window, he could see the cars of the afternoon shift pulling into the employee parking lot and the employees in their uniforms moving like a white wave toward the hospital entrance. He allowed himself a moment to speculate on what life would be like if he were responsible for nothing more than a manageable job, one in which he did not need to lie or manipulate people for that extra ounce of power or make decisions at whose dreadful consequences he could only guess.

Looking out the window from the confines of the hospital, Ranta thought that the spring day seemed a picturesque postcard of a foreign land. He was impatient to escape and, in spite of all he had been through in the last week, felt surprisingly strong. When his wife had died, he had wanted to die as well. He had even considered taking his own life at the time. Now he wanted very much to live to oppose Robert Lange. He considered Shakespeare's warning, "How oft when men are at the point of death have they been merry." It was the fight against the upcoming legislation that gave him a reason to hang on. He had a vague feeling that God had spared him to send him like David into the battle against the Goliath of the Washington establishment. He welcomed the fight. It gave a renewed purpose to his life. The realization that the odds were against him only made Ranta more anxious for the battle.

He had called party leaders. Just as he had suspected, the ones up for reelection in the fall were all going along with Lange on the Compassionate Care Bill. The only reason they supported the Bill was because Lange held all the reins of power. They hoped to ride his coattail of success into another term. Even the party chairman was on Lange's side. "Ranta," Jules Foster had said, "you know everyone's been taxed to death. Cuts in health care are crucial. It's the only viable solution. Anyhow, you shouldn't be worrying about that in your condition. Lie back and relax. If anything happened to you, we might have Ralph Prentice trying to fill your shoes."

Ranta had flinched at the thought. Prentice was the Speaker of the House, a man so dull that it was said when a TV reporter stuck a microphone in front of his face, you could hear the click of every remote control in the country.

Ranta had heard a rumor that some members of the opposition party were drafting a statement against the Bill, but, having been a loyal party man all of his life, he hoped he wouldn't have to cross over. Even for this. A few of the churches and some of the Jewish organizations were speaking out. He might see what support he could gather there, but the president had admonished the attorney general that if the churches and synagogues continued their action against the Bill, the government would initiate efforts to rescind their tax-exempt status.

Ranta had made his own statement from the hospital, "Since the Compassionate Care Bill isn't in effect, I've received the same good care as a forty-year-old." The remark was taken as a joke and hadn't received much publicity, but it opened the door a little. When he got out he could follow it up on the morning shows and the call-in programs.

The most unsettling thing had been the phone call a few days ago from the president's mother. In the whole time he had been in office, Ranta had never set eyes on her. Yet there she was on the other end of the phone telling him how important it was to see that everyone, young and old, got good health care. "And the mentally ill," she had insisted. "You must not forget them. I have called because I read the statements you have made against the Bill. You are a brave man to go against your party and your president."

"You're pretty brave yourself to oppose your son," said Ranta, surprised at the woman's conviction.

"I have hopes my son will change his mind," she answered somewhat enigmatically.

He wanted to tell her there was no chance of that, but he

merely thanked her for the call, wondering if she were a little dotty. There was talk about her never being seen in public, never appearing at political functions, and not even attending her own son's inauguration. At the time of the inauguration, the president's press secretary had said that Lange's mother had severe asthma and the January weather would have been too much for her. Ranta recalled reading somewhere that a librarian in her neighborhood had said on the day of the inauguration Maida Lange had come in for her weekly supply of books and apparently had been completely well.

After talking with Maida, Ranta had not been able to resist the chance to tweak the lion's tail. In a phone conversation with the president, he had casually mentioned Maida Lange's call. "How come your mother has a lot more sense than you have?" There had been a long, deadly silence on the line. The president's irritation had cheered Ranta. He decided that when he got out of the hospital he would run over to Alexandria where the woman lived and pay her a visit. He smiled with pleasure at the thought of how mad that would make Robert Lange.

A nurse wearing a white slack suit walked in with a small tray of medications. Ranta feigned a wicked look. "How come you girls don't wear skirts and little caps anymore like real nurses?"

"Caps and skirts don't make *girls* into nurses. Putting up with patients like you is the real test."

He laughed and took the pill from the little paper cup, gulping it down with a swallow of ice water that hurt his teeth. "What is this stuff you're poisoning me with?"

"You'll have to ask your doctor that."

"You done with your shift?"

"Thank the Lord."

He reached for his wallet and pulled out two tickets for the Kennedy Center Medal for Life Achievement gala. "Guess I won't be using these. They're just about the best seats in the house."

When the nurse studied the tickets, her mouth opened with disbelief. "The only cap I've got is a Washington Redskins' cap, but I'll wear it tomorrow if it will make you happy." She leaned over and kissed the top of his head and then fled, startling the Secret Service agents who were stationed outside the door of his room.

As soon as the door closed, T. Russell Ranta got out of bed and opened the closet. Pulling out his clothes, he rejoiced in the thought that in five minutes he'd be out of this dismal place. He would have the Secret Service agents give him a lift, and the first thing he'd do would be to pay a surprise visit to the president. He relished the thought of Lange's disappointment when he saw him walk into the Oval Office.

* * *

At the J. Edgar Hoover Building, a restless Randall Godden laid aside a plan for a sting operation to pull in a network of real estate crooks reselling the same pieces of property. He pushed his chair away from his desk and walked over to the window for another check on the weather. Tomorrow he was taking his son's Scout troop to the Shenandoah National Park. Below him at the E Street entrance was a long line-up of tourists with their children, waiting to get into the FBI building. What the children liked best was the firearms demonstration. They didn't want to be told that today's agents were more apt to use a computer than a gun to catch the criminal.

He remembered his own excitement as a boy listening to "The FBI in Peace and War." He had always known he was going to be an agent, but it had taken some doing. There hadn't been money for a college education and then he had married early. He worked at Sears selling appliances and finished up at the community college and the city law school. It had been eight long years, but once he was in the agency the promotions had kept coming. He knew he would never have the top job, but as far as he was concerned that was mostly show. He liked the excitement of nabbing the bad guys. There were people out there who would tell you there were no "bad" guys, only victims. Randall Godden had no trouble dividing up the world into good and evil.

Several times in the last few days he had thought about Ted Coulter's request for phony identification. He smelled something there. Godden considered having a chat with the Secret Service but he had no concrete evidence. Perhaps Coulter was doing just what he said he was doing—playing some sort of joke on a friend. Besides, Godden knew the Secret Service would not take kindly to the Agency muscling in on their territory. He decided he would say a word or two to T. Russell Ranta when Ranta was discharged from the hospital. The vice president was in a better position to keep an eye on Coulter. Ranta was the only man Godden trusted in the administration. It wasn't that the vice president always played by the rules; it was just that when he didn't he made sure everyone knew it.

Godden pushed Coulter out of his mind and let his thoughts return to the sting operation. He viewed it with a certain pleasurable enthusiasm. Fifteen years ago a real estate agent had cheated him on the purchase of his first house.

* * *

On his way from the Oval Office to the family quarters, Robert Lange turned to the Secret Service agent who was accompanying him in the elevator. "Weber, isn't it?" He tried to be conscientious about remembering their names. After all, they were prepared to give their lives for him, but there were so many of them and they were instructed to be unobtrusive in their appearance, which was simply another way of saying unmemorable.

"Yes, sir. Edison Weber."

"How long have you been assigned to the White House?"

"Six months, sir," Weber said in a clipped voice.

Robert Lange didn't miss the agent's reserved demeanor. It wouldn't surprise him if the agents thought he was something of a cold fish. He was always professional and never kidded around with them. Other presidents were not above a game of horseshoes, throwing a football, or even a hand of poker on Air Force One, but Lange had never been a man to make friends easily. As long ago as grade school he had reluctantly admitted to himself that he would never be one of the boys. His friends had sensed in him an agenda that had little to do with friendship and everything to do with looking for an advantage. There were a few astute children who recognized a wistful desire on his part to belong. However, Lange responded to their tentative efforts so clumsily that they soon gave up and left him alone.

A gift for friendship was the one thing his father had never been able to teach him; perhaps it was because his father had relegated friendship to that realm of sentimentality so distasteful to him. Friendship could get in the way of ambition. It was only after he began to campaign for office that Robert Lange learned how to substitute an artful affability for intimacy. The skill was simply one more thing he was willing to master to reach his goal.

The agents knew their boundaries and did not follow the president or the members of his family into the sanctuary of the family quarters. Robert closed the door of his bedroom with his usual satisfaction at shutting out the eternal scrutiny that made him feel like a rare bug under a microscope. There was little about Lange's bedroom that felt comforting or even familiar. In a frenzy of minimalism, and to the horror of the White House curator, the day they had moved in Paige ordered the traditional furnishings removed. In their place sat a steel bed sculpted to look like bare tree branches, some art deco chests, and a chair off to one side, upholstered in what had been a kilim rug. On the walls hung a solitary picture, an oversized canvas done by an artist who was a friend of Paige. It was a cityscape of a dilapidated neighborhood, the buildings either burned or boarded up, the only color the obscene graffiti scrawled on the ramshackle buildings.

Robert opened the bottom drawer of one of the chests and rummaged about under some sweaters until he felt the hard steel handle of his Colt revolver. Slowly he drew it out. When he was a senator there had been the usual death threats, and he had easily obtained a permit to carry a gun. It amused him to think of the covey of Secret Service agents scattered through the White House, confident that his life was safe in their hands, that as long as they stood guard, nothing could happen to him. Yet he knew his life was in his own hands. All he had to do was pull the trigger of the Colt or walk into the adjoining bathroom, take out his razor, and slash his wrists. He wondered idly how long it took to bleed to death.

Suicide always held a certain fascination for him. To distract himself at times from the suffocating protectiveness of the agents, he devised intricate schemes to do to himself the very thing they were paid to guard against. In the same way, he had always kept as a secret resource the possibility of a permanent escape from the demands made on him by others. As a boy, when his father's demands became unbearable, he would stroll along the Potomac, looking down at the murky water, thinking about slipping under it as you might escape through a doorway to some never-never land of release, through a looking glass or a wardrobe. During those trying times in his childhood, the only thing that kept him from the release of the water was the fear of what his mother's God would say to him. Despite all the training his father had poured into him, Peter Lange had failed on one point. He had never been able to banish entirely from his son's mind the image put there by his mother of a power greater than that promised to him by his father.

Since his mother's threat to expose him, Lange found escape more seductive than ever. Each compromise he made, each lie he told immured him behind higher walls of his own construction. He needed to hold the gun to assure himself there was still an easy way out. And of all days, he needed that sense of control today.

As he sat there, the thought of what was about to transpire

caused only a slight flicker in his conscience. This afternoon, at Lange's bidding, Ted Coulter would carry out a plan that would certainly shatter the life of the president's mother. It was not too late to contact Coulter, who would be in his car and easily available by phone. Yet Robert knew he would not make the call. His mother had become another obstacle in his path.

To assuage his troubled conscience, Lange summoned up an ancient grudge against his mother, one for which he had never forgiven her. The scene came back to him. The day of his father's burial he and his mother had returned to their home in Alexandria from the cemetery. There had been a handful of acquaintances at the cursory funeral parlor service, none of whom had made the trip to the cemetery to see Peter Lange laid to rest. The Langes had few friends. Over the years Maida had kept to herself, and Peter's time had been consumed by two things: the teaching of his medical students and the training of his son.

When they reached the dismal solitude of their house, Maida had called Robert into the library. He had gone reluctantly, frightened by his mother's pale face and burning eyes. He knew it was not grief he was sensing but the fierce anger of someone about to wreak vengeance.

"You are going back to law school, Robert?" she had asked in a controlled voice.

"If you don't mind being alone." For a moment he relaxed, hoping this was to be an ordinary conversation.

She made a gesture with her hand, dismissing such an idea. "It is time we had a talk. Robert, do you remember your younger brother?"

"My older brother," he corrected her. Robert could not recall what his brother had looked like, but he vaguely remembered a terrible ride to a hospital, and then his mother wearing a black veil. Once, he had asked his father what his brother had died from, but his father had brushed the question aside, clearly not wanting to talk of it. Robert had assumed the subject was too painful.

"No, Robert. Your younger brother. We have had lies in this house long enough. While your father was alive there was nothing I could do; he was too much for me. Now we will have the truth. What you will do with it must be your choice. You were not born in America. You were born in Germany. Your name is not Robert but Johann. When little Robert died, your father gave you his name so that you would appear to be a natural-born citizen of this country."

"You can't be serious. My father couldn't have done such a thing." Yet as she spoke he knew it was true. A childhood scene flashed through his mind. He could hear his father saying, "I'm going to give you the gift of a new name, Johann."

Lange turned on his mother. "Have you any idea what this means? It could change my whole life. Why in heaven's name wasn't I told?"

"It was your father's ambition for you, but I blame myself. I should have forced him to tell the truth, but he was too strong for me."

"Then why punish me with the truth now? It's too late. How can I announce to the world that I've been living a lie?"

"It would be better, Robert, if you asked yourself how you could go on living that lie."

Somehow Robert had known all along, but his mother had forced him to admit it, and in admitting it, he had to decide what to do with the truth. After the initial shock, he threw a few things in a duffel bag and took off, leaving his mother with no idea of where he would end up. He had hoped to leave both of his identities behind, and then Ted Coulter had found him and brought him back.

His mother had confronted him with the truth when he had no need or desire for it.

Then Ted Coulter had made him live that lie. Why should he not be content to leave his mother to Ted?

IX

As winter released its icy grip, the Washington weather softened. The buds on the cherry trees fattened. Daffodils pushed up to form frivolous borders around the serious gray granite of the Capitol buildings. Like children on the first warm day of school, the government workers left their coats behind as they scurried off to lunch.

On his way out of the office Ted Coulter paused at his secretary's desk. "I'm taking the afternoon off," he announced. "I worked until eleven last night trying to cobble together a final draft of the president's speech on the Compassionate Care Bill."

"I thought so. When I got in this morning I could hardly see your desk for the crumpled paper. You deserve the afternoon off." There was a touch of envy in her voice.

"Cheer up," Coulter said. "Tomorrow's Saturday. Have you got plans?"

"As a matter of fact I do. My date and I are going to the Washington Monument for the Smithsonian Kite Festival. Afterwards I guess we'll end up at Chief Ike's or the Pop Stop."

He hurried out the door. "Have fun," he said over his shoulder.

Coulter walked down the corridor of the West Wing, hurrying past the vice president's office, unwilling at that moment to have to face the man. He didn't want to see Bobby either. Nor would Bobby want to see him and be reminded of what Coulter was about to do. He greeted the various Secret Service agents, walked by the sentry box, and climbed into his sleek Lincoln. He had wondered whether the Lincoln was a little showy and if it might be better to drive his wife's station wagon. Elly wouldn't have questioned his taking her car, since every few months he got the oil changed for her. She hated waiting in service stations. "Those places are going to be the male's last bastion," she had said. He had decided the Lincoln was the better choice, since the police were more likely to leave it alone. They would recognize the car's official sticker and know that the driver wielded power and could get them into trouble if they detained him.

Coulter took Fourteenth Street to the George Mason Bridge and crossed into Virginia. In the trunk of his car lay a garment bag with an extra suit, a shirt, tie, socks, shoes, and a change of underwear. When Elly had inquired he had merely said, "There's a chance I may have to take off for New York. Our secretary at the United Nations has a tendency to give away the store. I'll let you know, but even if I don't go I won't be home until late."

"Ted, Sarah is having her recital tonight."

"Sorry, love, take the camcorder. I'll see it when I get home." He had a vision of half of Washington watching its children grow up on video.

Elly's own father had been a congressman, so he knew she would take a disappointment like that in stride. Ted guessed that his wife's complaint this morning had more to do with the feeling that he was keeping something from her than his long hours away from home. More than once she had accused Robert Lange of giving Ted a powerful position so he would be handy to carry out Lange's unpleasant jobs.

Ted sighed. Elly had always been his confessional. Whenever he needed her absolution, she had never withheld it. He dreaded this day, for he was about to do something for Robert Lange that he knew even she could not pardon.

As Coulter entered Fauquier County, his somber mood lifted somewhat. It was amazing how quickly he was able to leave the city behind with its burdens. The pleasant and rural countryside, with its acres of pasture and its low wooden fences meant for easy jumping in this hunt country, had a calming effect on him. It was the time of year when his mother began preparing for the spring steeplechases, but a call earlier that day had reassured Coulter that his parents would be tied up in Kentucky for two days at a horse sale. He was quite certain he could have carried it off without a hitch with them there, but they would have asked awkward questions. He found a certain irony in using their home, convincing himself it was only fair that they should play a part in what was required of him.

He pulled into Greengate's driveway with its *allée* of hornbeam trees and parked on the circular drive that swept like an enclosing arm around the entrance. He headed directly for the stables. He had disliked horses e ver since he had been forced on one at the age of five. When he arrived at the Virginia Military Institute, the school, knowing of his parents' interest in horses, had encouraged him to join up with the cavalry. He had managed to talk his way out of it. Part of his reluctance had been a fear of horses, part a sense of how ungainly his dumpling-like figure looked in a saddle. No one was more aware than he of his graceless and lumpish body. It was only when he was around Robert Lange that his self-consciousness about his appearance disappeared. Like some creature, ugly in itself but embellished by its surroundings, Ted Coulter profited from Lange's comeliness and charisma.

Greengate's stables, with its dozen formal stalls, its wash rack, foal room, tack room, and breeding room, were state of the art. Ben, who had been a groom there when Ted was a boy, was in one of the stalls busy with a hoof pick. He was eternally friendly and terrific with horses.

"Mr. Ted, how you doing?" he said, grinning at Coulter. If he was surprised to see Ted there he said nothing. He was a man who did his job well and considered anything else of little consequence.

"Fine, Ben. How are things with you? I understand Mother and Dad are off looking for another horse for you."

"Well, Trillium's Bud is on her last legs. I hate to see her go, though, reminds me how I'm getting on."

"You'll be here long after we're all gone. Mind if I have a look around? I haven't been in the stables for a while. The children have been after me to bring them down riding again. They're a lot better with the horses than I ever was. I'll report back to them."

"Help yourself, Mr. Ted." Ben was pleased at his interest. "Looking at horses is the most natural thing in the world."

Ted walked toward the end stall well out of Ben's sight. A horse stamped, nervous in the presence of a stranger. Ted reached for a currycomb hanging on the wall and drew it the length of the horse's body. The horse pulled away from the inexpert touch but Ted continued, gingerly keeping his eyes on the horse's hooves. After several sweeps he took the comb and shook it into a small plastic bag, which he sealed and stuffed in his pocket. He quickly checked the rest of the stalls and then said good-bye to Ben, who was now pitching straw. "Good to see you," Coulter called over his shoulder.

As Ted left the stables and walked toward the house, he saw Ben put down the pitchfork and look after him, as though there was something a little peculiar. After a moment Ben turned back to his job. Coulter was sure Ben thought it enough to understand horses—man was not worth the trouble.

It gave Ted an eerie feeling to be in his own room again. The room was changed. His mother, who had a hyperactive decorator urging her on, had redone the room a number of times since he had moved out the year he began law school at Virginia. Just now the room was meant to represent the French provincial countryside with the walls and draperies in a *toile de joie*. He was disappointed to discover nothing of himself remained in the room. Although to find the room just as it had been when he left, with its U-VA pendants and debating trophies, would have been even more unsettling. He washed his hands well, took the clean clothes out of the garment bag, undressed, packed the clothes that had been exposed to the horses in the bag, showered, and changed into the clean clothes. He kept the small, closely fastened bag of horse combings in his pocket. As he left the house he called to the house-keeper, Dena, "Tell my folks I said hello." He never made explanations to servants. His mother had taught him that.

He arrived at Maida Lange's home in Alexandria in less than an hour. He had first met Lange's mother when he and Lange were law students together. Coulter had liked Maida Lange but had never felt quite comfortable around her. She was one of those disconcerting people who seem to have the ability to see through you. The more you had to hide, the more she appeared to see. He sensed that, perversely, she dis-approved of him because of how much he admired her son. Coulter had sometimes caught Maida looking at her son with a tender, worried look, as though his successes troubled her. Ted thought it ironic that his own mother should want him to have the job that Lange had, while Lange's mother appeared to wish her son anything but president.

Unlike Ted Coulter's mother, who had not been in a kitchen in years, Maida Lange prepared cakes and cookies for the young law students, as if they were still hungry eight-year-olds. It was on one of those visits that Coulter had met Robert's father. Peter Lange had come home from his work at the university to find Maida sitting there, gazing wistfully at Lange and urging the students to eat. He had appeared so angry at this harmless scene, Coulter and the other students had hastily made their excuses and left. Not many months after that visit, the man had died.

Coulter had always viewed Maida Lange as a sad figure and someone totally benign. He had been completely taken aback when Robert Lange told him that his mother was threatening a kind of blackmail. A month ago Bobby had called Ted Coulter at two in the morning, summoning him to the White House. Coulter's immediate reaction to the call was to suspect anything from a declaration of war to some romantic involve-ment on Robert's part that was about to implode.

When Coulter arrived, Bobby had drawn Coulter into the informal presidential study in the family quarters and brushed these speculations aside. There in the small room with its familiar traditional furnishings—Paige had left the room's decor to her husband—Robert had said, "I've got to talk with you, Ted. There's something you don't know, something you couldn't guess." His face was pale and his hands clenched as though he were hanging on to an invisible support. "I have to have your absolute promise of secrecy. You've got to swear never to tell anyone what I'm about to tell you."

"Of course. You should know by now you can trust me." Coulter felt thrilling shivers run up and down his spine. It was impossible not to find Lange's agitation exciting. Ever since Lange had run away from law school, Ted Coulter had sensed Lange was holding something back, something fundamental that had shaped the course of his life. As he watched Lange, he knew he was about to learn what that secret was. Then and only then would his friendship with Bobby be consummated.

With his back turned to him, as though it were impossible to tell the story while facing Coulter, Lange told him what his mother threatened. He turned around and Coulter was startled to see tears in Lange's eyes. "You've got to help me," he pleaded. Coulter was so grateful for Bobby's trust he would have done anything for him. The president was a little wild, almost out of control. It was a different Robert Lange than Coulter had ever seen.

The president poured drinks for them, and then, before Coulter could reach for his glass, Lange suddenly snatched the drinks away.

"We have to be clearheaded. We have to make a plan. My mother is being irrational, so we must be rational. That's how we'll defeat her," he said, brushing his hair back as he paced around the room. "We have to get her away before she talks with the media. There must be someplace where we could put her. I don't want her hurt, but she must be kept out of the way. The woman is clearly mad. Just think what she would say! I would be finished."

"Maybe we could find a private nursing home," Coulter

suggested. "The owners might be bought off to keep her—"

"It would never work," interrupted Lange. "How would we convince her to go there? She'd never consent. And what would we tell the people who would be caring for her? And even if we managed it, how would we explain her absence? The media would notice and begin to dig. It wouldn't take them long to ferret the whole thing out. TV would have a field day."

It was the mention of television that made Ted Coulter remember the actress. "No, wait. I have an idea. There's this soap opera..."

"Don't be a fool," snapped Lange.

"No. I'm serious. An actress on a soap opera looks exactly like your mother. If your mother were..." Here Coulter paused, looking for neutral words. "If your mother were somewhere else, this woman could take her place."

*　　*　　*

It was only now, when he had to carry out the scheme the two of them had devised that night, that Coulter began to have second thoughts. Lange had ordered him to give Maida Lange one last chance, but after Lange's disastrous interview with his mother the night before, Coulter had little hope. He was sure he would have to go ahead with the plan, dangerous as it was.

What worried him was that Maida Lange was a very private person. How did they know she didn't have some heart problem? Suppose she died. At any rate, if something did happen, Coulter told himself, they couldn't possibly accuse him. He was only acting on executive orders. He concentrated on the importance of what he was about to do for the country and for the world.

When he arrived Maida led him into the house. She was still an attractive woman, but today her face was pale and resolute, like someone about to undergo an ordeal. "Mrs. Lange," he took her hand and squeezed it gently. "It's been a long time."

"Ted. Please come in. It was so nice of you to drive all the way down here. I hope you have good news for me. But first I have some coffee and a little cake for us." She led him into the library, where he settled into the chair across from the desk. While she went to the kitchen, he studied the room. The books were carefully lined up on the shelves. The desk was clear except for the folder Robert had described. The library was completely unlike the living room, which was strikingly original, beyond the achievement of his own mother and her retinue of expensive decorators.

Maida returned with a tray on which were arranged porcelain cups and saucers, starched damask napkins, and thick slices of a rich coffee cake he recalled nostalgically from an earlier time. She watched him closely as she handed him his coffee. "You don't have good news for me, do you, Ted?"

Coulter stiffened in his chair and took a deep breath. "Mrs. Lange, I wish you would reconsider. The Compassionate Care Bill must go forward. If it doesn't, there is no way your son will be reelected. His party will turn on him."

"Are you telling me I have a son who would acquiesce to thousands of murders in order to be reelected?" she said coolly.

Startled by her reaction, he saw at once that he had taken the wrong tack. Clearly, Maida would be delighted if her son were defeated. "I'm sure the election is not the president's main concern. Your son is good for our country. And 'murder' is rather harsh, I think. The Bill is simply an effort to use our resources in the best way possible—"

Maida stopped him. "You are familiar with the Nazi doctrine of *ein wertloses Leben*—'Life not worth living'?'" she asked. Without waiting for his answer she went on, "If we could all end our lives with a snap of the finger, Ted, there would be few left alive today. We all have moments when we wish we were gone. But we live on because we are in awe of the phenomenon of life bestowed upon us by God. We take a breath, we listen to our heart beat, we feel the warmth in our bodies. All that is a miracle, a gift from Him. You speak of resources, of efficiency. So did my grandfather—and he discovered the truth when it was far too late...."

As she talked Coulter noticed she was becoming short of breath. He must not have been as careful of his clothes as he thought. He would have to act quickly. "Mrs. Lange, the president has been completely forthright with me. I know about your grandfather, but those were unscrupulous men in aberrant times."

"No, Ted. Those were ordinary men in ordinary times. The terrible times came later—and partly as a result of the actions of those ordinary men."

"We have to make some hard choices. There are international crises all around the globe. Money is short. There isn't enough care to go around. Surely you wouldn't deny young children the opportunity for good health care?"

"We are wasting time, Ted. If you have come here to tell me that Robert is going forward with the legislation, then I have my statement prepared and I will call the papers immediately." One hand reached for her inhaler, the other reached for the phone.

"You win." Coulter tried to sound as though he were reluctantly giving in. "The president will do as you say, but how do we know the next piece of legislation that comes along will not make you threaten him all over again?"

"You have my word. This is the only thing I care about. Robert knows that. I have never interfered before. Politics is the last thing in the world to occupy me. Under men like you and Robert it has become an unprincipled game. I don't blame my son for all this, of course. It is my husband who holds the greater guilt for the damage that has been done."

"I've brought a copy of the Bill along," Coulter said. "We'll go over the wording of the triage section, and you can tell me exactly what it is you object to. Then we can make the appropriate changes. Since that's going to take some time, I'd appreciate a little more coffee, if you don't mind."

Immediately Maida got up, her severity gone. He saw that she did not entirely believe him, but he could tell she wanted to. She became the eager hostess. "There is a little more cake, too."

When she was gone from the room, Coulter reached for the inhaler and triggered it several times until he was sure there was no medication remaining. He let a moment go by. He told himself that he was taking these actions in the same way a Secret Service agent would shoot someone threatening the life of the president. Hers was a desperate act calling forth from him an equally desperate act. He took the little plastic bag from his pocket, opened it, and hastily shook it over the rug beneath Maida's chair. He tipped the remaining contents over the desk and blew the dander about.

When Maida returned, she was carrying a silver coffee pot. She reached for his cup, pausing midway. Her chest began to heave. He could hear her wheezing. She dropped the cup on the desk and reached for the inhaler. When she triggered it and nothing happened, she panicked. She put one hand on her chest and the other at her throat. Her breathing suddenly became rapid and shallow and then intermittent. She was gasping for air.

Coulter jumped up from his chair. He was terrified. He had expected a reaction but nothing this dramatic and life-threatening. "It's your asthma?"

She nodded, unable to speak.

"I'll take you to the hospital." He was desperate to get her out of the room. He threw his coat over her shoulders and, putting his arm around her, Coulter guided her to the door and down the walk to his car. She offered no resistance; instead she clung to him as she gasped for air. For a moment he considered going to an emergency room, but that would be dangerous. The media would find out and attempt to interview her. He would have to carry out his plan. If she died on the way to the Bunges', he would turn around and head for an emergency room, and simply explain that she had suffered an acute attack while he had been visiting her. He was appalled at how easily ready solutions came to his mind.

For a moment he almost wished she would die. It would solve everything. He winced at the thought of what her life was going to be like with that couple. But if she died he would have committed murder. He speeded up, keeping an eye on the rear window. She sat beside him gasping, trying to tell him that the hospital was in the other direction. Although it seemed to take hours, it was only minutes before they reached the small town and pulled up in front of Twin Oaks Nursing Home. He parked the car in the rear and hurried around to open her door.

"There's a nurse here who will know what to do," he said, but her frightened eyes told him that she no longer believed him. Even with the severe choking, she refused to leave the car. The door to the house flew open and the Bunges hurried out like convivial hosts welcoming expected guests. Together they lifted a terrified Maida from the car.

"She's pretty bad," Tom said. His affability had been supplanted with apprehension. "What if something happens?"

"Don't worry," Coulter assured him. "I'd get her away from here; you wouldn't be involved."

Liz was all business. "You just get her in the kitchen. I've got the adrenaline ready like you said."

Maida slumped down on a chair. Her chest heaved and there were frighteningly long seconds between each labored gasp. Liz jabbed a needle into Maida's arm. Almost at once Maida began to breathe normally.

As soon as she could talk she asked in a shaking voice, "Where am I? What place is this?"

Coulter, at once both self-conscious and authoritative in front of the Bunges, said, "I thought it would be much simpler to come here instead of a hospital. And you see, Mrs. Bunge has made you better." When Maida continued to stare in disbelief at him, he went on, "Mother, I hate to do this but it's the best thing for you. You have to be protected from yourself."

Maida looked from Coulter to the Bunges and back to Coulter. "Why have you brought me here? Why are you calling me Mother? I am Robert Lange's mother."

"Mother, please. Don't get started on that. I think it would be a good idea for you to rest for an hour or so." Turning to Liz, he casually asked, "Is there a place where my mother could lie down until she gets her strength back?" He turned back to Maida. "Once you've rested, I'll take you right home."

"Yes, of course," Liz said in a wheedling voice. "A nice room and the bed is all made up. If you'll just come up these stairs," she coaxed.

A weak and puzzled Maida looked at Coulter. "You would never have done this without Robert's permission." Her steady gaze forced him to look away. "I'm not surprised," she said. "If my son is capable of signing that Bill, then he is capable of this. But remember, if he would do this to me, just think what he would do to you if you became a liability to him."

As Coulter watched Liz lead Maida Lange away, the confidence he had felt in Lange's trust wavered. He steeled himself, telling himself Bobby would never turn on him.

When they were gone Tom asked Coulter, "How were you so sure she was going to have an asthma attack?"

"She has them when she gets upset and of course she was very reluctant to come with me. I'll bring her clothes tomorrow. Have you some sort of sedation for tonight if she needs it?"

"No problem," Tom assured him. "All our people get sleepy pills. That way we get our rest, too." He placed a beefy hand on Coulter's shoulder. "Don't you worry about a thing. We'll take good care of your mother."

As Coulter pulled onto the highway he called Lange on the secure phone. "It's done," he said in a shaking voice. "It wasn't easy." He waited to hear words of approval from Lange.

"No point in dramatics," Lange responded, his voice impersonal. "I'll see you here in the office in the morning. You'll take care of mother's house?"

After the president hung up, Ted Coulter wondered if he had already become a liability to Lange. Still, he knew from experience that the coldness was Bobby's way of handling emotional situations. He had seen it before. Whenever Robert found himself reacting to his feelings, he simply killed the feelings.

Coulter decided he could not face Maida Lange's home. He would go there first thing tomorrow and make a thorough search to make sure she hadn't hidden any evidence that might show up later. After that Sheila Covell could move in, the sooner the better. You never knew when the media might get the idea of doing a feature story on the president's mother. He only hoped the actress had studied her part.

* * *

Shortly after midnight Edison Weber, one of the Secret Service agents on the night shift, was surprised to see the president leave the family quarters and make his way to the Oval Office. Weber came to attention, but Robert Lange hardly seemed to notice him as he brushed by and closed the door of the office firmly behind him. Weber stared at the door. The door of the Oval Office had a peephole. He assumed it was installed at one time as a security measure, but agents were strictly forbidden to look into it unless they had an urgent reason. Weber wondered if overwhelming curiosity counted as an urgent reason.

It was not the president's habit to work in the Oval Office after hours. When he had work to do in the evenings, he usually did it in his study in the family quarters. At such a late hour, Weber decided someone must be going to join him, but when a half hour passed and no one turned up, his curiosity got the better of him. Making sure no one was coming, he looked into the peephole and saw Robert Lange sitting upright at his desk, his handsome face crumpled and ashen. The president was staring down at a Colt revolver that lay on the desk. Weber's first instinct was to rush into the office and snatch the gun, but how would he explain spying on the president? As he struggled with what to do, Robert Lange stood up and placed the revolver in the pocket of his coat. A moment later the office door opened.

Weber tried to arrange a smile on his face. "Working late, sir?"

"Always something, Weber. It is Weber, isn't it?"

"Yes, sir." Desperately he tried to think of a way of confronting the president. "Ever been through one of these things, sir?" He indicated the metal detector that stood in the corridor near the Oval Office. "Maybe you'd like to give it a try." Weber tried an offhanded laugh. It was his only chance to confront Lange.

"Some other time, Weber."

X

Sheila Covell read the name of the driver printed on the taxi licence. Mastur. One of the drivers of the limousine that used to pick her up and take her to the studio each day had had the same name. He had been from Pakistan. The cab lurched to a stop in front of the brick town house.

At the sight of the handsome old brick house with its elegant dark green door and shutters, Sheila's spirits soared. She had never owned a home of her own; the apartment hardly counted. She felt sorry for the woman who had to leave this house against her own wishes. Sheila honestly hoped the woman would soon be well enough to return. Ted Coulter had said the president's mother was being cared for in an excellent facility. Sheila had read that there was effective medication for the mentally ill these days. Hospitalization was often for short periods. Her hand trembled a little as she fitted the key Coulter had given her into the lock. The driver had already made his second trip and was holding out his hand. She tipped him liberally and dismissed him, glad to close the door behind her and have the house to herself.

Her first instinct in the empty house was to call out, "Is anyone here?" The responding silence encouraged her to begin to explore her new home.

The series of small rooms with their unique furnishings looked to her like stage settings, or perhaps like paintings. She admired the way disparate things were grouped to make a still life. Jumbled together in the living room were paisley shawls, damask and tasseled pillows, an ancient chest, a marble table, an old wicker chair, an eighteenth-century settee, and an etagere holding bits of porcelain. Oriental rugs worn to muted colors adorned the hardwood floors, and Austrian curtains of pale silk hung at the windows.

In the pocket-sized dining room, the papered walls displayed a collage of scenes from a formal garden. And in front of the window stood a wire stand crowded with ferns and flowering plants. Though she had never owned a plant in her life, Sheila instinctively tested the dirt in the pots with a tentative finger. Dry. It had not occurred to her when she accepted the job that there might be responsibilities. She knew she could toss the lot out if she wished, but she did not see how she could do that if she willed the woman to recover and return. She reminded herself that she was not the occupant but the custodian of this house.

Without pausing to take off her coat, she walked into the kitchen to find something with which to water her new dependents. There, too, she paused in wonder at the uniqueness of the place. Stacked on several narrow shelves were rows of cookbooks, and a pan rack from which dangled more pots and skillets than she could imagine using in a lifetime. The kitchen was painted a pale yellow, almost exactly the color of the weak spring sun that poured in the windows. Quickly she filled a tea kettle and set about satisfying the greenery.

The only room to disappoint her was the library, whose decor was in stark contrast to the rest of the house. It was obvious it had been inhabited by someone other than the woman whose original touch had put together the rest of the house. Everything in the library was orderly and unadorned. The desk was bare, the furniture heavy and traditional. Sheila was intimidated by the shelves full of books. She examined some of the titles: lives of world leaders, military strategy, history, foreign affairs. Coulter had said nothing about the books. She hoped she would not be expected to have read them.

She hurried back to the kitchen to make herself a cup of tea before exploring further. As though a hand were guiding her, she opened a cupboard to find a pretty blue ginger jar labeled "tea." When she poured on the boiling water the fragrance of the tea wafted toward her, astounding her more than anything else had that day. It was Formosa oolong, her favorite brand. For just a moment Sheila believed it was her house and that she might stay here forever. A mysterious pleasure and peace she had never experienced before seemed to envelop her, followed by the guilty feeling that she was usurping someone else's place. She had heard once about a bird, a cuckoo, that made its home in the nests of other birds.

This pleasure in the house surprised her. She had always told herself she was too busy to be tied down with a house, that she wasn't the domestic type. Her only disappointment was that Ava was not there to share it with her. "I have the money and the time and the house," Sheila thought. "All the things I longed for when Ava was alive and never had." She looked out of the window at the greenhouse and the narrow garden with its terrace. The promise of flowers was everywhere. Ava would have loved working in the garden.

Sitting in the kitchen thinking of her sister, Sheila felt very much alone. Her busy career had never permitted time for close friends. The soap opera took her entire day. Every evening she had pored over scripts, memorizing her lines for the next day's shooting. Weekends belonged to Ava. When Sheila had called her few friends to explain about a possible part on the coast, they had expressed pleasure, made a few remarks that suggested they considered her overly optimistic, wished her well, and rung off, seemingly relieved not to have to worry about her. It was enough for her friends to worry about how long their own jobs would last and what they would do when those jobs ended. Even Dan had been casual in his good-byes. "Great luck, darling, hope it turns out. Drop me a line. We all miss you here. Have you caught the show?"

She had to admit she hadn't. It wasn't from lack of interest, only a fear of how out of it she would feel if she saw it.

"Good thing," he said. "The woman who's taking your place is practically a nymphet. When they do close-ups of our love scenes, the contrast makes me look decrepit. I'm afraid it's another trip to the doctor for more tucks. It's been years since I've been able to wrinkle my forehead—now I won't be able to smile. Take care."

At her meeting two days ago with Ted Coulter, he had appeared preoccupied and despondent. At first she worried that he was going to tell her that he was withdrawing his offer. Instead, he assured her that everything was on schedule. Sheila supposed that in his position there were concerns that she could not even guess at. "Has the president's mother been hospitalized?" she had asked.

"Yes," he answered curtly.

"I hope things go well for her."

"Yes, of course, but we mustn't count on a quick recovery. In the meantime I think everything is in order. The house is ready for you. As I mentioned, Mrs. Lange did not drive, so there is no car. You will have to maintain that appearance, but taxis are available and there will be an allowance provided for that. From her calendar I gather Wednesday seems to have been her day to go to the library, usually after lunch. You've memorized the list of people who might phone and their descriptions?"

"Yes, she doesn't seem to have very many friends." The similarity to her own situation had struck Sheila.

"No, she kept very much to herself. Her house, her garden, her books, church, I believe, but you wouldn't have to go that far. That was about it. And of course her son, the president."

"It was very sad, their losing their first son. It must have made their early years in this country difficult." It had troubled Sheila to read of the loss in the biography of Maida Lange that Coulter had prepared for her. So deeply had she felt her way into the role of Maida Lange, it was almost as though the tragedy had happened to her.

Coulter had seemed anxious to change the subject. "You reviewed the material on Peter, her husband?"

"Yes, it's funny, but he reminded me of the kind of stage

mothers you see in the theater, women anxious to sacrifice their child just to fulfill their own ambitions. Was it that kind of vicarious thing with the father? He seemed so involved with everything the president did as a boy."

"It was more a love of America," Coulter hastened to say. "You know how enthusiastic about this country immigrants can be. And their lives in Germany after the war were extremely difficult, so of course they idealized their new country. During the president's campaign, the media tried to make something of his father's wish to see his son become president. I pointed out to them the dream that every boy can be president was the dream of a lot of ambitious fathers and mothers out there."

*   *   *

Sheila carried two of her cases up the narrow stairway. There were three bedrooms. She decided the one with the single bed and desk must have been the president's. A thrill ran through her. She had not paid much attention to politics and hardly knew what to think about Robert Lange, but she believed someday the house would become a kind of shrine, where tours would wander through while a guide pointed out, "This was the president's room."

There was little in the Spartan room to suggest what the boy had been like: a picture of a baseball team, a trophy won for debating, and, surprisingly, a scruffed teddy bear, an unlikely and endearing touch in the austere room.

The master bedroom was in the front of the house. It had twin beds, a pair of chairs, a dressing table, and a chest. She was disappointed to see there was nothing distinctive about the room. The dresser drawers were empty, but some of Maida Lange's clothes had been left in the closets. "For me?" she wondered.

As she looked about, she caught a glimpse of a strange woman in the mirror. Startled, she cried out. A moment later she realized she was looking at herself. Her hair had been gray for no more than a few days, and she wasn't used to it, nor the plain wool dress she was wearing.

For a moment she felt something like panic. She was a strange woman in a strange house; even her own appearance was unfamiliar. She worried that she would lose her identity altogether and never get it back. Suddenly the whole plan scared her. She didn't know how she would ever manage to live there, and couldn't imagine staying for one night, much less weeks and perhaps months or years.

Sheila knew she had only to pick up the phone and call the number Coulter had given her. He had told her she could leave a message at any time and he would get back to her as soon as he could. She would tell him she was backing out, leave the money he had paid her and the key to the house. In a matter of hours she could be back in her apartment in New York. "And then what?" she asked herself. She had no job, no prospects, little money, and no idea how long she could last.

Dismissing that thought, Sheila tried to recapture the thrill she had felt a moment ago at the thought of living in the house where the president had grown up. She tried to comfort herself with what a month ago would have been an inconceivable thought—perhaps she would be invited to the White House.

When she looked into the third bedroom, she found a single sleigh bed smothered in colorful cushions and a comfortable chair and footstool covered in a worn flowered cretonne. An enormous tiger eye maple chest stood against one wall. The windows in the room looked out on the terrace and a small garden. In the middle of the garden was a weeping cherry tree just coming into bloom.

Sheila dropped her cases in the middle of the room and sank down on the chair. For the first time since she had entered the house, she felt she might be able to live there.

XI

"We never get to go out together now. We're locked into this house just as much as she is." Looking out of the window, Liz Bunge regarded the unfolding April spring as useless. "We haven't even been up to the Capitol to see the cherry blossoms."

"We can go out separately anytime we want, Liz. Anyhow, it's worth it. He's paying us more than we ever made before." They spoke loudly to make themselves heard above the noise of the television set blaring in the other room. In the afternoons the wheelchair crowd gathered in the living room to watch the soaps. Liz often watched with them, which was why she had been so startled the night Coulter brought in his mother. By the time she had helped the woman upstairs, she realized Coulter's mother reminded her of the villainess that used to star on "Day into Night." The mother was older, of course, with gray hair, but the resemblance was remarkable.

"How long do you think we can count on her being here?" asked Liz.

After the first few days the woman hadn't been much trouble. In the beginning, just as Mr. Coulter had said she would, his mother insisted she was the president's mother. She was convincing, too. But as soon as she started talking about calling in the FBI and the Secret Service, they knew she was crazy. They had cared for other people with delusions just like hers. After a while she had calmed down, and now she was as good as gold, not in the least demanding. Her only requests were books from the library and a special kind of tea Tom had found over in Fairfax.

"I don't know how long, but the longer the better. In a

year's time we could have enough to turn this place into a bed-and-breakfast. Just think: a whole house full of people who could feed themselves."

"We'd need more money than that, Tom. I'm planning to put terry-cloth robes in all the rooms and little baskets of shampoo and lotions from Crabtree & Evelyn."

Just then they heard caterwauling going on in the other room. Tom said, "Must be the usual argument over which to watch: 'As the World Turns' or 'Another World.'" As the shouts grew louder, he reluctantly left his second helping of banana cream pie and made his way into the living room to restore order.

Liz gazed out the window at the unkempt, bedraggled yard. When the house was turned into a bed-and-breakfast, she would have a little garden with a fountain, she decided. On summer afternoons the water would splash softly, and all around the fountain she would plant roses. There would be a wrought-iron table and chairs, too, so that guests might have tea in the garden. Having tea was Liz's idea of gentility. Even now, tea was served along with a plate of doughnuts each afternoon at four to her clients. Tea was carried upstairs to the locked quarters as well.

Tom returned and picked up his plate with the remains of the pie. "They were all upset because the president's press conference knocked the soaps off the air. I'm going in and listen." Since the mother of the president's advisor was their client, Tom was taking an interest in affairs of state.

Upstairs Maida sat in her chair thinking that it was time to start the sweet peas that would climb the trellis near the kitchen window, where their fragrance would be carried by gentle breezes in to her all summer long. The roses needed uncovering and any winter kill pruned away. Most important of all were her more mature iris seedlings that ought to be transferred from the greenhouse to an outdoor bed.

To keep her sanity Maida went through a ritual of daily

tasks that she could not perform. It was necessary to be strict in diverting her thoughts. Almost immediately she had seen the uselessness of trying to persuade her captors to free her. At first she was puzzled at how easily the Bunges ignored her protests as well as the implications of her story. Soon she realized they had been well prepared for just such a story and warned not to believe it. She supposed Robert was paying them well for their collaboration. After her initial outburst she had simply decided to conform.

She understood that if she were to find a way out of her detention, it would not be through her jailers. They were like secretive children who had found a gold piece: they hid her away but took very good care of her. They coaxed her to eat, saw that she had an inhaler for her asthma, even provided her with a television set to break up the monotony of her confinement. They had gone out of their way to find her special brand of tea, and every few days she wrote out a list of books which Liz dutifully brought from the local library.

Sometimes Liz would return and apologetically explain that a book had to be ordered from another library. "It's just a tiny library, honey, but they're real nice. They've got something called interlibrary loans and they can send a request to any library in Virginia for a book, or even farther. So if there's something you want they don't have, just let me know."

Maida was amused at how Liz, who had obviously never dealt with books before, now enjoyed impressing the librarian with her requests.

It was this self-importance which Liz displayed that gave Maida the idea. On the request list Maida had handed Liz that morning was *Monastic Gardens of the Fourteenth Century*. She thought of the book with pleasure. Somewhere within its pages was the story of certain monks who rose early in hopes of getting to their chapel before God arrived. The thought of the monks creeping stealthily through their garden in the darkened hours of the morning hoping by their cunning to outmaneuver God always made her smile. It reminded her of the plight of mankind—this belief that if they were only clever enough they could outsmart God. And what did those pitiful efforts gain? Havoc. But that was not why she had requested the book. If someone were looking for her, that request might be seen as a cry for help. Maida knew it was a chance in a million but even those small odds gave her hope.

The world into which Maida Lange had been born, the world of Europe in the throes of World War II, was not a place where one had hope; one had only fear. Her childhood had been one filled with mysterious disappearances. Her father, Jurgen Liebig, had grown up in a house on the grounds of the mental institution where his father was the director. As a young boy Jurgen watched the population of the hospital slowly diminish. He was old enough to know why. Years later he joined the German army, and when Maida was only a baby, he was one of the youngest members to be rounded up and executed for collaborating in the officer plot to assassinate Hitler.

After the failed coup, Maida and her mother traveled to the ancient moated town of Lübeck to live with her mother's sister. Maida had grown up in that northern city with the cold winds blowing now from the Baltic Sea, now from the North Sea. The family lived on Mengstrasse in the shadow of the *Marienkirche*. That massive Lutheran church, with its stark interior and soaring steeples, had watched over her childhood. After school she often slipped inside just as Bach himself had once done, to hear the great organ played. The glorious sound reverberated through the vast interior of the church, thrilling and frightening her, for she was sure God resided there and listened with her.

When the war ended nearly a hundred thousand refugees from Eastern Germany had fled into Lübeck to escape the Communists. One of those refugees was Peter.

Maida possessed enough of her father's iron will that her imprisonment with the Bunges had not yet defeated her. She was convinced you could only succumb to defeat when you stopped loving. And she still loved her son. Whatever he did to her could not touch that. Love, she knew, was unconditional or it was not love. It was the way her God loved her. That did not mean she would not fight Robert, would not make every effort to take from him the thing he prized most—if it was the very thing that would destroy him.

Maida had always avoided television, but now, in her forced solitude, she was grateful to have the set. She kept it on the news channel much of the day. She had to know what her son was doing and whether her absence had been noticed. Eventually, her neighbors or someone would have to wonder at her sudden disappearance from the house. Newspapers would pile up, bills would go unpaid, and surely someone at the library would miss her regular Wednesday afternoon visits.

But as the days dragged on, no one came to rescue her. Her absence hadn't even been noticed. She was truly alone. Worst of all, it was clear that her son would go to any lengths to get what he wanted, even if it meant locking his mother away.

She blamed herself. She should have opposed Peter. She had been a helpless witness all those years while her husband tyrannized Robert, first breaking him, and then re-forming him into a kind of robot: his every breath and thought in the service of Peter's will. Every attempt on the part of the child to be himself was checked by his father. In his attempt to prepare his son as a leader, Peter had created a monster.

Countless times she asked herself why she hadn't kidnapped her son and, if necessary, escaped to the ends of the earth. She should have shouted the deception from the housetops when it first began. Now she had only one reason to survive: to find someone who would believe her story.

It was painful for her to look out at the world of green, sundered into shards by five iron bars across her window. She glanced at the television set which sat on her dresser. Liz had placed a crocheted dresser scarf underneath the set, and on the top of the set was a porcelain head of a kitten filled with paper flowers.

Maida was startled to see her son appear on the screen. He was standing at a podium in the East Room of the White House. To one side was the flag of the United States, on the other side the presidential standard. In the background stood two Secret Service agents scanning the room, their eyes darting back and forth, alert for any sign of danger. In front of the podium squirmed the corps of reporters, their hands waving frantically in the air as they tried to catch the president's eye.

Maida never got used to the sight of her son as president. She felt a certain pride in him, but she was also terrified of this product of her husband's obsession. Fielding the reporters' questions was a simple game for Robert Lange: he had been fielding such questions with his father since the age of twelve.

She watched as he answered the CBS White House correspondent. "I don't like that word 'triage.' Medicine has always had priorities. Just walk into any emergency room in the country. Some patients are more in need than others and they come first. Emergency rooms have a limited number of doctors and a limited number of nurses. They can't do everything.

"The same holds true for our health care system. We have to establish priorities. The people who will be productive have to come first. Those are the citizens who will accomplish most for our country. That doesn't mean we are denying anyone what they must have, as some have suggested, even in my own party." Here the camera panned to a shot of T. Russell Ranta who was standing to one side, scowling at Lange.

"It simply means," the president went on, "that if we place all of our resources into the care of the least productive people in our society, nothing will be left for those who must keep America strong."

At this a reporter from *The Wall Street Journal* interrupted, "Mr. President, sir, would you define for us who you mean by the 'least productive'?"

"No, I won't. It's not up to me. We have established a panel of experts in their respective fields. It will be up to them to establish criteria."

Maida recalled Ranta describing those experts as "boys of ice," sending the reporters, as he usually managed to do, to brush up on their Shakespeare.

"A follow-up, Mr. President, can you give us the names of these gatekeepers?"

"The most important aspect of this whole program is the anonymity of the panel. They should be able to make difficult decisions without being harried by special interest groups. The demonstration this morning in front of the White House by the Society for the Protection of the Mentally Impaired was exactly what I have been talking about when I insisted that the reign of special interest groups is finished.

"Incidentally, I don't like the word, 'gatekeeper.' That suggests a keeping out. On the contrary. This plan assures better health care for hundreds of thousands of citizens as health care costs are reduced for those who offer the least to our society."

"Mr. President." It was Marissa Templin from *The Times*. "The AARP says the elderly have had the rug pulled out from under their feet."

The president brushed back his blond hair from his forehead in a gesture that the presidential imitator on "Saturday Night Live" had down pat. "That's absolutely ridiculous. I have received hundreds of letters from the elderly congratulating me for freeing them from the prospect of having to spend their last days hooked up to tubes and machines. They are relieved to be rid of the torture of those extreme measures. As you know, we have already begun work on the building of Interval Homes all across the country. I would hardly call that 'pulling the rug out'."

The signal came for the conference to end. "Thank you, Mr. President." The reporters surged toward Lange shouting questions. He grinned affably and waved as he hurried away down the corridor, escorted by the Secret Service agents.

Maida stood in front of the television set unable to move. She did not know what was worse—the thought that her son did not believe what he was saying, or the thought that he did. Then, as she had every day of Robert's life, Maida Lange prayed for her son.

* * *

Ted Coulter followed the president into the Oval Office and watched him slump down into his chair. Coulter tried to gauge just how tired the president might be and how much he should tell him. Lange loosened his tie and began rubbing his makeup off with a wad of tissues. "How did it go, Ted?" he asked.

"Fine. Leslie and her staff from Health, Education, and Welfare are out there with them now. They're all getting the handouts we prepared. I suppose we can expect the special interests to scramble for air time on all the morning shows, but we've got our own people covering the three networks and CNN. That's not what I'm worried about."

The president straightened his shoulders in a battle-ready gesture. "What's up?"

Coulter turned his back to the peephole in the door. How did he know one of the Secret Service might not be a lip reader? "I had a call from your mother."

Robert jumped up from his chair. "What do you mean?"

"Calm down, Bobby. It's all right. It was Sheila Covell. I think it's best if we refer to her as your mother so we get used to it. That way we won't slip and make an embarrassing mistake. She contacted me because she was a little apprehensive. Ranta called her, said he was calling her back because he appreciated her support for the stand he was taking against the Bill. I don't think it's anything to worry about. After all your mother did call him."

"What did he want?"

"I guess he just wanted to talk. Covell said she made some general comments: didn't deny or affirm. As far as she could tell, he seemed to accept her as the real thing. He has only talked with your mother once before, so I don't think he would have been suspicious."

Robert walked through his study to the small kitchen and poured each of them a stiff Scotch. "We've got to keep them apart. Tell her under no circumstances is she to see him. You're sure you gave that house a thorough search?"

"I spent twelve hours there. I even shook out every book in your father's library. Apart from the folder—which I burned—I couldn't find a thing that would incriminate you."

Lange gave Ted an angry look. "I suggest you forget the word incriminate. You make me sound like a criminal. Is that the way you think of me?"

Coulter winced. One moment Bobby was amicable, ready to confide in him, anxious for his help. A moment later he was suspicious and hostile. He could never be sure of him. Lately, Coulter was becoming afraid that Bobby would turn on him someday and drive him away. "Of course I don't think of you that way." In a hurt voice he added, "I don't have to tell you what I think of you." Embarrassed by the affection he could not keep from his voice, he looked away and quickly changed the subject.

"By the way, something else she said. She asked if your mother had ever been invited to the White House. I suppose she wants all the perks of the position. I told her your mother had never come here."

Lange was his affable self again. "To tell you the truth, I wouldn't mind meeting her. Not that I don't trust you, but I'd like to judge what we've got for myself. Might as well keep her happy, that way we can be much more certain she'll do as we ask. Just impress on her the fact that visiting the White House won't be a regular thing. One time only and just a family dinner. Absolutely no publicity. We don't want any pictures going out. You and Elly come, too. Elly's never met my mother, so that's no problem. I'll have to talk Paige into the dinner." The president smiled to himself. With Paige it was always quid pro quo. He shrugged. With Paige there was always plenty of quid.

XII

Sheila tried to ignore the small pile of library books on Maida Lange's bedside table, knowing they would have to be returned. Coulter had said Wednesday was Maida's day for her usual trip to the library. The note on the calendar that hung in the kitchen was a nagging reminder. Sheila was not sure she could face people who knew Maida Lange. Tuesday evening she made herself look at the books, a Barbara Pym, a Graham Green, and something called *The Cloud of Unknowing*.

The English novels seemed to Sheila an odd choice for a woman who had such strong German roots. Pym and Green were both authors Sheila had read and this made her feel uncomfortably close to Maida. The other book appeared to be some sort of mystical thing and Sheila hastily closed it. If Sheila believed anything, it was that life was a series of narrow escapes. You had to depend on yourself to stay out of trouble. Who else was there?

Reluctant to face the trial of walking into the library, Sheila had considered mailing the books back, but that seemed out of character. Besides, the thought of a walk through the old town seemed pleasant to her. So the next morning after her usual cup of tea at ten, she headed for the library. In the yards along her way daffodils and forsythia had finished blooming. The tulips were just beginning to toss their colored heads to the bright spring sun. When people passed her without a glance, she began to relax and enjoy the walk. She was experiencing once again that slightly schizophrenic feeling she always had when she was moving from her own life into a new role. She knew that each time she made the transition it would become a little easier, a little more natural until, like her part in the soap opera, she could slip into the role without missing a beat.

Though it had been years since she had stepped foot in a library, as she opened the door she was surprised at how the memories of her childhood library came flooding back, reminding her of what a refuge it had been. Back then she had begun to spend her afternoons in the library to avoid her parents' bickering, but soon she was hurrying there for the sheer pleasure of the books. Each one was an open door offering her a different life into which she gratefully escaped, for all of the lives seemed more interesting than her own.

Sheila held her breath as she approached the library desk, reminding herself to use the slight accent she had been practicing. The librarian, a young woman with eager green eyes and a braid hanging down her back, immediately brightened when she saw Sheila. She turned away from her computer and put out her hand for Sheila's books.

"Mrs. Lange, we missed you last Wednesday. We were afraid you were sick. If you hadn't shown up today, I would have called to be sure everything was all right." She laughed. "Not that you don't have more important people looking after you. You know you're one of our favorite regulars. We can't get over how, well, how *normal* you are for being the mother of the President of the United States."

Sheila smiled and said a few pleasant words to the librarian, then excused herself to browse. After a few minutes, she selected a gardening book and then wondered what other books to take out. She recalled a play by Graham Green, "The Potting Shed," and chose that. The Pym book suggested other British women writers, so she picked out an Anita Brookner and an Iris Murdoch.

When she went to check out the books, the librarian smiled at her in a tolerant way. "You've already read this Brookner. Do you want it again?" she said.

Taken aback, Sheila mumbled something about not having had time to finish it before.

"I was waiting for you to come by today," the librarian said. "You know how every year on your birthday you present the library with a special book? Well, you'll be surprised at this, but the book you gave year before last, *Monastic Gardens of the Fourteenth Century*? Well, this morning we had a call for an interlibrary loan. It was on our computer of course. I was amazed that there was someone else around here who knew about the book. I mean it's such a rare book. Anyhow, I thought I ought to check with you to be sure it was all right to loan it out."

"Yes, of course. I don't see any problem at all. I'm pleased someone will be using it." Sheila gathered up her books and hurried out of the library. As she walked home she felt a mingled confusion and excitement over her first trip outside. She was playing the most important role of her life and she wanted to make it a success. She told herself she wasn't doing it for money, although she was being well paid. She was doing it for her country. Noble. She told herself she was doing something noble. She liked the word.

That afternoon Sheila studied the square of rosebushes, each bush set in its own straw hill. According to a gardening book she had consulted—Maida had a large collection of them—the straw had to be removed. Several days before she had visited the small greenhouse, which was full of seedlings. She adopted them as she had the plants in the house, faithfully watering them. Next to the greenhouse was a garden shed with various implements.

Now as she pulled the straw away with a rake, she breathed in the damp, rich smell of the newly exposed earth. Beneath the straw she found green shoots on the rose stems and even a few unfurled leaves, which she touched tenderly. When she had finished freeing the roses from their winter mulching, Sheila stood back, pleased at the result of her work.

According to the book, pruning was next, so she matched the shears with the pictures in the book and snipped away at what she guessed was "winter kill."

The whole process gave her immense satisfaction. She was dressed in a shirt and an old pair of slacks she had found in a closet and a straw hat from the shed. As she worked the sun warmed her back. A gentle breeze loosened the petals from the cherry tree and they fluttered over her like gentle fingers. In the tree an orange and black bird she couldn't name kept up the insistent warble of its territorial song.

Her happiness worried her. She was slipping imperceptibly into another woman's life which suited her perfectly. It was as though she had been searching all of her life for this small world. Sheila sensed that the woman who had lived as a recluse in this house possessed a strength of purpose that she, herself, did not have. Sheila was not only usurping the woman's home, but felt herself borrowing that strength. She warned herself to be wary, not to become too comfortable, for one day this "role" would end and she would have to return to her own drab life.

Her first days in the house she had found a notebook in Maida's cramped writing, listing page after page of her hybridizing experiments with irises. Each experiment was accompanied by careful notes of the results, all graded by the numbers one to five. As Sheila turned the pages she noticed that the painstaking and dedicated work had gone on for years. In the back of the book were letters from fellow members of the American Iris Society. Eagerly Sheila had checked the irises in the garden. They were only green spears with tightly wrapped buds, but one day they would shake off their paper shields to reveal themselves in all the breathtaking colors she had seen in Maida Lange's books: milky blues with lavender tongues, gold with green ruffles, sinister purples that were nearly black, and pure white blooms with lavish, drooping falls: the fleur-de-lis of the French heraldic shield. Sheila was eager to see it all.

She cared for the house, worked in the garden, read, and watched a little television. One Sunday morning she even gathered the courage to venture into the church that Maida frequented. Opening a hymnal she tried to follow the service. It was only when the organ played the familiar work, Bach's "Jesu, Joy of Man's Desiring," that Sheila was moved. Something about the visit to the church made her uncomfortable. Why hadn't anyone spoken to her? For some reason Maida Lange appeared alienated from the congregation, as though some burden or transgression kept her apart from the others. Sheila could almost feel Maida's guilt, as though she, too, were guilty of something. But what? For the first time she began to wonder if her impersonation of the president's mother was entirely honest.

All that was soon forgotten in the garden which gave her great pleasure. After an afternoon of digging and raking, she was finding that she could fall asleep at night as soon as the light was turned off. Day after day as she worked in the earth, a new strength found its way into her, invigorating her, giving her an energy she had thought never to regain. Perhaps because she had never had children of her own, this assisting at the birth of so many lives pleased her. Each small green thing that pushed up through the earth seemed a celebration of life.

Sheila could hardly believe a life like this could satisfy her, yet it did. These last few years she had worked her crazy schedule because she needed the money—there was no joy in the work. Much of what she did had been done by rote. The challenge had long since disappeared. Ambition had turned into survival. Her only release had been her weekend visits to Ava. Now it was as though someone had gently taken her unremitting job from her and told her she could enjoy her life. Often she wandered through the house from room to room touching things, telling herself that they belonged to her. Then the guilt would well up—for they weren't hers. She would think sadly of the woman whose home and garden she had claimed as her own.

Her isolation started her on an inward journey as well. She now had the time, and the peace and solitude, to reflect on her life, gather together all its disparate parts, and make some sense of them. She recalled her first days in New York. She had worked evenings waitressing at Schrafts to have her days free to make casting rounds. She never doubted for a moment that one day she would become a star. There had been small parts in summer theater and road shows but never the break, never anything that she hadn't snatched by sheer will and hard work, and these last years it had been hard work. Since moving into Maida Lange's home, she had dismissed her regrets and accepted what her life had been. A mantle of peace had settled on her, as though Maida Lange's peace were there for her to use like the dishes and books. The novelty of that peace left her stunned. She had even begun reading the strange mystical book in Maida's room looking for an answer.

Sheila glanced up from her work in the rose garden. A man was calling to her from the side gate, while a couple of other men deployed themselves discreetly about the perimeters of the garden. She recognized the man at once from television, T. Russell Ranta. He was an even more impressive man than his photographs suggested: six foot three or four with a sweep of silver hair and a ruddy complexion. Standing there he looked the picture of health, but hadn't she read somewhere that he had been critically ill?

"You're a little late getting to your roses, aren't you?" he said as he came through the gate, smiling at her. He held out his hand. "Sorry about my keepers." He motioned to the Secret Service men nosing about the shrubbery. "But I suppose you've gotten used to that on your son's visits."

Sheila tried not to appear anxious. She wasn't at all used to Secret Service agents, and Ted Coulter had been firm about her not seeing the vice president, but abruptly sending him away would certainly make him suspicious. She placed her hand in his and felt a warm strength in his grip. He held on to her hand for a moment or two more than necessary. She groped for an explanation. "I've been down with a cold, and I've just now gotten around to the roses."

"Don't know much about gardening. That was my wife's job. Where I came from there were only two seasons, winter and July. In the spring you had to take a pick ax to the ground to break it up, and the first frost came in August. We always had a big pile of corpses in the holding shed in the cemetery waiting for the spring thaw."

Sheila noticed he had used the past tense when speaking of his wife. She suddenly realized how much she had missed having someone to talk with. Forgetting about Ted Coulter's warning she said, "I've just about done all I can out here this afternoon. Come on inside and let me make you a cup of coffee or tea. Or would you like some sherry?"

"Sherry?" He laughed. "The last time I had sherry was back on the Iron Range when I was in high school. You could buy it for ninety cents a bottle. Tea will be just fine. The doctors are telling me to keep away from liquor."

She led him through the back door. "Let me take you into the living room," she offered.

He looked appreciatively at the kitchen, which was luminous with afternoon sun. "It's been a long time since I sat in a kitchen. If I won't get in your way I'll just settle in there at the table."

As she made the tea and arranged some English biscuits on a plate, she caught him watching her. Embarrassed, he turned his gaze on the collection of cooking utensils and decorative odds and ends: a blue pottery jar, canisters in stripes of green and gold, a tea pot in the shape of a cat.

"Bells in your parlors, wild cats in your kitchens," he grinned at her.

"Iago in Othello," she said.

"So you know your Shakespeare?"

"Not all that well," she told him, warning herself to be more careful. She had no idea whether Maida Lange cared anything about Shakespeare. Obviously, playing the part of someone else was not going to be as easy as she thought. How did you erase everything that was a part of your own life? Suddenly, she felt uncomfortable lying to T. Russell Ranta. He struck her as a man who appreciated the truth.

"I learned Shakespeare early," Ranta said. "They mined iron ore up on the range, and the schools got most of the company's tax money. They brought the best teachers from all over the country up there. The kids were first generation. Lots of them couldn't even speak English when they got to school, but most of them went on to college. The discipline was pitiless. There's a story that the janitor left a pail of water in the corridor, and rather than break lines, the kids all stepped in and out of it as they filed to class."

As they sipped their tea Ranta looked across the table at her. "I guess I came by because I was a little puzzled at your tone over the phone. When you called me a couple of weeks ago, you seemed so strongly on my side. I mean, *you* called *me*. But the other night you seemed hesitant. You didn't want to talk about the Compassionate Care Bill. I guess what I wondered was, did the president get to you? That boy of yours can be pretty persuasive. No offense, but I've seen him step over people who got in his way. I certainly hope I didn't get you into any trouble by mentioning to him that you had called me?"

When Ranta had phoned her Sheila had little idea of what he was talking about. He had mentioned something called "triage." She had looked the word up after their conversation and could make no sense of what he meant. Since then she had paid more attention to the news. Evidently, money for health care was running out. From what she gathered about this new Bill, there were groups of people who would be denied care, and babies failing to meet certain criteria would not be allowed to be born. When she understood someone like her sister, Ava, would not have met those criteria, she immediately detested the Compassionate Care Bill.

"I saw you the other night on TV talking against the Bill," she said. "Do you think it's going to pass?" She had admired the way the vice president had refused to allow his inquisitor to skew the questions or to cut him off when the commentator objected to what he was saying. At one point Ranta had called the interviewer "Sonny."

"I'm afraid so, unless a miracle happens—and there are no miracles in politics. You have to have faith for miracles to happen, and to have faith you have to believe. In politics no one really believes."

"When I watched you the other night you sounded very much as though you believed. You convinced me."

"I thought you were already convinced."

She saw her slip and hastily said, "I mean if I hadn't already believed, I would have been convinced by your talk." Sheila felt a need to confide in the comforting man sitting across from her. "Many years ago a good friend of mine had a sister who was developmentally disabled. She was very fond of her sister. They were close. The sister meant everything to her. I can't bear to think of legislation that would have said my friend's sister would not have been entitled to a license to exist."

He was surprised at the passion in the woman's voice. "This friend of yours lived in Germany?"

Sheila went blank for a moment and then recovered. "Yes, in Germany." She began to doubt whether she could carry off the part she had been assigned. The vice president was no fool. If she weren't more careful he might become suspicious.

"Please don't think I'm criticizing you for not openly opposing the Bill," Ranta said. "Ordinarily I'd admire your loyalty. It's just that I'm caught in the same predicament. I ought to be loyal to the party and support the president, but on this issue I can't. It goes against everything I believe in." He appeared to forget for a moment that she was the president's mother and leaned toward her, covering her hand with his. "Can I tell you something in absolute confidence?"

She nodded. Coulter had warned her not to "get involved" with T. Russell Ranta. She was only being friendly, she told herself. Besides, it was hard not to be impressed with the fact that the Vice President of the United States was sitting in her kitchen, about to confide in her.

There was something else, too. As long as she could remember she had been on her own. She sensed that T. Russell Ranta was a man who would never turn away if you went to him for help. He was a man who would willingly take on the burdens of others.

"If your son goes ahead with this abominable Bill—and it looks like he's going to—I will have to resign. If I fight the president on this legislation, it will finish me in politics, so I might as well get as much bang out of the gesture as I can."

"Why does defeating the Bill mean so much to you?"

"You have to know where I come from. When I was growing up the Minnesota Iron Range was a pretty unbuttoned, freewheeling place. We made our own decisions about our lives. People had come there from all over Europe to settle in the towns and work in the mines: Swedes, Italians, Montenegrins, Slavs, Jews, Irish, and Finns like my folks all came because they wanted their freedom. Now we've got this petty tyrant—excuse me, I forget he's your son—trying to tell us who can live and who must die. I'm not going to stand for that. The trouble with your son and Ted Coulter and the whole bunch of them is that they lack the moral character to stand up for what is right. They've been corrupted by their own power and shortsightedness. They believe this government is the only thing on earth that can solve all the problems this nation is facing."

He reached for another biscuit, drank down the rest of his tea, and grinned at Sheila. "How would you like a boat ride on the Potomac? I've got a little cruiser that I take out when I want to get away from my jailers. I promise I won't say one word about politics. We'll just act like two normal people. You can tell me about your garden and I'll tell you about the Minnesota Iron Range. What do you say?"

Sheila hesitated, trying to think what the president's mother would do. In spite of Ted Coulter's warning, wouldn't it be perfectly natural for her to be friends with her son's vice president? And the thought of spending an afternoon on the water with this man was an irresistible one. "Yes, I'd love to do that."

"I'll pick you up tomorrow afternoon around four."

As soon as Ranta left, Sheila had second thoughts. Coulter would not like her seeing the vice president. He had told her to keep her distance from Ranta. Still, she reasoned, Coulter needed her more than she needed him. How could he possibly fire her? She could go to the press with her story and expose the president before the whole world. She knew it was something she would not do, but Coulter could not be sure of that.

Minutes after Ranta left, the phone rang. It was Ted Coulter. She felt like a child caught with its hand in the cookie jar. To her relief he sounded unusually friendly. "I assume you aren't doing anything Saturday night?"

"No," she said.

"Well, you have an invitation to the White House for dinner. It's a small affair. Just the president and his wife, and myself and Mrs. Coulter. The president is anxious to meet you."

"I'd love that." She was genuinely excited. "How will I get there?"

"The White House will send a car for you at six sharp. See you then."

He hung up before Sheila thought to tell him about her plans with T. Russell Ranta. She smiled to herself, "I'm working my way up: the vice president Thursday and the president Saturday."

When she returned to the garden she began to think again of Ava. For all the difficulties and complications over the years, she was grateful for her sister's unshakable love. Without her sister she would have been as self-absorbed and brittle as Dan. She felt more uneasy than ever about taking Maida Lange's place. For the first time, it occurred to her that Ted Coulter might not have been telling the entire truth.

She stood with the rake in her hand, not moving, letting the breeze blow away the leaves from the little pile she had just gleaned. She asked herself if the vice president was right in thinking the president might destroy someone who got in his way. Would he destroy his own mother? If that were true the enormity of any possible complicity in his evil frightened her.

Sheila began raking again, trying to lose herself in her garden work. In the middle of a circle of boxwood, green shoots were just emerging. She examined the shoots, trying to distinguish between flower and weed. In the center of the bed was what looked like an ancient statue of a saint. He was wearing a monk's robe and his hands were extended. He seemed to be reaching out to her. Sheila remembered the name of the book the librarian had mentioned, *Monastic Gardens of the Fourteenth Century*. She supposed that was a book that Maida Lange would have enjoyed.

* * *

On his way back to the office, T. Russell Ranta thought over the afternoon. There was an elegance and ease to the way Maida Lange moved, almost as though she had been trained in those movements. Ranta had a nagging thought that something was wrong, but he was unable to sort out his misgivings. Her dissembling over her phone call puzzled him. He decided politics was making him paranoid. Here was an attractive woman whose company he enjoyed. Why question that? He had never been one to run around with twenty-year-olds. "Old Lear had it right," he thought. "Ripeness is all."

XIII

On Thursday morning Darron Sullivan, Special Assistant to the President for National Security, arrived at the Oval Office three minutes after the president. In the early days of the administration he had tried to be there before Robert Lange, but no matter what time he arrived the president was already there waiting. Sullivan got the message.

Now he came at the same time, 7:03 A.M., reconciled to finding the president waiting expectantly behind his desk. As soon as he was seated, a steward brought in glasses of orange juice and a pot of coffee. As the steward was arranging glasses and cups, the conversation was general. Sullivan said, "You'll be throwing the first pitch out soon, Mr. President."

Before the president could answer, the door opened and Coulter walked into the room. "Morning, sir," the steward said, standing aside to let him pass. Sullivan gave Coulter a less than welcoming look. Everyone in Washington knew Coulter as the president's pit bull. Right behind Coulter came Douglas Sarlund, the President's Chief of Staff, who was extremely jealous of the advisor's close relationship with the president. Sarland frowned suspiciously at Coulter. The last person to arrive was the vice president.

Ranta finished off a glass of the freshly squeezed orange juice in one gulp. He surveyed the room. "You look like a bunch of crepe hangers this morning."

The moment the steward closed the door behind him the president turned to Sullivan. "Let's hear the bad news."

Sullivan sighed, his hangdog look suggesting he felt a responsibility for the absurd things other countries did. "I'm afraid, Mr. President, that's about all we have this morning.

Since the coup, Obronsky has the Russian parliament in his pocket. It looks like he might get their permission to retake the Baltic states. Estonia, Lithuania, and Latvia are arming. Of course, it could just be a threat like the Cuba incident—an attempt to blackmail us for more money—but we'll have to watch them closely."

"I don't suppose you want my opinion," Ranta said, greedily eyeing Coulter's untouched glass of orange juice. "I say let's preempt them. Not a penny of aid to Obronsky, who is desperate for it, and we can beef up NATO maneuvers in the Baltics. If there is anything those Russians know, it's who means business and who doesn't." Ranta glanced sharply at the president. It was no secret in Washington that the vice president thought Lange had a fatal tendency to take no action when action was required. "What we have to do for a change is take the initiative instead of continually reacting to Obronsky's mischief," Ranta added.

Sullivan looked gratefully at the vice president.

"Your advice is always appreciated, Ranta." The president's tone was dismissive. "Okay, Sullivan, I hope that's the extent of the bad news."

Sullivan flushed and shuffled through his papers. "I'm afraid something more serious has come up. In fact, we almost awakened you early this morning, but we thought it best to round up all the information we could first. It's Saudi Arabia. They want our help. The fundamentalist regime in Egypt is deploying troops in the Sinai. Of course they're being supplied with plenty of arms from Iran, who obtained them from Russia. The problem is there are enough fundamentalists right there in Saudi Arabia to provide a dangerous fifth column. The Saudis have approached the Israelis for help as well—not troops, of course, that would only infuriate the fundamentalists, but weaponry. If the Saudis are willing to make some concessions to their own fundamentalists, Egypt says it will back down, but it looks like the king is holding firm."

Ranta downed Coulter's orange juice. "Let's get one of our

carriers..." He turned to Lange. "We still have a carrier, don't we? Get it in the Mediterranean off Port Said."

The president turned angrily to Ranta. "We can't be in two places at once. We'd be lucky to have the defenses to meet *one* of these crises. Sarlund, schedule a meeting with the Chief of Staff and Kinney at State for this morning. And, Sarlund, let's see if we can keep the media out of this for the moment. Is *that* all, Sullivan?"

Sullivan looked like a student who had angered his professor with a poorly prepared lesson. China had issued an edict that would all but nationalize the Hong Kong businesses, but Sullivan decided he'd talk with Ranta about that.

When Ranta left the Oval Office Sullivan hurried after him. Coulter, staring peevishly at his empty glass, said, "There's one up side."

"It escapes me." Lange detested optimism.

"When people see how much we are going to have to put back into defense, they'll understand why we have to scale back on health care."

"I don't know," Sarlund said. "Ranta's been working the Senate. He still has IOUs there. What's worse, the grass roots groups opposing the Bill are becoming more vocal."

"I know," the president agreed. "Every time I look out of the window, I see a new parade of them picketing outside the White House. Last night I heard one of them made it over the fence before he was stopped. The sooner this Bill is passed the better, or it will get away from us." He stared coldly at Coulter. "I think rather than spending your time sitting in on these security sessions, you might be out there working on the opposition."

"Yes, you're right," Coulter said, trying not to notice the smug look on Douglas Sarlund's face.

* * *

Ranta spent the morning closeted with Darron Sullivan.

Together they worked out counter moves to Obronsky's threats. Ranta decided to take their initiatives to the Foreign Affairs Committee where he had friends. If he worked it right, the committee chairman could be convinced to go on the national news that night and push those initiatives forward. The president would have to go along, or the whole nation would see just how indecisive Robert Lange was.

Ordinarily, on a day like this Ranta would remain in his office working, so that by the time night came his exhaustion would allow him to sleep, safe from the loneliness that hovered around him in his empty house like a plague of sharp-needled insects. Instead, he left his office in the early afternoon with a bounce in his step.

His secretary gave him a quizzical look. "You don't have an appointment. I can't believe you're leaving this early. You must have a date," she teased.

* * *

Ranta opened the door and helped Sheila into the small sedan, taking the hamper she had packed. "Not much of a date if you have to provide the food. I should have thought of that. Hope you weren't expecting a limousine," he said. "Never take them. They make me feel like I'm on my way to my own funeral." He settled in beside her and signaled the Secret Service agent, who doubled as his driver, that they were ready to leave.

Sheila stopped herself just in time from telling him she had had enough of limousines all those years of being driven to rehearsals for the soap. Instead she said, "I feel like a child let out of school."

"You have a reputation for being something of a recluse. I suppose you want to avoid being one of the media's little toys."

"I've never been comfortable in the public eye." Sheila smiled to herself. For years she had appeared daily before millions and thought nothing of it.

When they reached the marina Ranta led her down the narrow wharf to a sport cruiser. "You weren't expecting one of those?" He pointed to a large yacht in a nearby slip. "I always seem to be apologizing, but I wanted a boat I could handle myself."

"You must be something of a recluse yourself."

"Under the circumstances that's hard to arrange." Nearby five Secret Service agents were boarding an open boat. One of the agents offered to help him remove the canvas cover on his own boat, but Ranta motioned him away. "You fellows mind your own business. And keep your distance. As far as I know there are no Russian subs cruising the Potomac." He pulled in the lines and eased the boat out of the slip.

Sheila settled down, enjoying the warm April sun. A few sailboats skimmed along the river, their sails almost indistinguishable from the swatches of white clouds scudding across the blue sky.

"Only the second time I've had her out this year," Ranta said. He smiled down at Sheila. "I'll be honest with you. When I first met you, I wanted to spend time with you so that I could get to know more about Robert Lange. Your son never lets his guard down. It's hard to know what he's thinking. If you'll forgive me I do have one question. Would Dr. Lange have approved of the Compassionate Care Bill, or would he have agreed with you?"

Without thinking Sheila said, "Oh, I think he would have agreed with the president." She did not know why she was so sure. Then she remembered Coulter telling her it was Lange's father who had formed him.

"Like you, his father came from Germany?"

"Yes," Sheila said, feeling a little unsure of where the conversation was going.

"All the stories I've read about your son's childhood suggest your husband had always planned to have his son become president."

Sheila tried to recall Coulter's words, "As a child during the war, Dr. Lange saw firsthand what the chaos of unreason could do, what misery and terror it could accomplish. When their city became a part of Eastern Germany, his family had to flee from their home and leave everything they possessed behind. He dedicated his life to rationality, to the idea that if a reasonable man became the leader of a nation, the state would act reasonably." She was aware that in repeating what Coulter had said, her words sounded hollow, too much like a speech. Desperately she tried to think of a way to change the subject. Ranta's questions were becoming dangerous, forcing her into unknown territory. She smiled up at him. "I thought you said we weren't going to talk politics today."

"You're absolutely right. I'm sorry. Let's enjoy the scenery. There's Mount Vernon," he said, pointing toward the shore as he slowed the cruiser to view the mansion.

She looked at the gleaming white building set on the broad green lawn, watched over by great trees. Its pillared east front overlooked the shores of the river. She had seen Washington's house pictured more times than she could count, but this was the first time she had actually seen the house. "It's impressive, isn't it?"

"Glad you think so. No one bothers much with old George these days. Heroes are an anachronism. An embarrassment. It wouldn't surprise me if someone in Hollywood were putting together a movie that would cut him down to size."

"Didn't Shakespeare humanize the kings of England?"

"Humanize, yes, but not trivialize. We're getting too serious. Let's have a little fun." Ranta opened the throttle. The prow surged upward and the cruiser shot away from the Secret Service boat. "What they don't know is that I had a high-output engine installed in this thing over the winter. Look at them." He roared with laughter as he looked over his shoulder at the agents falling farther and farther behind. One of the agents was waving her arms, obviously not amused at Ranta's antics.

Sheila laughed, not so much at the plight of the agents as

from the pleasure the vice president was taking in their discomfort.

"What do you say we keep going and lose ourselves in the Bermuda Triangle? Don't you ever have dreams of escaping from your life?"

For a moment she couldn't answer, for that was exactly what this whole charade was about. She had an impulse so strong she could hardly resist telling this man the truth. She wanted his friendship to be with herself and not with the other woman she was being paid to impersonate.

He saw her hesitation and misunderstood it. "Sorry, why should I assume everyone else is as fed up with their life as I am?"

"I would have thought you loved politics."

"I do when my hands aren't tied. Just now I don't seem to be able to accomplish much that's worthwhile. There are a lot of people in Washington, and I'm afraid your son is one, who wouldn't have minded if my heart attack had been fatal. Cicero said people who look for happiness in power or wealth will be disillusioned. Cicero should have included politics in that list."

He was smiling but Sheila heard the bitterness behind the words.

Soon a helicopter appeared over their heads. Ranta laughed. "The boys called it in. Couldn't stand having me out of their sight." He eased the throttle on the boat, giving the frantic Secret Service agents a friendly wave. "We were going to forget politics. The river air is giving me an appetite. What's in that hamper?"

On her way to the library Sheila had explored a gourmet food store. After Ranta's invitation she had returned and made a few purchases for their outing. Now she proudly opened the hamper and drew out a loaf of french bread, slices of paté, a hearts of artichoke salad, eggs stuffed with caviar, and a sumptuous-looking strawberry torte.

Ranta looked hungrily at the generous display and grinned

down at her. "You know this is the first time in months I've felt really hungry. But I owe you one. I'll let you treat me today if you let me take you to dinner tomorrow night. I'm enjoying your company."

Sheila hesitated only a moment. "I accept if you promise the Secret Service won't have to sit at our table. And shouldn't they taste this food before you eat it?" she said, smiling at him.

"Only if it was prepared by your son." They both laughed at the absurdity.

* * *

It was still early evening when the vice president dropped Sheila off and then headed to a caucus meeting. She carried the empty hamper to the kitchen, then checked the wall calendar on which the president's mother had jotted down garden reminders. Something about the conscientious notes on the calendar and the careful entries in her hybridizing notebook had puzzled Sheila. How could they be the work of a confused and disturbed woman, a woman who had to be hospitalized? It didn't make sense.

She looked out at the garden, at the monk with his outstretched arms. She had to hunt for her glasses, and then it took her a minute to find the library number, but at last the librarian's voice responded on the other end.

"Alexandria library, Sue speaking."

"This is Maida Lange. I wonder if you might be able to help me with something?"

"Of course, Mrs. Lange. What can we do for you?"

"Could you tell me where the request came from for that book I donated to the library?"

"If you don't mind waiting a moment, I'll bring it up on the computer."

Sheila's knuckles were white from clutching the receiver. She hoped she hadn't overdone the accent.

"Yes, here it is. The interlibrary loan of *Monastic Gardens of the Fourteenth Century* was sent to the Singleton Library, and the request came from a Mrs. Bunge. Since it's such a valuable book, I took the liberty of getting the address of the person who requested it. It's the Bunge Nursing Home on Oak Street in Singleton. I've already sent your book. I hope that was all right?"

"Yes, of course," Sheila reassured her. "I was just curious. I'm glad someone else can enjoy the book. Thanks so much for your help." Sheila stood looking out into the garden. Suppose Maida Lange was in that nursing home? It seemed unlikely, but Sheila had to find out.

XIV

Sheila awoke before daylight with a sense of relentless resolve. She could no longer sit back and pretend that she was doing a service for her country when she might be part of a devious plot. From somewhere in her Sunday school childhood she recalled the phrase "sins of omission." She knew for her own peace of mind she would have to discover the truth. The clock in the kitchen seemed to stand still. When eight o'clock finally came she called the Alexandria Cab Company.

To avoid the morning commuters on their way into the Capitol, Sheila waited until a little after nine o'clock to have the taxi come for her. It didn't seem wise to risk renting a car in Alexandria where she might be recognized. Somehow the information might find its way back to Ted Coulter, who would certainly wonder what she was doing with a car. He had pointedly told her that the president's mother did not drive.

The National Airport was only minutes from Alexandria. The taxi dropped her off at an airport car rental, and by ten she was behind the wheel of a rental car. She had no alternative but to use her driver's license to rent the car, and for a moment she felt relieved to slip back into her own identity. The girl at the counter gave clear directions for getting out of the capital, but in her distraction Sheila found herself going the wrong direction on the expressway. She had to get off and back on before she was over the bridge and into Virginia. Studying the Virginia map provided by the agency, Sheila discovered Singleton was no more than a short drive from Alexandria.

The town was nondescript with its single traffic light and its cinderblock post office. It had seen its best days, like the hundreds of small Michigan towns she had left behind years ago. No jobs were to be had here: its school's graduates had to move on to find work in some crowded and impersonal city. Though they left the town behind in search of better opportunities, all their lives they would recall the town's old shade trees, its lilac bushes heavy with blossoms, its sidewalks worn from years of bicycles and skates, and they would wonder if they should not have stayed.

Sheila was reluctant to draw attention to herself by asking directions to Oak Street. Instead, she drove around crosshatching the streets until she came upon the street a block west of Main Street. The nursing home surprised her. From Ted Coulter's description she had imagined a large, professional, well-kept facility. Instead, she saw a decaying Victorian house desperately in need of repairs. "She can't be here," Sheila thought, relieved that she would not have to continue her search. Yet she parked the car a few doors down from the house. Tying a scarf around her hair and putting on sunglasses, she got out of the car to walk casually by the nursing home, taking in the dingy curtains and torn screen door. Without pausing she continued along the sidewalk, lingering by a nursery school to watch the noisy exuberance of the children on the playground.

Next door to the nursery school was a bed-and-breakfast, where a young woman was planting geraniums in an ornate cast-iron urn. Sheila paused and, smiling at the woman, said, "What a handsome urn. It must be very old."

The woman looked up. She was dressed in jeans and a man's plaid shirt. Her hair was tied with a frayed ribbon into a ponytail, and there was a smudge of dirt on her face. "Well, it came with the house, so I'm not sure. A lot of people have offered us good money for it, so I guess it must be old." Thinking Sheila's question might be an offer she added, "We wouldn't consider selling, though. Do you live around here?" Her question was one of curiosity and not suspicion.

"No. To tell you the truth I was interested in the nursing

home down the street. We're looking for a place for my husband's mother, but before I talked to the owners I thought I would take a look for myself. Maybe ask around. You can't be too careful these days. I don't suppose you could tell me anything about the home? Sometimes neighbors know more about these things than the authorities." The line of inquiry came easily to Sheila. She had asked the same questions when she was looking for a place for Ava.

"We don't see much of the residents there. They're mostly old people, a lot of them in wheelchairs. The Bunges run it. They seem nice enough." There wasn't much conviction in the woman's voice.

"Do they take in people with mental problems?"

"Oh, no. All the neighbors wondered about that at first. Mrs. Bunge told us they aren't equipped to handle those kinds of people. It's just sort of custodial. If this Compassionate Care Bill they're talking about goes through, I don't know how much longer people like the Bunges will have customers. I guess they're doing pretty well though. I saw carpenters there last month. Whatever they did, they did in the back of the house. I wish they would do something to the front of the place to spruce it up. It sure is an eyesore and people say it brings down the rest of the neighborhood." Sheila nodded sympathetically and turned to go, but the woman put out a hand to stop her.

"If you do decide to put your mother-in-law there, you or your husband might need a place to stay sometime when you come to visit her. Here's my card. Would you like to come in and take a look at our place?"

Sheila took the card. "Another time. Thanks. And thanks for the information."

Before going to her car Sheila passed by the nursing home again. Not seeing anyone at the windows, she walked quickly into the backyard, which was a tangle of weeds. The only effort at gardening appeared to be concentrated on a small square of dirt, where a few prematurely planted petunias had succumbed to a late frost. Sheila doubted if the creator of this crude landscape would have been the one to request a rare book on monastic gardens. The back door opened and Sheila hastily turned to leave, first glancing up at what the carpenters had been working on—sturdy iron grills on three of the windows.

* * *

The return taxi had to fight the Friday afternoon rush escaping from the capital for the weekend. Sheila was dropped off just in time to change for her dinner with the vice president. Although she had no solid proof, she was convinced now that she had been hired to take the place of the woman who was imprisoned behind the bars of the nursing home. The more she thought about it, the less Ted Coulter's story added up. If the president's mother had deteriorated to the point that she was simply too disturbed for anything but custodial care, why would he choose this place? And if she were that sick, would she be alert enough to request a book from the library? Unless...

The thought chilled Sheila. Unless it's all a sham. And the book is a cry for help!

On her way back from the nursing home, she had decided what to do. She would keep her date with the vice president. She would risk being honest with him and tell him what she suspected. She would tell him about her own involvement and beg his forgiveness. If she came to him voluntarily, she hoped he would see that she was innocent.

She rifled through Maida's closet, looking for something a little less fashionable than her own dresses. She tried to imagine what Maida Lange might wear, something European and somber, she guessed. Hanging toward the back of the closet was a simple black suit, well cut. With her own Valentino silk blouse it would do very nicely. She found a pin, an opal encircled in gold, in a small jewelry box. She would add that to the suit, somehow sure it was what Maida would have chosen, but putting on the clothes of the president's mother made her feel as though she were taking the clothes from the body of a dead woman. She shivered at the thought.

Twice she had almost picked up the phone to cancel her date with Toivo. She smiled. What an odd name... but he had insisted she call him that. The discreet and chastened appearance in the mirror reassured her. "Somehow," she told herself, "I will find a way to tell him. Maybe, just maybe, he'll forgive me."

XV

Le Lion d'Or was crowded. Ted Coulter had asked the maître d' to seat them at the table set aside for prominent government officials, but the maître d' had apologized, explaining that it was *tres malheureux* but this evening the table was reserved for the vice president. With many words of contrition, the maître d' ushered Coulter and his wife to a comparatively private table off to the side. "This will be more *intime*," he said.

Coulter felt rather irritated at having to defer to Ranta. The man was becoming an increasing problem. He managed to get all over Washington stirring up the special interest groups. Yesterday his picture had appeared in *The Post* at a press conference, where he had somehow managed to get the Right to Life people together with NOW. Right to Life had opposed the Compassionate Care Bill from the beginning. NOW opposed it because national census reports showed there were more elderly women than men, therefore under the Bill more women than men would be denied care.

Elly Coulter leaned across the table toward Ted. She spoke softly, knowing the diners around them would certainly be straining to hear any political tidbit that was said at the table of the president's advisor. "Ted, this is our first chance to talk without the children around. Is something bothering you?"

He opened the menu and pretended to study it. "Elly, you've been after me to take a night off for weeks. Now are we going to enjoy it—or will you spend the whole evening doing your Dr. Freud thing?"

"But something *is* bothering you. I can sense it."

He gave up the pretense of looking at the menu. "Of

course there are things bothering me. Read the papers. The world is a mess and I'm not in a position to just shrug my shoulders. Bobby and I have to make difficult decisions, and then we have to shoulder the responsibility when we get blamed for them."

Annoyed at his evasive response, Elly leaned closer and lowered her voice even more. "You've been dealing with crises for two years without waking up in the middle of the night and pacing back and forth like a caged animal. Don't you understand? I'm not prying. I only want to help you."

All of his defensive anger disappeared. Elly Coulter was one of those disconcerting people whose innocent stare made you feel as though you were lying to a child. He longed to tell her the truth, to share with her some of the anxiety and guilt he felt, to receive her assurance that he was right in what he was doing. Yet he knew she wouldn't approve.

Sitting there, Coulter thought of how cold and dismissive Lange had grown toward him lately. This morning, right in front of the Secretary of State and the Joint Chiefs of Staff, the president told Ted there was no need for him to sit in on the meeting. Coulter stalked out of the room, his face burning with humiliation. He knew that every time Robert Lange had to look at him, Lange was reminded of his mother. For a brief moment Coulter peevishly comforted himself with the knowledge that at any time he had the power to destroy the president. Right that minute he could get up from his table and walk the two or three yards to the table where CBS's anchor was having dinner. All it would take would be one sentence. But Coulter knew Bobby had nothing to fear. Bobby was absolutely convinced of Coulter's fierce loyalty—and, of course, Coulter had to admit Bobby was right.

He decided the least he could do was to make this evening pleasant for Elly. He smiled across the table. "Look, don't worry. There are a few problems in the administration I can't get a handle on, but time will solve them. There's no point in hashing them over with you. Just trust me that things will

resolve themselves." Elly was silent. Frustrated, Coulter blurt-
ed out what he had been brooding over all day. "I don't think
Bobby wants me around anymore. I've been seriously thinking of resigning." The moment he said the words he realized
how little he meant them, but a smile lit Elly's face and he
didn't take them back.

"That's the best news I've heard in years. Ted, that's the
first time I've ever heard you raise a question about Robert
Lange. Sometimes I think he's more of a rival than a mistress
would be."

For a few moments Ted Coulter contemplated the
immense satisfaction he'd feel in telling the president that he
could make his own arrangements for his mother. Let him
deal with the Bunges. See how he liked it. Let him climb
those servants' stairs and unlock the door and face his mother.
All the while Coulter was indulging his wounded pride, he
knew the daydream was only a fantasy. He would never aban-
don Robert Lange.

* * *

As they walked through Le Lion d'Or to their table, Ranta
kept a possessive hold on Sheila's arm. When they were seated
she said, "You're looking very pleased with yourself."

"You can't see him from where you're seated, but there's a
man across the room who isn't too happy to find me here
tonight. As a matter of fact he's looking quite livid. I guess I
didn't realize how much I've been getting under his skin lately."

"Who is he?"

"We call him the bootlicker. He's the man who does all the
president's dirty work for him. But let's not spoil our dinner
by talking about politics."

"Politics is your life." She smiled at him. "Why shouldn't
we discuss it? Tell me, what do you think of the president?"
She would lead up to her suspicions by gradually coaxing
Ranta to talk about Lange. Then she would tell him the truth,

tell him who she really was, and ask him to find out if Maida Lange was being held against her will in the nursing home. She was only sorry her confession would have to take place in a crowded restaurant, although having other people around them might soften the kind of outburst she feared from Toivo.

"Surely you don't need to have someone else tell you about your son?"

"I'm interested in how others view him."

"I don't want to hurt your feelings, but I'm afraid your son and I have our serious differences. We're both ambitious, but I could imagine myself living another life; I don't believe your son ever could. Unlike Caesar, his ambition is made of sterner stuff. That makes him a rather formidable enemy.

"I don't say he isn't intelligent, and he's read just about everything, but somehow it doesn't seem to stick. It's as though he thinks the world is just ten minutes old, some sort of blank slate on which he can write whatever he pleases.

"Of course, he'd have plenty to say about me. I'm sure he thinks I'm mired in the past with a bunch of fossilized principles and worn-out beliefs." He paused. "I'm afraid I'm being rather insensitive, but when someone asks me what I think, I tell them."

"You don't know how important your opinion is to me," Sheila said, glad for his honesty.

"I don't think I've ever seen your son relaxed. He always appears to be preoccupied with the next thing on his agenda. But I don't intend to spend the whole evening discussing Robert Lange when I have the company of a lovely woman to enjoy. Let's just have a good time." He signaled the waiter and ordered dinner and champagne to accompany it. "Do you care for the theater? There's a new production of 'Timon of Athens' playing at the Kennedy Center."

"Yes," she smiled up at him. "Yes, I've always been fond of the theater." Hurriedly she added, "Of course only in a modest way. I really don't know much about it. Timon is certainly a man who discovered the politics of friendship, if you can put friendship and politics together. Several years ago I saw Brian Bedford do a wonderful Timon." She remembered taking Ava to the small Canadian village of Stratford for a weekend. They drove through miles of rich farmland until they finally came to the quaint town. The English heritage of Stratford was evident everywhere in the profusion of flowers and a river called the Avon with swans gliding about.

As though he had been reading her mind, Ranta said, "I saw the production in Canada. My wife and I used to make yearly pilgrimages to Stratford for the Shakespearean plays." His face seemed to cloud with memories. "We used to stay in country inns and do all the antique stores. That was her passion. In those days I could travel without being recognized. I suppose it was the production Bedford brought to New York that you saw."

Quickly Sheila said, "Yes." The thought that the two of them might have been at Stratford at the same time, perhaps sitting close to each other, silenced her.

She saw that Ranta was puzzled by her silence. The awkward pause was broken as the waiter arrived with the champagne. "I haven't had champagne in years," Sheila lied and smiled brightly across the table.

"Nor have I," Ranta said. "It's an occasion for both of us. I'll tell you something if you promise to keep it a secret. Up on the Iron Range I was in the high school dramatic club. I think I really always wanted to go on the stage. I suppose there are those who consider me more of a ham actor than a politician, but as I see it the two are the same. You, on the other hand, strike me as a woman who values her privacy, someone for whom acting in front of an audience would be torture."

Sheila gave him an earnest look. "Yes," she agreed. "Acting would be the last thing I would choose." It was true. She would give anything in the world if she could just be herself with this man. Before the evening was over, she would tell him the truth.

* * *

Across the room Elly asked, "Who is the woman with the vice president? She's very attractive." From the moment T. Russell Ranta and the woman he was escorting had walked into the room, Ted's attention was riveted on what was going on at Ranta's table.

"It's Bobby's mother."

"The president's mother! With Ranta! You can't be serious. I thought she never went out in public. Are you sure it's her?"

"Of course I'm sure. I used to stop at her house with Bobby when we were in law school. She has no business with that fool."

"Ranta is much too shrewd to be a fool.... Why shouldn't she go out with him if she likes? He's a widower and she's a widow. I think they make a handsome couple, and they're obviously enjoying each other's company. In fact, they look like a couple of infatuated kids."

Ted turned on her. "That's ridiculous. They hardly know each other. And how does it look for Bobby to have his mother appear with Ranta? He's betrayed both the president and the party with his rogue attack on the Compassionate Care Bill. It was a sure thing until all the weirdo organizations started rallying around him."

Elly regarded him thoughtfully. "I don't want to be disloyal, but I have some questions about that Bill myself. Anyhow, we know a lot of people who disagree about politics and stay happily married. Ted, I wish you wouldn't glower at them. Other people are beginning to notice."

Coulter got up from the table, his face distorted with anger. Hastily Elly reached for his arm, trying to stop him. He pulled away and in the struggle knocked over a wine glass. A waiter hurried over to the table and began dabbing at the puddle. As Coulter strode toward the vice president's table, a photographer suddenly materialized from the restaurant's vestibule and raised a camera to his eye.

* * *

The vice president was startled to see Ted Coulter approach their table looking as if he could eat nails. Ranta tried to guess what was going on. He knew it couldn't be his opposition to the president. They had already had that out. He decided it was his being here with the president's mother. Ranta had known Coulter would be miffed; he hadn't dreamed the man would be enraged.

"Well, Coulter, nice of you to come over to say hello. You must know Mrs. Lange."

"Yes, we're old friends." Coulter stood glaring down at her. "I must say I'm surprised to find you here tonight, Mrs. Lange."

Sheila, with her back turned to the Coulters' table, had not seen Ted Coulter until he stood beside her. She quickly looked up at the sound of his voice. The color drained from her face. Her hand holding her coffee cup started to tremble.

It was obvious to Ranta that she was afraid of Coulter. Coulter, he decided, was the one the president had sicced on her to get her to keep quiet about the health Bill. She had been so positive when she first phoned him, Ranta was sure she had been warned off.

"The vice president was kind enough to ask me to have dinner with him." Sheila's voice was unsure, defensive.

Ranta, furious at Coulter's rude bullying, impaled him with a sharp stare. "How come Bobby's letting you off the leash tonight, Coulter?" Ranta knew Coulter hated anyone to refer to the president as "Bobby"—anyone but himself.

Coulter spoke through clenched teeth. "I just wanted to say hello to Mrs. Lange and remind her that we have a little date." He turned away and strode back to his own table where the waiter was laying a napkin over the wine stain.

"Didn't know you knew Coulter that well." Ranta watched Sheila's tense face. "I wouldn't have thought he was someone whose company you'd enjoy."

Sheila, looking pale and confused, finally managed a weak response, "He called me yesterday to invite me to dinner at the White House tomorrow evening."

"You mean your son didn't bother to invite you himself?"

Sheila appeared flustered. "Well, he's terribly busy these days. Of course the invitation came from him. Ted simply was confirming the arrangements." She lay her napkin on the table and reached for her purse. "It's been a wonderful evening, Toivo, but I'm a little tired. I'm not used to so much excitement. I think we had better leave."

"Yes, of course." Ranta signaled to the waiter. The maitre d' would total the bill, add a generous tip, and put it on his account.

In her nervousness Sheila dropped her purse. Ranta bent to recover it. Looking up he caught her in an unguarded moment. There was panic on her face. He began to loath Ted Coulter.

When they reached her home, aware of the Secret Service watching him, probably with high amusement, he hung by her doorway like a boy on a first date. He hoped she would invite him in for a drink, but she merely thanked him for the evening. Still hopeful he asked, "About that play at the Kennedy Center, shall I get tickets?"

"That's very kind but I'm afraid I'm really not up to it." She took several quick breaths, holding her hand to her chest. "I have asthma. There are so many things I'm allergic to, I'm afraid I'm much better at home. But thank you for a wonderful evening."

Before he could say another word she closed the door behind her. He stood there for a moment. He doubted she was having an asthma attack. If she were, it was certainly Coulter who had brought it on. Tomorrow he decided he would give Godden at the FBI a call to see if he had anything on Coulter. It was probably his imagination but it wouldn't hurt to check.

* * *

On the other side of the door Sheila collapsed into a chair, certain that her performance had been a disaster. All of her professional career, Sheila had been conscientious in preparing thoroughly for her parts. She was the first at rehearsals and the first to memorize her lines. She knew she would never be a great actress, but at least she tried to be a competent one.

But tonight she had clearly failed, committing one gaffe after another. The thing that troubled her most was that she had not been able to tell Toivo the truth. She had been afraid he would think she was only confessing because she had been caught out by Ted Coulter. He would never believe that she had meant to tell him that evening. She could not go to the police or the FBI; they would immediately want to know what her involvement was. She knew the penalty for kidnapping. She would be considered some sort of accessory. Yet she couldn't simply disappear and leave an innocent woman locked up. She had to help her! She tried to think if there might be some way to get into the nursing home and release the prisoner. She recalled the iron grills at the window and knew that was impossible. Elaborate care was being taken to imprison whomever was behind those bars. In the morning she would have to call Toivo and tell him the truth. She was sure he would never want to see her again.

Sheila started up the stairway, anxious to get out of Maida Lange's clothes. As she always did with her own clothes, she automatically checked the pockets of her jacket before taking it off. Something was in the pocket. She drew out an envelope addressed to Mrs. Peter Lange. The return address was a German hospital in Berlin. She only hesitated for a moment before taking out the letter. Unfolding the official looking paper, she was disappointed to see the letter was written in German.

XVI

Robert Lange could not say why he had always been mistrustful of his closest friend, unless it was because Ted Coulter thought too highly of him. How could he trust in the judgment of someone who was so foolish as to idolize him? No one knew better than Lange how few qualities there were in him to admire. Just now his feelings toward Coulter were more than mistrustful. The president was furious with his advisor, who was standing in front of his desk, summoned by an early morning phone call. "I want you over here," Robert had shouted into the phone.

The two people Robert Lange was most anxious to keep apart had found each other. And their meeting had become a media disaster. *The Washington Post* lay open on the president's desk to a gossip column captioned:

FIRST MOM DATES VICE PRESIDENT

An improbable couple sashayed into Le Lion d'Or restaurant last evening. The rebellious vice president, T. Russell Ranta, escorted the reclusive president's mother, Maida Lange. No one can recall the last time Maida Lange was seen in public. Often rumored to be ill, Mrs. Lange looked the picture of health last night as she and the vice president exchanged smarmy glances over champagne. The only interruption to this idyll came when Ted Coulter stomped across the room to snarl what appeared to be some disagreeable words at Ranta. Perhaps he was chastising him for not supporting the Compassionate Care Bill. Coulter then stomped back to his table where Elly Coulter, probably nervous about the little terrier she's tied to, had knocked over a glass of wine.

Robert Lange glared at his advisor. "Just tell me why you had to create a scene." The president's lips compressed inward so that his mouth became a grim line.

"I guess I lost it. When the two of them came in together after I had told her—warned her actually—to keep away from Ranta, I couldn't believe my eyes. He was like the cat that ate the canary, so cocky and smug."

"You promised me Sheila Covell would do exactly what we wanted her to. She's supposed to be playing the part of my mother, not some glamorized actress traipsing around to high-profile D.C. restaurants and getting her name in the paper. Can you imagine my mother doing something like that? Can we trust this woman or not?"

"Don't worry, Bobby, I'll take care of it. It's just a little misunderstanding. I'll stop over and talk with her today and straighten things out."

"Ted, if you had ignored the whole thing no one would have guessed who she was. I want you to leave Sheila Covell to me. And you can forget about coming to the White House for dinner with us tonight. After the scene in the restaurant, your presence would only draw the attention of the media. I'll talk with Covell myself."

"I've already told Elly we'd be coming. She's been looking forward to it. What am I supposed to say to her?"

"I'm sure you can make some excuse. To tell you the truth, Ted, I'm beginning to wonder if you still have what it takes to handle the advisor's position. The whole point of your job is being able to stay calm when the heat's turned on. You're supposed to cool the media off, not throw raw meat to those hungry dogs. I'm leaving my mother to you. Do what you have to. I don't want any trouble in that department. If there is a hitch there, Ted, I'm warning you, you're finished."

Lange knew he was asking for trouble. Ted Coulter could finish him with one phone call. He took pleasure in courting danger, a certain thrill in seeing how close he could come to destroying himself. Recklessly, he allowed himself to push the danger even farther.

"Another thing. Why did you set up a meeting for me in the Rose Garden with the Association of Private Campground Owners?"

"You said you wanted to be seen to be more friendly with small businesses," Ted choked out. "And they do have sort of an outdoor environmental tie-in."

"You're losing it, Ted. Let me tell you something. You're just like everyone else. You think I sit in this office as a sort of puppet with you pulling the strings. You think I serve at your pleasure and for your convenience so you can brag to those pretentious parents of yours that you're close to the President of the United States. Well, I have a surprise for you. Any day now I might decide I've had enough. I might walk out of here the same way I walked out of law school and go and live my own life. Only this time you won't be able to find me and drag me back. And you'll have to deal with my mother alone."

Listening to his own voice, his explosion of rage had alarmed Robert Lange. He turned his back on Coulter to keep him from seeing the fear on his face. "Just get out of here," he snapped.

He heard the door close as he dropped into his leather chair. The red light on the phone was flickering, letting him know an important call was waiting. After a deep breath, he picked it up and resumed the presidency.

* * *

Ted Coulter slunk from the office like a whipped dog with its tail between its legs. The Secret Service agents who were hovering outside of the Oval Office stared at his flushed face with open curiosity.

Coulter fought to keep tears from his eyes as he stumbled into his office and slammed the door. He had risked everything for that man! If Maida Lange ever got to the police, he, Ted Coulter, would be accused of kidnapping. It would ruin not only him but Elly and the children as well. All his pandering for power and recognition was about to destroy him.

And what would his parents say? Leaning against the door, he trembled with resentment and fear. For a moment, standing in front of the president's desk, he had relived his dishonorable dismissal from VMI. Once again, he was the disgraced cadet before the Honor Court. Coulter had clenched his fists to keep himself from reaching over and strangling Robert Lange.

Over the years he had often stood back and watched as Lange discarded people who were no longer useful to him. It had never occurred to him that one day it could happen to him. That Bobby could turn on him. Last night when he told Elly he might resign, he had merely been toying with the notion that he could be free of Bobby if he wished. Even as he had said it, he knew he didn't mean it.

The feeling of power he had once pretended to have over the president was gone. He could go to the media with his story, but he was just as guilty as the president, and Lange knew it. Robert Lange would lose the presidency, but he, Ted Coulter, would be arrested on criminal charges. Lange could deny knowing anything about the plan. And there was no conclusive evidence to incriminate him.

He remembered Robert's words, "I'm leaving my mother to you. I don't want any trouble in that department." Coulter knew if the Bunges discovered Maida Lange's true identity, they wouldn't hesitate in the least to blackmail him. He tried to imagine facing Elly after the truth was discovered. He couldn't take any more chances.

Packed away in the attic of his Georgetown home were several boxes, oddments Elly had inherited from her parents: a set of Haviland dishes they were saving for one of the children, Elly's mother's wedding dress, an expensive croquet set from England, and Elly's father's 950 Beretta, which neither he nor Elly's father had bothered to register. Like a birthday child, he saw himself breaking open the various boxes until he found the one that contained the perfect gift.

* * *

"Try one of these, Tom." Tom Bunge gratefully selected three warm muffins from a basket Liz passed to him. "I'm practicing for when we own our own bed-and-breakfast. Each morning I'm going to serve a different kind of muffin along with gourmet coffee. So far I've made bacon muffins, chocolate chip muffins, orange muffins, oat bran muffins, banana muffins… these are gingerbread muffins."

Tom, who had spent the morning in town shopping for groceries, a task Liz had delegated and which he enjoyed, now settled down with the muffins, a steaming cup of coffee, and *The Post*. He read the paper in strict order: the front page headlines, the sports section, the comics, and the business page, where he faithfully checked on the five stocks he was planning to own one day. As he plodded conscientiously through the paper from front to back, he prided himself on being informed. For Tom Bunge, the very act of knowing what was going on was as good as being on the scene. He had an opinion on everything. He was wholeheartedly in favor of the Compassionate Care Bill. It was true there would be fewer older people, but those his age would have more benefits. He viewed the world as a finite pie and kept a diligent eye on the size of his slice.

He took a huge bite. "These are the best you made yet," he said to Liz, who grinned. "Aren't you going to take some upstairs?" He was aware of the prestige conferred on his establishment by having in residence the mother of the Advisor to the President of the United States. He was careful to do his best for her. Not to mention the sizable cash payment they received every month. That she had to live locked up behind iron bars on her windows he considered unfortunate—but since her seclusion was necessary for the good of the country, better here than elsewhere.

"In a minute," Liz answered. "It always bothers me, the expression on her face when I come in."

Tom was bent over *The Post*, his third muffin arrested midway between his plate and his mouth. "Hey, honey, look here."

"What's the matter?" She leaned over his shoulder and followed his chubby finger pointing to a picture caption: First Mom Dates Vice President. "Don't it look just like her?" Tom said. "It's eerie. No wonder she thinks she's the president's mother."

"Isn't it strange, though, that those two should look so much alike. It seems more than a coincidence," said Liz as she looked more closely at the picture.

"What do you mean?" It was a sore point with him that Liz often arrived at a conclusion more speedily than he did.

"Well, one of these women is the mother of the President of the United States and the other is the mother of his advisor. It would be weird if they both looked alike." After a moment she said, "You remember when she first came I told you there was this actress on the soap that looked just like her and how she wasn't on the program anymore?"

"So?" He was trying to catch up.

"I have this funny feeling. Maybe Mr. Coulter isn't telling us the truth. I mean, his mother reads lots of books and seems perfectly okay in everything else she says, except when she talks about being the president's mother. I mean, what if she really is?"

"She couldn't be. This lady is." He pointed to the photo.

"I think we should show her the picture. Maybe she can tell us something that would explain it."

Together they climbed the stairs, Tom carrying a plate of muffins and *The Post*, Liz balancing a cup of hot oolong tea. It was a tentative procession, for they were beginning to be apprehensive of what they might learn from their secluded guest.

* * *

Maida looked out at the greening trees through her barred windows. The approach of spring saddened her, for every unfolding of leaf and flower was an indication not only of time passing but of time lost. Each day of her imprisonment was a forewarning of other lonely days that would come and go. She found it ironic that she was the first casualty of her son's proposed health plan. She was a martyr to the cause. And no one would ever know that Maida Lange had been sacrificed on her son's political altar.

She had been sure that she would be missed, but somehow, between them, Robert and Ted Coulter had successfully managed to arrange things so that no one had noticed her disappearance. At first this depressed her, but after thinking about it, she saw that hope, like faith, was something one holds on to despite circumstances, not because of them. After that the flicker of hope began to glow again.

The Bunges had respected her privacy and made a practice of knocking before coming into her quarters. She supposed it was some kind of polite homage to their most important resident. She heard the key turn in the lock. First Liz and then Tom entered. They carefully placed their offerings on the sitting room table. Maida was surprised to see the two of them together. She was further puzzled to find them hanging about rather than disappearing downstairs after a word or two as they usually did, for they were obviously uncomfortable in her presence. She was glad to make them uncomfortable and anxious to be rid of them, for their oppressive presence choked her small room. As long as they remained in the room with her, Maida's small vestige of hope disappeared.

Tom handed her *The Post,* which she refused with a shake

of her head. "Look at the picture here," he coaxed. "It looks just like you; only it's the president's mother."

Maida snatched the paper from his hand. It was her. The woman was an exact likeness, and she was wearing one of Maida's suits. On the lapel of the black suit was the opal pin that had belonged to her aunt. She looked at the Bunges. "Is this some cruel trick?" She was grasping for breath and reached for her inhaler. With all the new computer technology, perhaps they had simulated her portrait and attached it to some other woman, but where had the woman found those clothes?

"Now don't get upset. That's bad for your asthma," Liz said. "You can look at the date. It's today's paper, so there's no way we could have done it. I was saying to Tom it's no wonder you think you're the president's mother with how much you look like her."

Maida felt her chest contracting until she could hardly breathe. She studied the photo. Her phone call to Ranta had been her first contact with the man. Apart from television, Maida had never met the vice president nor had he ever met her. Because of his outspoken attacks on the Compassionate Care Bill, she had thought he was someone she could trust, but he, too, must be involved with this sinister plot.

She turned to the Bunges. "Don't you see now that everything I said was true?" For the first time she saw a glimmer of doubt in their faces. Suddenly she recalled something from the days when Robert used to visit Ted at Greengate. "Ted Coulter's parents live in Fauquier County, less than an hour from here. Their number must be in the phone book. I used to talk with my son when he was visiting there."

Years before, Maida remembered reading that the Empress Elizabeth of Austria had visited a Viennese asylum to be confronted with an inmate who insisted that she was the true Empress Elizabeth and that the Empress was an impostor. Now Maida knew what the Empress must have felt.

Tom went down the stairway slowly. From the living room he could hear the TV blaring away. He took out the phone book and soon found a number listed under Coulter, Theodore. Mr. Coulter himself? No. Tom had seen him named as Theodore Coulter, Jr., and he had learned from a newspaper article that he did not live in Virginia but in Georgetown with his wife and children.

The phone was answered almost immediately. "Yes?"

Faced with so curt a response Tom was momentarily taken aback. He managed to stammer, "Is Mrs. Coulter there?"

"This is Mrs. Coulter. Who is this?"

"Are you Theodore Coulter Junior's mother?"

"Yes. Who are you? Are you a reporter? Has something happened to my son?" He hung up and, slowly ascending the stairway, returned to what he now realized was the room of the president's mother. As he opened the door, both women looked at him expectantly. He looked at Liz, his face pale.

"You were right," he said, his voice almost a whisper. He looked at Maida with new respect.

"I knew it—as soon as I saw the picture!" Liz said. "There was this actress that looked just like you on 'Day into Night.' She stopped appearing on the show a little before you came here. Do you think that's her?"

Maida considered the possibility. "Yes, they could have arranged that. They certainly have the money to pay her off. She could be living in my house right now and wearing my clothes. Ted Coulter and my son must have been carefully planning my imprisonment for weeks. If that's true, the two of you will be involved in a kidnapping plot that is sure to get out eventually. Think what will happen to you then."

"Excuse us," Tom said nervously. He and Liz tiptoed from the room, carefully locking the door after them. Slowly, quietly, they descended the stairway into the kitchen. They looked at each other across the kitchen table.

"Do you believe her?" Liz asked.

Tom returned to his muffin. "I don't know." He nibbled thoughtfully. "I guess I have to believe her, partly. All I know is we might be in big trouble. I think we should let her go.

Maybe she's telling the truth, and maybe she isn't, but I don't think we can risk taking a chance."

"What if Mr. Coulter goes to the authorities about Ohio?"

"Whoever she is, he wasn't telling us the truth, so he's in trouble himself. I doubt he would want to draw attention to what he's done."

"What will we do if she tells them we kept her locked up?"

"I've got an idea about that." He stuffed the last bit of muffin in his mouth, washed it down with cold coffee, and looked for a pen and paper. Laboriously he scribbled down a series of phrases in mock legalese: will not hold them responsible, of my own free will, completely absolved from any wrongdoing. Tom Bunge had little respect for following the law, but held great stock in its protection.

Returning to the small room upstairs, he handed the paper to Mrs. Lange. "What we want from you," he said to Maida, "is to sign this. If you do we'll let you leave. I've got somewhere to go first, but after I get back we'll give you money and call a taxi for you."

"How do I know this is not just another trick?"

"Look, we got ourselves into a mess, and we just want to get out of it as soon as possible." Tom handed her a pen. "Now, you sign that and in an hour or so you'll be free to go."

"There's one thing," Maida said. "I don't want Ted Coulter to know you've let me go. You've got to promise not to call him. He's capable of doing anything for my son."

"That's fine by us," Liz said. "Right now, Mr. Coulter is the last person we want to talk with. He lied to us and he's gotten us in a lot of trouble. If I was you I'd keep my distance from him."

* * *

Tom Bunge drove his van along the *allée* of hornbean trees and pulled onto Greengate's circular drive. The immensity of the house and its surrounding grounds intimidated him, but he also felt pride in the elegant surroundings, for he felt an affinity with them. He sat in the van for a moment, rehearsing what he was going to say. Beside him lay a ragtag arrangement of wilted multicolored carnations he had purchased from a local florist.

The bell was answered by a woman dressed in a tan uniform with a neatly pressed white apron. She sized him up with all the prejudicial judgment of those who themselves have experienced discrimination. He took a deep breath and said, "Tell Mrs. Coulter I got a delivery here in the van for her."

"You can give it to me."

"I got orders to give it to Mrs. Coulter personally. It's flowers from her son."

The maid, relenting a little, disappeared into the house, closing the door firmly behind her.

A moment later a thin woman appeared. She was wearing checked slacks and a silk blouse. Her white hair was pushed back by a blue velvet band, and her slim arm was weighted down by a tangle of gold bracelets, whose clinking rattle sounded to Tom like the jangle of expensive coins.

"If you're Mr. Ted Coulter's mother—Mr. Coulter that's advisor to the president—I got some flowers for you from your son."

She stared at him with obvious impatience. "Certainly I'm Mr. Coulter's mother, but I don't understand. What does his position have to do with his sending flowers?"

Tom pulled the arrangement out of the van and thrust it at the woman. "We don't ask questions; we just follow orders. Have a nice day." He climbed into the van and headed back to Singleton.

When he returned he described the woman to Liz. "She's his mother for sure, but she's not what you'd call a real warm person."

* * *

Ted Coulter looked up to see Elly opening the door to his study. "I couldn't imagine where you were," she said. "I was looking all over for you. Your mother wanted to talk with you."

"I was up rummaging in the attic."

"What in the world were you doing up there?"

"Going through a box of old books I've stored up there for years. Nothing important. What did Mother want?"

"To thank you for some flowers and to ask why you sent them. I got the impression she thought they were a rather pathetic arrangement, but you know how your mother can be."

"I didn't send any flowers. There must have been some mistake."

"Your mother doesn't make mistakes," Elly said in a mocking tone that was rare for her.

Coulter wasn't really listening. He was thinking that he would have to get bullets for the cartridge, maybe go somewhere and test the gun. It hadn't been fired in years.

Elly brushed off the attic dust from his coat. "I thought when you came home early today from the White House you might have resigned?" She looked questioningly at him. "I guess you weren't serious last night."

"I couldn't leave Bobby at a time like this. There's too much going on. Just this morning he said how much help I was." In his eagerness to convince himself, Coulter didn't notice the disbelief that spread over Elly's face. "When he wants something important done, I'm the one to do it. There's no one else in this treacherous town he can depend on and he knows it. One of these days I'll be writing the memoirs of my time in the White House."

Elly winced. "There hasn't been much about your job these last months that would make for a very cheerful book." She watched as Coulter locked his briefcase. "Ted, are you feeling all right? Your face is flushed." She tried to feel his forehead but he brushed her hand aside. "Bing is pleased that you're going to be here for his birthday dinner."

"A twelfth birthday is a milestone." He tried to recall himself at that age, but all the intervening years got in the way. "I have some things to work on now, Elly, and after dinner I'll have to go out for a couple of hours. There's a meeting..." His voice trailed off. He found he was too distracted even to invent a meeting, and yet in Washington that evening there would be hundreds of meetings. For years he had despised their tedium; now he would give anything to be going to one. The tedium of a long meeting seemed a blessing compared to having to carry out the errand he had set for himself.

He was relieved when Elly closed the door of his study. He had to be alone to go over his plans. He had to have a clear head to go through with it. He told himself he was doing this for Bobby, and when Bobby discovered how clever he had been, he would be sorry for the way he had treated him that morning.

*   *   *

Randall Godden sat back in his chair and stretched his arms above his head. The speaker button on his phone was punched down, and T. Russell Ranta's voice boomed out into his office. He got up and closed his door before replying to Ranta's question. "Sure I can keep quiet about something, Mr. Vice President. That's why they put me in this job. If I wanted to tell what I knew about the people in this town, I could get a ten million dollar advance on a book contract. What do you have in mind?"

"I have Ted Coulter in mind."

Godden laughed. "You sure you aren't after the man just because he ruined your little party last night? I saw *The Post* this morning just like the rest of Washington. Is there any truth to the fact that you're going to be the president's step-daddy? You should be able to tell him what to do about the Compassionate Care Bill then, maybe take him to the wood-shed if he doesn't mind you."

"Listen, Godden. This is no laughing matter. Maida Lange

is a very nice woman, and it was the first time I had taken her out in public. Thanks to all this publicity it will probably be the last time. Just forget all that. The thing is Coulter overreacted last night. I mean, I'm no buddy of the president these days. Everyone knows that, but Coulter plain freaked out. This morning I heard he came skulking out of the president's office like a whipped puppy."

"To tell you the truth, it's funny you should call, Mr. Vice President, because I've been keeping an eye on Coulter." Godden depressed the button on the speaker phone. "Look, this isn't going to go any further, is it?" Godden had always been able to trust Ranta, but Godden had not attained his position by taking chances. One thing he was absolutely sure of was that if Ranta gave his word he'd keep it.

"I'm not going to say anything. Anyhow, no one's talking to me these days. The president has put out the word that I'm anathema because of my fight against his Bill."

"Some of us around here are taking that Bill a little hard ourselves, but I make it a policy to stay out of politics," said Godden. "That's why I'm still here. What I wanted to tell you is that Coulter came by here last month asking for some phony identification. Said it was to play a joke on someone. I didn't buy it, but the guy's got the president's ear, so I did him a favor. You never know when you might need one in return. That's the way things work here, but I don't have to tell you that. Anyhow, the more I got to thinking about it, the less I liked it. So I did a little looking. Right after his request to me, Coulter made some unofficial trips to New York, skipping school from the White House without any explanation. We don't know where he went. We didn't follow him. That stuff's all up to the Secret Service, and they'd hit the roof if they knew we were encroaching on their territory."

"Could you bug his phone?"

"You know better than that. You were in Congress when they tied our hands."

"So what can you do for all the money the country pays you fellows?"

"Last time I looked it wasn't all that much," retorted Godden.

"I'll tell you something interesting, Godden. The president's mother mentioned last evening that she was having dinner tonight at the White House with her son and the Coulters. This morning I happened to be down in the basement of the White House where Irene Carrick, the director of scheduling for the president, has her office. We were having a little chat. She can get a readout on that little black box of hers, so she knows where the president is at any time, day or night. I looked over her shoulder. Sure enough, there's the president's mother's name listed for dinner at 7:00 P.M., and right underneath are the Coulters' names. But the Coulters' names were crossed off."

XVII

Sheila wandered distractedly from room to room straightening pictures, plumping pillows, occupying herself with meaningless tasks while she tried to find the courage to make the call that she knew would change her life forever. The house that had been such a pleasure to her had now become a horror. Everything she looked at reminded her of her intrusion, her complicity. Her only hope was Toivo Ranta. He would know what to do, how to rescue Maida Lange. She told herself she had to move quickly. It was already noon.

She had been awake all night, sitting in the chair by her bed reading one of Maida's books, *The Cloud of Unknowing*. Sheila had done very little praying in her life, but the book said a single word was enough. "If you were to hear your deadly enemy in terror cry out from the depth of his being this little word 'fire' or 'help!' you, without reckoning he was your enemy, out of sheer pity aroused by his despairing cry, would rise up, even on a mid-winter night to help him put out his fire or quieten and ease his distress." The book asked, "How much more would God respond to a cry of despair?" She had spoken that word. Just as she had borrowed Maida's clothes, Sheila found herself borrowing Maida's faith.

Now she sat at the library desk, her hand on the phone. Still she could not dial the private number that would connect her with the vice president's office. She stared mindlessly at the books that surrounded her in the library. Her eyes rested on a German dictionary. Grateful for anything that would delay the call, she mounted the stairs, retrieved the envelope from her dresser, and carried the letter downstairs. She looked at the German:

Berlinen Algenmeines Krankenhaus

Sehr geehrte Frau:

In Beantwortung ihres Briefes möchte ich Ihnen mit-teilen, dass wir einen Mikrofilm der Krankengeschichte Ihres Sohnes Johann haben. Die Aufzeichnungen ergeben, dass kurz nach der Geburt eine Dextrocardie diagnostiziert wurde. Keine anderen Abnormalitäten wurden festgestellt und der Junge war ansonsten völlig gesund

Mit Hochachtung

Dr. med. Gustav Schmidt

Paging through the Germany dictionary she found that "Beantwortung" meant "reply." Evidently Maida had requested some information. The word "Mikrofilm" was easy. She recalled "Johann" was their older son's name, the boy who had died. But why would Maida make inquiries so long after his death?

It took over an hour to translate the brief letter:

In reply to your letter, let me assure you we have a microfilm of the medical record of your son, Johann. This record shows that he had a dextrocardia which was diagnosed shortly after his birth. No other con-genital abnormalities were found and the boy was in excellent health.

The word "dextrocardia" meant nothing to her. She hunted through the shelves for Dr. Lange's medical dictionary she had seen a few days ago while browsing through the library. "Dextrocardia," she read, "location of the heart in the right hemothorax." "Thorax" was the part of the trunk between the neck and the abdomen. It must mean that the child's heart had been on the right side rather than on the left, which was its normal position. Subconsciously she had known all along what that word meant. Why? Then she remembered the article.

To learn more about the Compassionate Care Bill she had bought a news magazine. Sheila had thumbed through it without much interest other than revulsion for a piece of legislation that—had it been in effect when Ava was born—might have been the means of her sister's death and would certainly send several actors she knew who were struggling with AIDS to a lonely life of incarceration. She had glanced at a few other news items and then turned to the theater and film reviews at the back of the magazine. Now she hurriedly thumbed through the magazine's pages, unsure of what she was looking for.

It contained the usual articles: speculation on Russia's next move, another royal scandal, the pros and cons of the Compassionate Care Bill. There it was at the end of an article on the Bill. It was just as she now recalled. A brief note said that the president himself had made use of a government health plan by going in for his annual checkup at Walter Reed. After a battery of tests, he was pronounced in excellent condition. "All you can say," the doctor joked, "is that his heart isn't in the right place." The article went on to explain that Robert Lange had been born with "dextrocardia," a rather rare but completely benign condition he had had since birth.

Sheila put the magazine down on the table and got out the phone book. Running her finger along the names of doctors, she came to a listing of pediatricians. She picked one at random and dialed. It was easy for her to emulate the half-aggressive, half-wheedling voice of an investigative reporter. She once had played that role in a sitcom that had never gotten beyond the pilot. When a secretary answered, Sheila said, "I'm calling from *The Washington Post*. I'd like to ask Dr. Holly's opinion for an article I'm doing."

"What did you say your name was?" the secretary asked.

Sheila quickly scanned the articles on the front page of the paper and picked the name of the first woman reporter she saw.

"One moment, please, the doctor will be right with you."

"What can I do for you?" The doctor's voice was wary. "I'm afraid I don't have much time. I'm busy with a patient right now."

"I'm doing an article on dextrocardia, Doctor. There's been some interest in the phenomenon since it was mentioned in the report on the president's health. I could either use or not use your name, just as you like. I could simply put 'authority on childhood diseases....'"

"Oh, you can use my name if you want. What would you like to know?"

Sheila knew the man was hooked. What doctor wouldn't want his name on the front page of *The Post* quoted as an expert? In a casual voice she said, "I gather it's not a serious problem."

"Not at all. It's a cardiac malposition—a location of the heart anywhere other than its usual position in the left hemothorax. Dextrocardia simply means the position of the heart is a mirror image of its usual site. You don't see it that often, maybe one in thirty thousand—but don't tie me down to those figures. Very occasionally there are complications that might need surgery but that's the exception. You usually discover it when the patient comes in for an x-ray for something else."

"Is it a disease you would find in a sibling? I mean if one child has it, might another child in the same family be likely to have it as well?"

"No, it's not familial," said the doctor, glad to display his expertise.

"So if two children in the same family both had it, it would be just a coincidence?"

"Yes, and an unusual one."

"Thank you very much, Doctor. You've been most helpful."

"You're very welcome. Have you got the spelling of my name correct? That's two ls."

Sheila hung up but she continued to clutch the phone. How did you call a vice president?

XVIII

As his driver took him into the familiar streets of Alexandria, T. Russell Ranta felt uncomfortable. Although his retinue of Secret Service agents was mercifully smaller than the president's entourage, on this occasion Ranta found them particularly intrusive. He cringed at what they must be thinking of his visit in the late afternoon—during office hours—to what they must consider, after the picture in *The Post*, his lady friend, even if she happened to be the mother of the president.

Her phone call had come at an awkward time, just as he was putting together some notes for his upcoming television interview on the Compassionate Care Bill. Of course he was pleased to hear from her again, but she had sounded agitated on the phone. He was disappointed, afraid he had misjudged her. The last thing he needed was a relationship with a hysterical woman who would call him away from crucial business for some neurotic reason.

As he rode along gathering his thoughts, he saw school children on their way home. In the warm spring afternoon they had shed their jackets and sweaters. Some of the older children were zooming by on rollerblades. A friendly baseball game was going on in a vacant neighborhood lot. Ranta sighed. Some things never changed. In northern Minnesota spring did not come until June, and then it came in a single explosive day so that everyone on the Iron Range was rapturous with relief. The Finnish rite of spring arrived on June 21, the first day of summer, when all the Finns held a special dance at their club in Mesaba Park.

Half the Finns at the club were loyal members of the

Finnish Communist Party. His wife's parents had been old-line Communists. His own family were Lutheran Finns who didn't go to dances and who considered the Communist Finns Russian traitors. At his wedding the two families had not spoken to each other until the vodka had been passed around twice.

As soon as the black limousine pulled up in front of the small brick home, the front door opened and Maida stood there expectantly. Ranta winced. What would the Secret Service agents make of that—elderly lovers enjoying an afternoon tryst? He shrugged. What did he care anymore? He was glad to see her.

She led him into the library, a room to which he took an instant dislike. Its orderly rows of dry books reminded him of Robert Lange. "I trust this is important?" He sat down in one of the leather chairs with his coat on, a signal that he didn't intend to stay long.

She handed him a magazine article and what appeared to be a letter from a physician. "I would never have called you if it wasn't important. Toivo, look at this letter. With the help of a German dictionary I was able to translate it."

He glanced at the paragraph in the magazine she had checked and then at the letter, which he read twice. "It appears both of your sons had the same anomaly." His voice was dismissive. It was hardly a good enough reason to call him from the White House in the middle of the afternoon. Then, recalling the death of the president's brother, he said more gently, "Forgive me. I had forgotten you had lost your older boy."

"I called a pediatrician today. He said it would be extremely rare, almost unheard of, to find siblings with dextrocardia."

Ranta dropped the magazine and the letter on the desk and stared at her. Ever since he had walked into the house, he had been aware of some change in her, but he had been unable to place it. Now he realized that the slight German accent that had been there on their other meetings was absent in her speech. "You said you translated it 'with the help of a German dictionary.' Surely you can't have forgotten your native language?"

"German isn't my native language. Toivo, let's get out of this room." She shivered. "It seems so menacing in here. I have coffee for us in the kitchen. You might as well take off your coat. There's something you have to hear and it will take a while."

Seated across the kitchen table from him, Sheila warmed her hands around her coffee cup. The late afternoon sun lit the kitchen but she couldn't stop shivering.

He reached across the table and put his hand over hers. "The longer you wait the more difficult it will be. I don't think you would have called me if you didn't trust me." T. Russell Ranta was aware of something decidedly strange, as though he had walked into the wrong house and was about to learn something which he had no desire to know. Had he not seen how desperate she was to unburden herself, he would have stopped the telling.

The words rushed out. "I never meant to do something dishonest. Ted Coulter told me I would be serving my country. And I needed work. I had been fired from my television job, and at my age TV roles are nearly impossible to get. I see now that they had me fired on purpose, so that I would fall into their plans."

He stared at her, unable to follow what she was saying. "Maida, none of this makes sense to me."

"My name isn't Maida. It's Sheila Covell. I'm an actress. Ted Coulter saw me on TV and realized how much I looked like Maida Lange. He had me fired, and then he came to my apartment and told me that the president's mother was senile or mentally ill or something. I don't quite remember how he put it. But he said she had these delusions, and that she would say terrible things about her son, the president. He said she had to be hospitalized before she publicly embarrassed the president."

"What you're telling me is incredible, a monstrous deception." He tried to find his way back to reality. "Surely it would have been a simple thing to find a suitable place to care for her. The mentally ill are no longer pariahs. At least they aren't until Lange passes his legislation."

"Coulter said that if she disappeared with no explanation, the media would become suspicious. They would try to find out where she was. A nurse or her doctor or some attendant would be bribed by the press to give her location away. He said all the supermarket tabloids would print these delusions about her son and people would believe them and it would be dangerous for the country. To protect her they planned to hospitalize her under another name while I took her place."

Two words circled around and around in Ranta's head: deceit and treachery. They were old-fashioned words from another time, Shakespearean words, certainly not words from this liberal age when nothing was so heinous that it could not be explained away as the result of an onerous childhood. This woman whom he had begun to care for was involved in deceit and treachery. Ranta withdrew his hand.

"Toivo, if it were just that, I wouldn't be so upset, but that's not the worst of it."

"What could be worse than that!" He listened with growing alarm as she told him about the library book and how she found the nursing home where Mrs. Lange was being held.

"It was horrible, a run-down place with iron grills on the windows. I have no idea what I've done or how much I've hurt Maida Lange."

Ranta had seen too much of life to accept the excuse of innocence so easily. He would never permit others to shirk responsibility for their actions. He believed the woman was an impostor who had tricked him, and not only him but the whole country.

And yet, he cautioned himself, as soon as the letter raised her suspicions, she had gone in search of Maida Lange. At least he supposed she had, and then she had called him. She could have simply said nothing, gone on with the deception, kept her "job." Or she could have disappeared, leaving Maida Lange to her son and Coulter. No one would have suspected her. Everything was happening too fast for recriminations; time for that later.

"You think Maida Lange is in that nursing home?" It was strange pronouncing that name, knowing it didn't belong to the frightened woman sitting across from him.

"I don't know. But we have to find out."

"You don't even know if she's still alive."

"Alive! What do you mean?" Sheila stared at Ranta. She was horrified. "You mean I might be responsible for murder?"

"Hasn't it occurred to you that if what we suspect about the president is true, the reason she was removed from her home was because she could, at any moment, have exposed the president's secret? Something must have happened to make her threaten to tell the world her son was constitutionally ineligible to be President of the United States."

Ranta recalled Maida Lange's voice on the phone and her distress over the Compassionate Care Bill. Suddenly he was filled with remorse. Was it possible that he, himself, had been the one to put her in harm's way? He remembered the impulsive phone call when he had enjoyed needling the president about her call in a childish desire to get under Lange's skin. But to imprison one's own mother over some legislation was unconscionable, inhuman. But then Ranta had never thought Robert Lange was human. The whole time he had been in office with him, Lange had always seemed to Ranta like some robot programed for the presidency.

Lost in his disturbing thoughts, Ranta forgot there was another person in the room until she cleared her throat. Startled, he looked up. "I'm afraid I've forgotten your name."

"Sheila, Sheila Covell."

Her voice was so low he could barely hear her. "Sheila, I'm going to take this letter with me. You must not say a word to anyone about it. I'll be direct with you. What you have done is far more serious than you can imagine. By your willing involvement, you enabled them to do what they wanted with Maida Lange, perhaps even kill her." Across from him Sheila began to cry. In a stern voice he said, "Stop that and listen to me. You are not to tell anyone about this letter or about the nursing home. Until I get in touch with you, you are to go on acting as though you are the president's mother. If Lange or Coulter suspect you know what they're up to, they very well might get rid of Maida before we can reach her—and then get rid of you. Both of your lives are going to depend on just how skillful an actress you are."

With a start Sheila remembered where she had been invited that evening. "Two hours from now I'm supposed to have dinner at the White House. I'll have to call and tell them I'm not well."

"You'll do nothing of the kind. When Coulter saw you last night you were fine. A call like that would just make them suspicious. You will go and you will behave as though nothing has happened."

"I can't," she whispered.

"If Maida Lange is still alive, her life may depend on how well you play your role tonight." A plan was beginning to form in his mind.

"Why can't you just tell the FBI to go to the nursing home?"

"We have to have a reason for breaking into the nursing home, something more than your suspicions. To do a search we have to have some proof of all this. This is the President of the United States we are dealing with. Just give me a few hours. In the meantime, I'll see that they put a surveillance on the nursing home immediately. For now we have to assume Coulter and the president have no idea you or anyone else is suspicious of them."

Ranta looked across the table. Sheila looked so pitiable, so guilty, he gave her a thin smile. "In the end you might do your country a great service. That letter may save a lot of lives." T. Russell Ranta had been in politics all of his life and, even at this extraordinary moment, he could not entirely forget that with Robert Lange out of the way it would be much easier to defeat the Compassionate Care Bill.

Amazingly, in all the confusion of the evening, it had not occurred to him that if Robert Lange were no longer president, he, T. Russell Ranta, would hold the highest office in the land. He had always been a man who enjoyed power, but he had never been one who enjoyed stepping over the bodies of others to achieve it.

"Don't volunteer anything about my being here this afternoon," he warned her, "but if they ask about it you must admit it. The Secret Service agents talk to one another, and one of mine may mention my visit to one of Lange's. If it does come up, tell them I phoned to ask you out, and when you refused to see me again, I came by to find out why. Tell them you got rid of me." In a sardonic voice he added, "You should have no trouble inventing some story."

She flushed. "Are you suggesting lies come easily to me?"

He regretted his remark, but after all that he had just learned in the last hour, what else could he think? "You'll have to admit I would have plenty of reason to believe that."

XIX

As T. Russell Ranta's small motorcade made its way from Virginia to the FBI building, it faced the Saturday traffic streaming out of the city. The drivers, intent this pleasant spring afternoon on escaping to the countryside, scarcely noticed the vice president's motorcade. Ranta regarded the escapees with envy. Their minds were a million miles away from their jobs, thinking about the weekend: hiking along the river, accompanying their children to soccer and baseball games, an afternoon at the mall.

What would they say if they knew their president was about to be arrested, if they realized there would soon be one more corrupt public figure for the media to blow the whistle on and discard? One hero less for young people to look up to and emulate. Today's reporters destroyed the living heroes; the revisionist historians destroyed the dead heroes. "Glory," Ranta thought, "that 'circle in the water.'"

Ranta experienced a wave of nausea at the idea of what a merciless media would do to Robert Lange: the indignant columns, the smug editorials, the TV shows where reporters questioned reporters in one rapid-fire interview after the other. When the mayhem of malicious publicity was all over, the country would be more cynical than ever. And it would be more difficult, perhaps impossible, for someone to gain the kind of trust needed to lead the nation. Ranta had always disliked Robert Lange; now he hated him for the deception he had perpetrated. Prison would be too good for him, but he was having second thoughts about exposing the man to the predators. That kind of feeding frenzy would undermine the very foundations of the country. It would serve no good.

Vindictive anger never served the claims of justice. As they pulled up in front of the FBI building Ranta thought of another way.

Ranta told the Secret Service agents to wait downstairs. "If I'm not safe in the FBI building, then we're all in trouble." A few minutes later he walked into Randall Godden's office just as Godden was taking off his coat. It looked more like a warehouse than an office. Godden's desk was covered with listing heaps of files. Statute books with their daunting legalese titles were stacked in disarray against a wall. A table held a chronological display of the evolution of the computer—nearly every model known to man. The jumble offended Ranta, who was a clean desk man.

Godden apologized for his work clothes. "I was up on a ladder cleaning out the eaves when you called. You sounded like you meant business, so I hurried over here as fast as I could."

"Sorry I had to call you in on a Saturday, Godden." Wasting no time, he handed a paper to Godden. "Take a look at this letter and the translation."

Godden took out the case that held his glasses and fished them out. The first time he read the letter, he didn't notice to whom it was sent. He looked inquiringly up at Ranta, and then read through the letter again, this time noticing its recipient. "It's to the president's mother. This is about the older son, Johann. Everyone in Washington knows the president had an older brother who died as a child."

"But it's the president who has dextrocardia," Ranta pointed out.

"Yeah, so it runs in the family."

"That's just it. It would be extremely unusual for two siblings to have it." On his way into the capital, Ranta had used the car phone to check out Sheila's findings with a retired pediatrician who had once headed the pediatrics department at Washington's largest hospital. The man was an old friend and could be trusted to keep a confidence.

"I don't like to disagree with you, Mr. Vice President," said

Godden, "but that's exactly what this letter says. By the way, what is dextrocardia?"

"It's a condition in which the heart is on the right instead of the left side, a sort of mirror image of the normal position of the heart. Look, can you find out at what hospital Robert Lange's father practiced?"

"Sure. That would be in the president's file. We know everything there is to know about him. You, too, including the fact that your wife's parents were Communists. But I don't get any of this."

"Do it."

Godden switched on the newest of the assortment of computers and punched in a code. After a minute he punched in the word "father." He scrolled down a page and then another. "Evidently after accepting a teaching position, the father had only a limited practice at George Washington University Hospital."

"All right. That's probably where he would have taken his child when the boy became ill. Call the hospital for the boy's records. Tell them you need any x-ray reports."

"Listen, Ranta. Excuse me. I mean, Mr. Vice President, but fooling around with the president's family records could get me a front-row ticket before a grand jury. Besides, the Secret Service doesn't like to share its little toys."

"Godden, if what I suspect is true, the fewer people who know about this the better. That includes even the Secret Service."

Godden sighed and thought for a moment, then he reached for the phone. "The rare pleasure of being one up on the Secret Service is an irresistible inducement. It's worth the risk." He spoke into the phone. "Get me Donna Metzer in the record room of the George Washington University Hospital." He turned to Ranta with a superior smile. "I've got someone there who isn't too finicky about giving out a little information.

"Donna? It's Randall Godden. Great, and how are you?

Look, could you do me a little favor? I need the medical records of Johann Lange." He consulted his computer screen. "Would have been hospitalized there November 19, 1965. Sure, I'll hang on." While he waited he looked up at Ranta. "I hope this isn't some crazy political vendetta I'm getting mixed up with." His doubt dissolved when he saw the intense look on Ranta's face, a look that had crisis written all over it.

Ranta watched while Godden made notes on a dry cleaning receipt he dug out of his pocket. When the receipt was nearly covered with Godden's minute writing, Ranta pulled out a legal pad from the desk, tumbling a stack of files and causing Godden to shoot him a reproachful look. "Read that x-ray report again, will you? Thanks. No need to fax it. It's just a routine check. I wouldn't want this call mentioned to anyone. What's on for Sunday? Well, I owe you one. I'll see that Brian doesn't get any emergency calls." Godden hung up and turned to Ranta. "Discretion runs in Donna's family. Her husband is one of our best agents. It looks like you're on to something, Mr. Vice President. When little Johann was admitted into the hospital, the x-ray they took showed a normal heart. No mention of dextrocardia. It doesn't make sense."

"It does if you remember Article II of the Constitution of the United States: 'No person except a natural-born citizen or a citizen of the United States at the time of the adoption of this Constitution shall be eligible to the Office of President....'"

"Do you think...?"

"It's exactly what I think."

Godden stood up, his mouth still open in amazement. "What we should do is get all of the facts together and then take it to the Secret Service and the attorney general. After that it will be up to the powers that be. Impeachment, I suppose, if you can impeach a president who has never legally been a president. But I'm not going to do a thing until I know exactly what I've got. Have you any idea what this could mean if word of it leaked out and it wasn't true? They'd have my head on a platter." He looked at Ranta. "I hope you know what you're talking about."

"Right now we have something else to worry about."

"Something else!"

"The president's mother is missing."

"Missing. What do you mean? She was out with you last night at that classy restaurant you execs like to frequent." He grinned salaciously. "What exactly did you do with her, and why are we talking about her at a crucial time like this?"

"This isn't a joking matter and that wasn't the president's mother. You're going to be busy all night, so just relax and listen to the rest of what I've got to say. When I've finished we have to figure out a way to let the president off the hook."

"Let him go after all this?" Godden was incredulous. "Now I know we're not talking politics."

"I won't pretend I wouldn't like to nail Robert Lange—for what I think he's done to his mother if nothing else—but the country can't afford the kind of scandal we'd have if the truth were known. What we have to do is put a twenty-four-hour watch on his mother so no harm comes to her. When we're sure of what's going on, we'll find a quiet way to go in there and get her without alerting anyone. When that's taken care of we'll confront the president, present him with a *fait accompli,* get him to veto the Compassionate Care Bill, and then send him on his way—as far from the White House as possible. I have to believe the president would prefer that route to public humiliation."

XX

Finding herself at the North Portico of the White House, Sheila Covell forgot her fear for a moment and experienced a childlike excitement. The floodlights, meant more for security than aesthetics, illuminated the most famous residence in the world, transforming it, like the Lincoln and Jefferson Memorials, into a kind of apostatized shrine levitating there on sacred ground. For a moment Sheila forgot the corruption and the wickedness behind the facade of the mansion.

The driver opened the door of the presidential limousine and stood to one side as she climbed out. All the way up the driveway, past the watchful entry booths and Secret Service agents, she dreaded the moment when she would be face-to-face with Robert Lange. She was greatly relieved when the door opened and the president's wife stepped out to greet her. Seeing several Secret Service agents in the background at once reassured and frightened Sheila. She wanted to believe as long as she was here nothing could happen, and yet what would these same agents do if they knew she was impersonating the president's mother? She felt like a wanted criminal walking into a police station. The White House, which had appeared a fabled palace, might turn out to be a lethal trap if she wasn't careful. She was afraid if she walked through its doors she would disappear forever.

Quick as a serpent's tongue, Paige Lange extended her hand to Sheila and as quickly withdrew it. She was as tall as Sheila, but her body had a thin, consumed appearance, worn away by an energy that crackled and bristled in her rapid movements and rushed speech. Sheila, who had taken considerable time even in her anxiety about her appearance, was quite surprised to find the First Lady in jeans and a sweater. Her red hair was pulled tightly back, accentuating her high cheekbones and giving her face a pinched look. There was a friendly smile on her thin lips but no warm welcome in her hooded green eyes, which took only seconds to rake over Sheila and dismiss her.

Paige Lange's likeness appeared in papers and magazines almost as often as the president's. While the president tolerated publicity as a necessary evil, his wife thrived on it and sought it. For years she labored at her paintings, getting nowhere, while others, whom she believed had less talent than she did, received the important shows and had articles written about them in *Art Monthly* and *The New York Times Magazine*. If critics noticed her work at all, they invariably labeled it "eclectic."

Paige freely admitted to herself that there was an element of truth to this charge. If she saw an artist recognized and acclaimed, she found herself imitating the artist's style, hungering for the same recognition. But by the time she had mastered that particular style, another artist with a completely different approach would have been singled out by the critics. It was like running in place.

"I've been looking forward to meeting you," Paige said with a mocking smile.

Sheila flinched at the coldness of the words. "Of course," she thought, "Paige Lange would have known her husband's mother. Like the president, she understands I'm an imposter."

Once inside, a white-jacketed man took her coat. Sheila tried not to stare at the familiar stairway where heads of government from all over the world were photographed descending with the president and his wife in magisterial state. The awed look was not lost on Paige, who offered, "I'll give you the quick tour. I hope you don't want to go downstairs and ogle at the portraits of the First Ladies or snoop in the china room?" She grasped Sheila's elbow and guided her expertly from room to room, keeping up a brisk commentary on everything. "The Blue Room, very nice bow windows. The East Room. You see it all the time on TV. Receptions, concerts, press conferences, all that kind of thing take place in this room. A number of presidents who died in office have lain in state here."

Sheila couldn't help noticing in each of the rooms the contrast between the traditional furnishings and the contemporary paintings interspersed between eighteenth- and nineteenth-century art. Next to stately portraits of presidents and romantic Hudson River scenes hung huge, brash canvasses composed of sweeps of bold color or enigmatic subtleties of white on white or black on black. When they reached the Green Room— "Rug designed by Tiffany studios, Italian marble mantelpiece, the coffee urn belonged to John Adams"—there was a canvas positioned over a delicate Duncan Phyfe console that featured a life-sized and rather vulgar nude of a woman.

"The paintings seem to be an interesting mix of different periods," a startled Sheila said.

Paige studied the portrait dispassionately. "I had a brawl with Elwood Brighton over that one. He still blushes whenever he sees it. He's the White House curator. The little prude had the nerve to accuse me of purposely displaying the art from New York galleries in return for their promise to display my work. What's the matter with doing friends favors? Don't think that doesn't go on all the time in my husband's office." With a wave of her hand, she motioned Sheila to follow as she continued her hurried tour.

In the State Dining Room Sheila paused to read the inscription carved on the mantel: "I Pray Heaven to Bestow the Best of Blessings on the House and on All that shall hereafter Inhabit it. May none but Honest and Wise Men ever rule under This Roof." Paige watched her, the same mocking smile playing over her lips. "And do you think your son lives up to that description?" she asked.

Sheila could not keep the revulsion out of her eyes as she looked away. Early on in the tour Sheila's wonder in her surroundings shriveled in the cold breeze of Paige's haste and cynicism. Fear crept back. The shadowy, ubiquitous presence of the Secret Service agents felt more ominous than protective; the rooms more stage set than home, suggesting that any minute a troupe of costumed actors would appear and commence a performance that was sure to have a tragic ending.

"Had enough?" Paige inquired.

Sheila shuddered and agreed readily.

Sheila's uneasiness was confirmed when Paige marched her to the elevator. "We'll go upstairs to the family quarters. Your son had some business to take care of, but he'll be ready for us now." Each time she repeated the phrase "your son," there was derision in her voice. An agent stepped into the elevator but Paige waved him away. "We'll manage ourselves." As the elevator door closed, Sheila caught a glimpse of a brace of agents starting a rapid ascent up the stairway.

Enclosed in the elevator and alone with Sheila for the first time, Paige said, "Of course you know I've met Robert's mother. There is no question of my being fooled. After all, I have an artist's eye for faces. Robert told me everything. He trusts me implicitly. We have a very nice arrangement. I just didn't want you to think you were getting away with anything. Once we get off of the elevator, a steward will be creeping about, so we'll keep playing our little charade." In a heavily ironic voice she added, "Remember, it's for the good of the country."

Before Sheila could answer, Paige shot her a look that warned Sheila to be careful, then she swung open the elevator door and swept out into a corridor. Sheila followed along, suppressing an urge to run in the opposite direction. She was alarmed at the thought of someone else knowing of her deception, but there was also some comfort in no longer having to pretend with Paige.

A moment later the Secret Service agents, showing no discernible fatigue from their hasty climb, arrived and took their station in the hallway. Paige gave them a dismissive look. "They're not allowed in the family quarters," she said, as though they were poorly trained puppies.

Heading for the west end of the corridor, Paige paused in front of a series of portraits of various heads of foreign states: the Canadian, Israeli, and British Prime Ministers; France's and Italy's presidents; and the premier of China were all there, captured in a style that was not unlike Picasso at his most whimsical.

"I did them all," Paige said with a kindergartner's pride in her own imperium. "They all come here fawning over Robert, wanting something. Part of the payment is sitting for a portrait by me. When our second term is over I'll have an exhibition of the whole collection. Robert's going to try for the National Gallery."

Unlike the formal downstairs rooms, the family sitting room into which Paige led Sheila was comfortable, almost cozy. A fire glowed in the fireplace; the draperies and chairs were covered in a floral chintz. Newspapers and magazines lay scattered about, and Paige's miniature dachshund, which had been stretched out on the floor, was now advancing toward Sheila with a playful curiosity. A television set, placed unobtrusively in a large mahogany secretary across the room, was switched on and watching it was Robert Lange. He rose as Sheila entered the room and walked leisurely over to greet her.

For a disoriented moment Sheila found herself thinking that the tall, attractive man with the frank blue eyes, the blond hair falling over his forehead, exuding confidence and power was surely the dream of every mother. More startling was the recognition that even more than in pictures she had seen of him, he did indeed resemble her. But of course, why wouldn't he? Maida and she could pass for twins. Immediately, reality tugged at her and the man's size became threatening, the eyes deceitful, the boyish forelock falling over his forehead a practiced affectation meant to disarm.

For a second he looked in the direction of the steward, and then in what was meant to appear a spontaneous gesture, he put his arms around Sheila and kissed her. "Well, Mother," he said, "we finally got you here. Paige and I certainly have looked forward to your visit. Come over here and sit next to the fire. I'm sure you're chilled. The evening's turned rather cold. I'm sorry to say the Coulters had to cancel at the last minute. Ted had to do a little something for me. Now, what can we get you to drink?"

A Filipino steward in a white coat was placing a tray of carefully crafted appetizers on a table. The steward waited for her order, trying not too obviously to evaluate the woman who was known for being so mysteriously elusive. "Some wine would be fine," Sheila said, eager for anything that might help her to compose herself.

"Unlike state dinners," Robert said, "in our own private quarters we can give the French trade balance a little boost. How about a nice Montrachet? I seem to remember that was your favorite." He couldn't stop staring at her, obviously startled by her marked resemblance to his mother.

Sheila wondered if the sight of her pushed into his reluctant consciousness the thought of his own mother and what he had done with her. She managed to reply, "That would be lovely, Robert." Sheila had bitten her tongue to keep from saying "Mr. President." She wondered if his mother would have called him Bobby? As much as she hated Robert Lange for what he had done, she found herself more comfortable with him than she did with Paige, who simply sat there with a simpering, superior grin. He, at least, was working at playing his part. It was like any performance. You did your best with the actor who gave the most back; playing against an indifferent actor was uphill work.

Only for a moment did Robert Lange's implacably poised expression change. The dachshund reached Sheila and began sniffing at her ankles. The president swooped down on the dog and, picking it up with one hand, handed it to the steward with an order to take it away. Lange's face was flushed and he looked like he was trying to restrain himself from handling the dog more harshly. He apologized to Sheila. "I'm afraid we forgot how sensitive your asthma is to dog dander." His expression appeared clouded by some distant memory.

When the steward returned, he busied himself opening a wine bottle and filling crystal glasses set out on a butler's tray while the president chatted on comfortably about Washington happenings. When the wine was served, Lange casually turned to the steward and suggested, "Carlos, you go along. We'll help ourselves. Give us a call when dinner is ready."

The steward had clearly enjoyed bustling about with the trays and glasses and now appeared like a child dragged from a party. It took him a long time to put his playthings away and depart.

As soon as Carlos closed the door behind him, Paige stood up. "I must say, I admire your superb performance, Sheila," Paige said in a mischievous voice. "I think I would have been fairly intimidated by all these trappings and," she grinned at her husband, "the royal presence. But of course, acting is your business."

Robert gave his wife a friendly pat. "I can't think of anything that would intimidate you, Paige," he said in an admiring voice. "But let's continue to play the game, shall we? No more 'Sheila,' even when we're alone. It's Maida."

As though she had received some subtle signal from her husband, Paige announced in a tone of dismissive relief, "I'm going to leave this tender reunion between mother and son for a few minutes. I've some important calls to make."

With Paige gone Robert turned to Sheila. "Both Ted and I have been quite impressed with the excellence of what Paige calls your 'performance.' I know it can't have been easy for you; it hasn't been easy for us." He leaned forward, his voice confidential, his expression one of great sadness mingled with brave resolve. Sheila was at once fascinated and appalled by the skill of his acting. No wonder in this age of television campaigning the man had won election after election.

"I'm sure you can imagine how devastated I have been over my mother's illness. A physical illness would be one thing—although I certainly wouldn't wish that for her—but the mental difficulties would have serious national, even international, implications should the media get hold of them. Her delusions are bizarre. Without getting into the nature of her psychosis, I can tell you it has to do with deranged ideas about her childhood as well as hallucinations about me. The doctor believes it may relate to the deprivations she experienced as a child in Germany. Unfortunately, there doesn't seem to be much we can do to help her except to make her as comfortable as possible."

Sheila thought of the shabby house with its barred windows. She tried to cover her anger by bringing out the usual platitude, "It must be terribly difficult for you. Of course I'm glad to help in any way I can."

He caught the slight hesitation. Perhaps sensing some reserve in her reply, Lange turned on his regal smile and in a practiced gesture carelessly swept a fallen lock from his forehead. Leaning toward her he said in an earnest voice, "I hope you realize how crucial what you are doing is to the welfare of our country. I've been thinking of the man who pretended to be Churchill in World War II to mislead the enemy. Who knows how many thousands of lives the man saved? I'm not suggesting anything quite so dramatic here, but given the mounting political pressures all over the world and the importance of our country's leadership, you can surely understand how vital it is to avoid a storm of destructive publicity against the President of the United States."

Only her promise to Toivo and her concern for Maida Lange kept Sheila from lashing out and calling the man across from her a liar and worse. In the theater she had learned to keep inappropriate emotions from straying across her face, but she didn't trust her voice.

When there was no response, Robert continued, "We have one small difficulty. I think Ted Coulter made it quite clear that you were not to see the vice president, and yet you were at the restaurant together." He gave her a quizzical smile; behind the smile lurked a menacing threat.

"I'm sorry," Sheila said. "I suppose I was just carried away by having the vice president ask me for a date." She tried to make her reply light and even laughed a little, as though the spectacle of a woman her age dazzled by a date was absurd. "I'm afraid I didn't understand how strongly Mr. Coulter felt. Of course I won't see Toivo again."

"'Toivo' is it?" Robert said. He paused to look at her thoughtfully. "Well, as long as you understand the rules. Just now Ranta is making a great deal of trouble for us, and having him seen with my mother while at the same time I'm trying to discredit him sends a confusing message to the public. And it's very important that they not be confused.

"If it's the spotlight you like, I can promise you something better. I doubt this 'acting' is going to be necessary much longer. I heard yesterday from the private facility where Mother is that she is doing very poorly. In addition to her mental condition, she's seriously ill with acute asthma. They think her days are limited."

Sheila felt the dampness break out on the palms of her hands and across her forehead. How much time did they have before something happened to Maida? For a moment she considered accusing him, telling him that the FBI would be watching his mother, but Toivo had warned her not to say anything. Her accusations might precipitate Maida's murder. Once she climbed into the limousine, she, too, would be vulnerable. She had no idea how many people Robert Lange had involved in his evil scheme; after all, the president had the resources of a whole country at his service.

"I'm sorry to hear about your mother," she said. Then before she could stop herself, "Just where is she?"

Lange looked at her sharply. "That needn't concern you. If the worst should happen and she should pass away, we would let you know immediately. You would leave her house at once, and we would bring my mother home, announcing that she had died. That would, of course, free you of any further responsibilities. Needless to say, you would be handsomely compensated for your valuable help.

"I can promise a boost for your career in exchange for your continued discretion. I have several excellent contacts in Hollywood." He went on to mention a producer and two directors, one of whom had just won an Academy Award. "I can almost certainly guarantee someone with your talent a substantial part in a movie."

Sheila forced herself to appear excited and grateful. "That would be marvelous," she said. As she spoke she tried to figure out what the mention of Maida's illness and possible death might mean. Were they getting ready to kill Maida? And would they really let Sheila, herself, go, after all this?

Certainly there was little time left. With growing anxiety she wondered if that was the real reason the Coulters had not come. If anyone was going to harm Maida Lange, it would surely be Ted Coulter. The casual words, "Ted had to do a little something for me," took on a sinister meaning. She would have to leave as soon as she could without raising suspicion.

She saw Robert Lange watching her closely, as though he were trying to read in her face the progression of her frightening thoughts. She was trying to collect herself when Paige ambled languidly into the room, an impatient look on her face suggesting she had allotted them enough time for their mischief. Carlos, a step behind her, announced dinner and began to bustle about gathering the trays and bottles, obviously happy to be back at the party.

Before they could make their way to the family dining room a telephone rang. Robert narrowed his lips into a thin line. "I gave orders that I wasn't to be bothered unless an emergency arose." He picked up a phone placed discreetly on a Chippendale console.

"What do you want, Rodgers? I wasn't to be disturbed tonight."

"Durwood Rodgers, the president's press secretary," Paige explained to Sheila.

"Now that you've got me, what's it about?" Lange snapped.

Sheila watched the president's face tighten. "George Washington Hospital? I'm sure it's just routine. I suppose some reporter is doing another in-depth biography of me and my family, but you were right to call." He hung up and turned to Sheila and Paige. "Sorry, but something has come up. I have to get down to the Oval Office. They can send my dinner down there. You two go ahead." He gave Paige a starched smile. The look he directed at Sheila frightened her. There was regret in it, as though, against his will, he was forced to take some action against her. "You two will probably have a better time without me." Before either of them could answer he was gone.

Paige gave Sheila a cold smile. "I hope you know something about art because I don't know anything about the theater and I couldn't care less."

For Sheila, the thought of spending another five minutes with Paige, much less sitting across a table and having dinner with her, was impossible. All she could think about was Maida Lange and the imminent danger she might be in. Sheila was desperate to get home and call Toivo. "Actually, I seem to be developing a migraine headache. Unfortunately they also make me rather nauseated. Would you mind terribly if I just skipped dinner?"

"Not at all. I'll have a quick snack and get back to my painting." Paige looked off into the middle distance and said, "It's the only time I feel really alive." She appeared almost irritated to find Sheila still there, an impediment to her work. "I'll call your driver." And then, since Carlos was still there, with only a tinge of sarcasm she added, "You must spend more time with Robert; after all, he's your only son."

XXI

Ted Coulter pulled up to the curb and, opening the door of the car, held out the New York strip steak he had taken from the kitchen freezer. The motley dog was a mix of some sort, possibly beagle and spaniel, with the eager trust of a well-loved pet. Coulter was relieved to see the dog wore a collar with a name and address. "Max." Perhaps the dog belonged to some child. He would feel better knowing that later, when the dog was picked up, the owner would be notified. He tossed the steak onto the floor of the backseat and the dog eagerly scrambled to retrieve it. Coulter slammed the car door and drove off as the dog hunkered down on the floor and gnawed on the frozen steak. "Good doggie," Coulter said aloud. "Good Maxie."

In the early spring evening the town of Singleton appeared more appealing than Coulter recalled. The trees had leafed out and hung like great green balloons above the houses. The beginning of the warm days and prolonged twilights kept homeowners busy in their yards at spring tasks: putting in bedding plants, giving the grass its first cutting, raking up the few errant leaves left over from the fall. The smell of burning leaves drifted into Coulter's car window, and its acrid, nostalgic odor filled him with an aching wish to be any other place in the world than where he was. He was overcome with the melancholy knowledge that even with all his present culpability, never again would he be as innocent as he was at that moment.

It was nearly eight o'clock when he turned onto the Bunges' street. He slowed the car as he approached their house, telling himself that it was not too late to turn back. Yet he had rehearsed the deed so often in the last hours, its performance seemed almost anticlimatic. He parked the car far enough from the house so the Bunges would not see the expression on Maida's face when he put her into the car.

He was self-conscious as he approached their door. The weight of the gun in the pocket of his suit jacket seemed the weight of the world. Though he wore a raincoat, he feared that even a casual observer would detect the suspicious bulge. It was unlikely that he would have to use it. He would merely tell Maida Lange that her son had had a change of heart and she was going to her home. It was only when she reached the car and saw the dog that he might need the threat of the gun to keep her in the car for as long as it took. He had already discovered an obscure trail where he could park until the dog's presence had the "desired effect" on Maida. At no time had he used, even to himself, the word *death*.

As soon as he pushed the bell, he saw the curtain at the window move slightly. Since they had obviously recognized him, their delay in opening the door puzzled him.

When at last Tom Bunge greeted him, Coulter stepped jauntily inside, meaning to disarm the Bunges with his breeziness. "Well," he said to Tom, "I thought you might be outside doing some raking. How is Liz tonight?"

The clients were all lined up in the living room in front of the TV watching a rerun of "Golden Girls." "If you don't mind, Mr. Coulter, we'll go into the kitchen. Liz is back there."

When they reached the kitchen Liz was effusive. "Sit right here and let me get you some coffee and scones. I've made about every kind of muffin there is, but now the bed-and-breakfast magazines are saying you got to change to scones, which aren't so different from biscuits."

Coulter stopped listening. The thought of food sent a wave of nausea through him. He thought he might be sick and moved closer to the sink, trying to get his panic under control. After a moment he managed to say, "No, thank you. I just finished supper. How is my mother?"

"Never better." Tom's smile had a cunning slyness. "Let me hang up your coat."

"No. I'm just going to stay for a minute or two. I have a little surprise for you. I'm going to be taking my mother with me this evening. There's a new medication that her doctor is anxious for her to try. It means a short hospitalization. After that we have high hopes that she'll be well enough to return home on her own." Coulter was desperate to be free of the two intimidating presences. They were so close he could smell their yeasty odor, as though they were both excessive products of Liz's deranged baking skills.

"Well," Tom said, his voice unpleasantly wheedling, "this is such short notice. We had all the expense of fixing up the room and stuff. We had counted on the money for her being here for a while."

"That's no problem." Coulter pulled out an envelope with a thick wad of hundred dollar bills and began counting, relieved to be able to solve even one problem.

Liz started to say something but Tom quickly interrupted her. "Thanks. That's very generous." He tucked the money well down into his pocket. "I guess your mother must have had the same idea as you." There was a mixture of fear and satisfaction in his voice.

"What do you mean?" The smugness in Bunge's tone alarmed Coulter.

Tom took his time. "I mean she wanted to take off."

"Well, I know she hasn't been happy with this arrangement—not that you two haven't done all you could to make her comfortable—but now she'll be able to go back to her own house."

"You mean Greengate?"

Coulter's jovial mask froze.

Tom took his time, thoroughly enjoying Coulter's obvious discomfort. "I went to Greengate this afternoon and met your real mom. She's a classy lady. You haven't been too honest with us, Mr. Coulter."

Liz shoved *The Post* with its picture of Maida Lange and the vice president at Coulter. "Maybe you don't think we're too bright," she said, "but we can put two and two together."

Coulter saw that Lange had been right. If he had not marched over to Ranta's table and made a scene in the restaurant, Sheila Covell's picture would not have appeared in the paper. He stood up. All he could think of was getting out of there as quickly as possible.

"I don't know what you two are talking about. I'll just go upstairs and get my mother. I hope you haven't forgotten that I'm in possession of some information on the two of you that would interest the authorities." He knew they would have to be paid off, but he never doubted that they were for sale.

Tom stood in front of the stairway, his enormous presence blocking Coulter's way. "I suspect the authorities would be interested in why the president's mother was here. If it comes to that, we got a whole lot more on you than you have on us. Liz guessed who that woman in the picture is—"

"It's that actress that was on TV, isn't it?" Liz interrupted. Her voice was hopeful, as though she were excited at the connection she had with the magical world of entertainment. "I wouldn't mind meeting her—"

Tom interrupted. "We don't have to meet her, or have anything more to do with what you're up to, Mr. Coulter, except to remind you, you've put us through a lot of trouble and we'll be looking for a little something to make up for it."

For a wild moment Coulter wondered if he had enough ammunition in his pistol to do away with these two huge, oppressive people who were suffocating him with their presence and their threats.

"Has she seen the picture?" he asked.

If Maida had seen it she would be wary of him, perhaps refuse to come with him. Would he have to do away with her right there, and, if so, what about the Bunges? He wondered how much money it was going to take to buy their silence. He could threaten to implicate them if they said anything. After all, they had held Maida Lange prisoner here. Surely that was against the law. He felt as though he were clutching the end of a piece of string while the ball itself bumped irretrievably down an unending stairway.

Desperately he tested their gullibility. "You're quite right. Your guest is the president's mother. The woman in the picture is an actress. However, all of this was planned with the full knowledge of the Secret Service. This is classified information, and I really shouldn't be telling you any of this." He saw with relief that he had their attention. Their diet of nonstop TV created a hunger for plot, the more farfetched the better. "Because of her mental instability, Maida Lange has actually tried to harm her son physically. The president was in grave danger. Of course it is all part of her delusions about her son and no one else is in danger. After careful consideration, it was thought that bringing her here was the best way to handle it. Now we are hoping with this new medication that she will improve and be able to resume her old life.

"I want you to know that the president and the Secret Service are extremely grateful to the two of you. I can promise after all of this is taken care of, you will receive proper recognition for everything that you have done. Of course we'll want to reimburse you for all of your trouble—and stress."

Tom regarded Coulter doubtfully. "But you said it was your mother and it wasn't."

"Yes, of course. I was under orders from the Secret Service. We couldn't possibly have let you know who she really was. It was crucial that her identity be kept a secret. As it turned out you were too clever for us." He shook his head at them, as though their cleverness was beyond him. "However, the important thing to understand now is that this must remain absolutely secret. You are part of a clandestine government operation, and if you were to speak one word of any of this, the government would have to take legal action against you."

Tom and Liz exchanged surprised glances. Tom said, "You mean this is some sort of secret government plot? And we've been part of it?" There was excitement and wonder in his voice. The words rushed out. "Mr. Coulter, I have to apologize for not trusting you, but how were we to know? When we found out she wasn't your mother and that she might really be who she said she was, we were afraid if we were caught holding her we'd be in serious trouble. We had no way of knowing that the government was behind everything. I wish you had told us because that would have made a difference."

"Well, now you can stop worrying." Coulter tried to sound reassuring, but he had an uneasy feeling that the Bunges were hiding something from him.

"That's not it," Liz said. "We were really afraid to have her here. That's why we let her go."

Instantly, Coulter shoved Tom's bulk out of the way and raced up the narrow stairway. When he reached the landing, he found the door into Maida Lange's rooms unlocked and open. Although he knew it was useless, he searched the rooms, flinging open closets and looking behind doors in a frenzied hide-and-go-seek.

Liz and Tom followed him upstairs. "She's not there," Tom said, "I gave her some money and called a cab about an hour ago." When he saw Coulter's face go livid he added, "I hope the Secret Service isn't going to be angry with us?" He imagined agents with machine guns swarming all over their place.

"Where was she going?" Coulter demanded.

"She didn't say." Tom's voice was worried, apologetic.

Coulter tried to think. She could go to the media, the police, the White House. Anywhere she went she would cause trouble, and the worst thing of all was that he would have to admit to Bobby that even in this he had failed miserably.

"I'll look for her, but remember what I told you about not saying a word. After your stupidity in letting her go, I can't answer for what the Secret Service might do to you. I'll try to intercede. I warn you, though, if so much as one word leaks out I'll see you both end up in jail."

The noise and shouting had proven more interesting than

the television, so that as Coulter rushed out he had to push his way through the curious elderly residents gathered at the door.

Minutes after Coulter left, a gray Taurus pulled up to the curb and parked thirty feet or so from the Bunges' house. "Did the agency say what the surveillance was for?" the driver asked.

His partner, her mouth full of food, shook her head. She swallowed a few times and said, "They wouldn't give me any information. Just that it was top secret and to let them know immediately if anyone arrived at the house or left it." She handed the driver a lukewarm can of Coke and a slab of pizza on which the cheese and tomato sauce had congealed into a glutinous alloy.

"The pizza's cold," the driver whined. "Oh, well. It goes with the job."

* * *

Ted Coulter felt tears running down his cheeks, blurring the median of the highway into a wriggling snake. He guessed Maida Lange would return to her own home. She was stoical, not a woman to make a scene. He knew that if she did anything, she would do it in her own time. Maida Lange's home in Alexandria was on his way to the White House. Stopping there would delay for half an hour having to tell Bobby what had happened. If he was lucky and found her there, he could still carry out his plan. He would hold her prisoner with his gun, tie her up, and then bring in the dog. When it was over he would rush her to the emergency room, explaining she had succumbed to an acute asthma attack. Bobby need never know that she had escaped.

He still had Sheila Covell to consider, but she was having dinner at the White House and it would be at least another hour before she left there. By then he would have taken care of Maida Lange. He could return later to deal with her.

He knew he had to succeed. The President of the United States was counting on him. Coulter could forgive Bobby for the recent displays of anger toward him. He knew Bobby was under tremendous pressure. He was the most important man in the world, and he had chosen him, Ted Coulter, to be his second-in-command.

Coulter tried to cheer himself by remembering that on Bobby's very first evening in the White House, Bobby had invited him and Elly to spend the night in the Lincoln Suite. They had been up until two in the morning crisscrossing Washington making brief appearances at the inaugural balls. The four of them, Paige and Bobby and Elly and Ted, had all climbed up on the great rosewood bed like schoolchildren and talked until nearly dawn. He had never seen Bobby so spontaneous, so giddy with excitement and grand plans.

There had been only one bad moment that night. After Bobby and Paige had gone to their own room, he had picked up the phone and dialed his parents' number. When his mother answered, he said, full of pride, "I'm calling from the White House, Mother."

"I don't care where you're calling from, Ted," his mother's voice was irritated, impatient, "do you have any idea what time it is?"

Ted Coulter told himself that all through history men had made sacrifices for the things in which they believed. They had fought and killed for those beliefs. What did it matter if you killed on the battlefield or somewhere else, if you were doing it for a good cause? It was imperative that Bobby remain the president. Nothing else mattered. He, Ted Coulter, had been unimportant, but now he was indispensable to Bobby and to the country. Everything depended on him. He had to go through with it.

The dog scrambled over the front seat, the steak bone in his mouth. He settled down beside Coulter, resting his nose on Coulter's thigh. Coulter reached down and patted the dog's head. "Good boy, good Max." The dog's soft fur felt comforting under his hand. It really takes so little to make a person happy, he thought. Why, then, did everything seem so difficult?

XXII

Maida asked the taxi driver to drop her off a block from her home. As she made her way along the backs of the houses to her yard, the streetlights flickered on, illuminating the canopy of trees with their heavy trappings of leaves. She was giddy with freedom. The common, usual flowers and hedges in her neighborhood appeared exotic. From time to time she stopped to touch their tender surfaces. When she reached her own yard, the familiarity of it reduced her to tears of mourning for all the lost days she had been without it.

Quietly she slipped between the hedge and into the garden shed, where she ran her hand along the wall until she felt the hook with its key. More than once the back door had blown shut while she was working in the garden, leaving her locked out of the house. The small key secreted in the shed had been her backup.

She couldn't resist a quick look in the greenhouse. Even in the dim light she could tell the rows of seedlings were healthy. Someone was caring for them, but they should have been planted in the garden by now. She stood there in the growing darkness trying to imagine what those seedlings might become one day, but in her heart she knew she might not be there to see them bloom.

As she made her way quietly toward the house, she was startled to find all the straw had been raked away from the rose beds. For a moment she thought she might have done it herself before she had been snatched away, but no, it would have been too early. For a moment she found herself disoriented. She began to think she might be losing her mind, perhaps imagining all of the bizarre things that had happened to her.

She noticed a light on in the library and another one in the living room. The upstairs was dark. She looked through the windows at the lighted rooms. It was her home and still she felt like a voyeur. With wonder she saw everything was just as she had left it.

She had little time to waste. Soon they would discover her escape and come after her. She knew it was naïve to think that all she had to do was go to the authorities. Her son *was* the authority. The newspaper picture of the woman wearing her clothes, and the signs that someone had been living in her house so robbed her of her own identity that she was afraid to go to the police, afraid they would not believe her. Robert could claim *she* was the imposter, that the woman who was taking her place was his *real* mother. After weeks of being locked up, looking into the windows of her home, Maida felt so much the outsider that she did not think she could convince anyone.

She hesitated to ask for help for another reason. She trembled at the thought of facing her son. In spite of all that she had suffered, she could not let herself believe he would do this to her. During her weeks of imprisonment her last hope had been to seek out the vice president, to appeal to him. But when she saw the photo in *The Post* of the only man she trusted escorting her double, that hope, too, disappeared.

However dangerous it might be, Maida decided to risk a face-to-face confrontation with her imposter. As long as this usurper went about as the president's mother, she, Maida Lange, no longer existed and might as well be dead. Before she could pass judgment on her son, she had to know what they had told her double. No matter how terrible the lies she learned, she no longer had the strength or the will to destroy her son. She would continue to pray for Robert. "No, Johann," she corrected herself. Prayer was all that was left to her.

For a moment she clung to a wisp of hope that her son might yet change. But first he must admit his guilt, his deceit.

Maida shook her head. What were the chances of *that* ever happening? Everyone these days seemed eager to rid themselves of guilt—without admitting to any wrongdoing. There was no remorse, no contrition. Instead, everyone was a god, equally right in their wrongdoing. It was frightening to think of living in a world where redemption was considered obsolete and true repentance old-fashioned.

She slowly turned the key and cautiously opened the back door, waiting a moment to listen for any sound. Silently she inched her way along the familiar hallway, feeling like an intruder in her own home. She searched one room after another, the kitchen, living room, library. No one was there. Most surprisingly, nothing had been changed. Surely it was a good sign that whoever this woman was, she could live intimately, congenially all these weeks amongst Maida's things.

She mounted the stairway, pausing between steps to listen for the least sound. The bedroom she had once shared with Peter was empty; so was Robert's room. The guest room where Maida had slept since Peter's death was the one the imposter had chosen to make her own. It was here that Maida found herself displaced. The woman's clothes were scattered haphazardly over the chairs and bed. An untidy pile of magazines and papers was on the bedside stand. Unfamiliar bottles and jars were jumbled together on the dressing table. The whole room was suffused with the heavy scent of an unfamiliar perfume.

Hastily Maida turned away. She would not meet this woman in a room where the woman was so much in place. Quickly she shut the door and hurried downstairs. She went to the kitchen and boldly put on the kettle. When she opened the cupboard, she discovered that her supply of Formosa oolong had mysteriously been restocked. She took her cup of tea into the living room and sat down in a dark corner of the room to wait, not so much a presence as a shadow. She comforted herself with the thought that whatever happened to her would happen in the familiar confines of her own home. The dark silence reminded her of her childhood visits to the great silent cathedral of Lübeck. In the days immediately after World War II the Marienkirche was still in ruins, yet God never deserted the church and over time it had been rebuilt. Now, even with her life in ruins, Maida knew God had not deserted her. She felt His presence in the silence but she was terrified of what He might ask of her.

* * *

After Sheila was settled in the limousine, she thought over the evening, trying to remember if there was anything she might have said or done to make Paige or Robert Lange suspicious. Perhaps her early departure was a bad idea, but then Paige was bored with the prospect of having to entertain her alone and had clearly wanted her to leave. Besides, she didn't trust Paige, who seemed to take pleasure in embarrassing her. Sitting across a table from Paige with the White House staff serving them a formal dinner would have been torture and certainly would have provided further opportunities for her to commit some faux pas and, perhaps, even give her new and frightening knowledge away. There seemed to be little that Paige missed.

She tried to recall the exact words the president had said to whomever had phoned him so that she could tell Toivo. The president had looked upset after his phone call. Sheila knew it had been a mistake to call Toivo by his first name, but the president had seen their photo in *The Post*, and their familiarity must not have come as much of a surprise to him. She prayed that Toivo would call this evening to tell her that Maida Lange was all right. After that, all Sheila wanted was to get as far away as possible—and yet she longed to be close to Toivo, a combination that was impossible. After her confession of her involvement, Toivo must despise her.

The Secret Service agent who drove her was subdued, perhaps sensing in his passenger's early return that some awkwardness or even unpleasantness had taken place. When they reached her home his voice was routine as he asked, "Would you like me to go in with you and check your house, Mrs. Lange?"

"No, thank you. I'll be fine." Hearing herself called "Mrs. Lange" added to her mounting anxiety. She dreaded entering Maida Lange's house, where she now so clearly did not belong. For a brief moment she thought of asking the man to stay with her for a while.

The agent walked up the path with her. "If you'll let me have your key I'll open the door for you, Mrs. Lange."

Sheila handed over the key. She noticed the agent stealing a glance at her face. She was sure the porch light would reveal how frightened she was.

After opening the door for her the agent paused for a moment. "I'd be happy just to have a quick look around. I don't want to alarm you, but you can't be too careful these days."

Every moment counted. She had to call Toivo at once. As firmly as she could she said, "Thank you, but I'll be just fine." She watched him return to his car, then she walked into the house alone.

Toivo had given her a number where she could reach him anytime. By now he might be able to reassure her that Maida Lange had been safely rescued. She walked into the living room on the way to the library phone and saw the apparition of Maida, sitting in the darkened corner, her mute spectre more a phantom than a human presence. Silently Maida rose from her chair.

Sheila's hand flew to her mouth to stifle a scream, thinking it was the ghost of Maida come to seek retribution. Then, seeing that it was really Maida, she burst into tears of sheer relief. "You're safe. Thank God, you're safe."

For a moment the two women stared, shocked and confused at confronting their mirror image. Maida was the first to recover. She smiled coldly. "I would not have thought you cared much about my safety."

"You have every reason to believe that, but I do care. Please believe me. They told me lies about you."

"Lies? What lies?"

"I… I thought I was doing something vital to save the president—and the country."

Maida nodded. "I can almost believe that. It sounds like Robert. His sense of importance was always exaggerated."

Desperate to explain herself, to excuse herself, to apologize, Sheila groped for words of contrition. "Until tonight, when I went to the White House, I had never met your son. Ted Coulter was the one who made all the arrangements. I was an actress on television. When he saw how much we looked alike, he had me fired. So when he offered me a job I was eager to take it. He told me you were insane and that you were spreading wild lies about your son that would do terrible damage to him if the media got hold of them. He said you were going to be placed in a private hospital and that by taking your place I could help prevent a national emergency that might have dangerous repercussions around the world. Now I see what a fool I was to believe him. I suppose the drama of it all appealed to me."

Maida shuddered. "Ted Coulter was always a nasty boy, always anxious for any crumb of approval Robert tossed his way. Even in law school I regretted he was Robert's friend."

"None of that matters now," Sheila said. "I found the letter from Germany and I gave it to the vice president. I expect to hear from him anytime. He was going to go to the FBI. It's what you would have wanted, isn't it?" asked Sheila.

Maida hesitated. "I only wish there were some other way. There isn't. I was going to do it myself if Robert didn't promise to veto his Death Bill." She struggled to get her breath. "I'm glad it was you and not me. I'm… not so sure I would have been strong enough…."

Sheila watched as Maida gasped for each breath. "Is something wrong?"

"It's my asthma." She groped in her purse for her inhaler.

"Robert is really your older son, Johann?" Sheila asked.

"It was my husband's grandiose idea. Ever since we left Germany, Peter wanted his son to become president one day. It was an obsession. When my second son, the real Robert, died, my husband refused to give up his lifelong dream. So he switched their identities and raised Johann as Robert. I can't blame my son, even for what he has done to me. But I cannot allow him to use his power to inflict harm on countless others. If, as you say, the vice president has alerted the authorities, there is nothing more to be done."

Sheila warned Maida, "Toivo fears you are in great danger because of what you know. Certainly what Ted Coulter did to you makes him culpable. He would have every reason to wish you dead. The first thing I have to do is to call Toivo and get someone here to protect you." As Sheila started for the library, she heard a noise at the rear of the house. "That could be Toivo." She hurried toward the door, anxious to open it to Ranta's reassuring presence. Now that Maida Lange was safe, perhaps he would forgive her for her part in impersonating Maida. Suddenly she stopped, too frightened to move. Why was he coming to the back of the house, and where were the Secret Service agents who always accompanied him?

Maida caught up with Sheila. "By now my son might have learned I've managed to get away." As they stood beside each other waiting uncertainly, Ted Coulter opened the door.

He was obviously startled to see Sheila. "What are you doing here? I thought you were at the White House." Coulter had a gun in his hand. He was holding it in an awkward manner, as though he were not only unused to a weapon but actually afraid of it.

Sheila was terrified, her body immovable stone. In her years on television guns had been pointed at her more times than she could count, but that had been make-believe. This was real.

"Go into the library," Coulter ordered, waving the gun at them. Nervousness made his voice hoarse. In the library he motioned for them to sit down while he stood behind the desk, his face gray, a tic pulsing in his cheek, his hand trembling as he held the Beretta. He regarded them like a schoolmaster with two recalcitrant pupils.

Maida showed no panic, only a kind of stoicism. She glanced apologetically at Sheila. "I was not very clever," she said. "I left the door unlocked when I came in." Only the heaving of her chest as she tried to catch her breath gave away her fright. "Ted, there is no reason to keep this woman here. If she is found in this house there will be questions. You don't need her anymore. Let her go." Maida used her inhaler but it did no good.

"No," Sheila said. "I won't leave." She knew that as long as there was a witness in the house Coulter would hesitate to hurt Maida. Yet another, wiser part of her knew that she, too, was in danger. Still, she would not leave Maida to face Coulter alone. If she hadn't allowed herself to be seduced by the promise of money and adventure, Maida's life would not be threatened now. Suddenly a picture of Ava came into her mind. It seemed important to remember someone who loved her.

Coulter looked reprovingly at Maida. "Why couldn't you have left Bobby alone? You know nothing about all of the pressures he is under, all of his problems. You were willing to destroy him—and he is your son."

Maida stared back, her eyes cold. "I don't want to destroy him." She tried to expel her breath. "I want to save him. All his life he has been forced to live a lie. I only want to make him recognize the truth!" Maida appeared spent, her breathing labored.

Ted stared at her as though he were trying to think his way out of the maze in which he was trapped. "You are coming with me." Outside he could hear Max barking to be let out of the car. To Sheila he said, "If you had just done what we told you, none of this would have happened. You know too much. I can't let you go now." He leveled his gun at Sheila, then hesitated.

Maida saw the indecision. With her last breath she pleaded in a hoarse whisper, "My life is over, Ted. I'm ready to die. I have many questions to ask of God but I won't have the death of this woman on Robert's conscience. Or on yours." She made one more desperate effort to get out her words. "You are a fool to throw your life away for Robert. He doesn't deserve your loyalty. You have never understood him. Only a part of him loves power. A part of him hates the world for stealing his childhood. The one time he tried to escape, you interfered. He never forgave you for bringing him back after his father's death. I believe he hates you more than his father."

"You're lying. Bobby depends on me." The stricken expression on Coulter's face suggested that Maida's words only confirmed what he had already known. He lay the gun on the desk but kept his hand on it, as though if left unattended it might escape. An interminable minute passed. Suddenly Coulter snatched up the gun and ran from the room.

Maida was choking. Her hands clawed at her throat. She reached for the phone but she was unable to get a word out.

Terrified Sheila asked, "What is it?"

Maida whispered, "Robert. Warn Robert."

Sheila watched horrified as Maida struggled helplessly to expel the air from her lungs. Frantically Sheila dialed 911 and waited with her arms around Maida. All those days when she had tried to take Maida's place, she had never come close to the woman. Now Sheila felt the two of them were inseparable. She quickly gave the address to a woman whose calm voice infuriated her. "Send an ambulance, immediately."

She heard pounding on the front door. It couldn't be the ambulance so soon. She ran to the window, terrified Coulter might have returned. She saw the Secret Service standing by a limousine. Desperate for help she ran to the door and flung it open to admit Ranta and another man.

She wasted no words but led them into the library. A moment later the lights of an ambulance flashed yellow and red through the windows of the house and two paramedics rushed through the open door. Ranta hastily hustled Sheila out of the library. "They mustn't see you. Hurry." He led her into the kitchen.

"I found her here when I got home," Sheila told him. "Then Coulter came. He had a gun. Maida started to gasp for breath and then she just collapsed. It's my fault. I got all of us into this."

Ranta held her. "That kind of talk is useless. Where is Coulter?"

"I don't know," Sheila said, her whole body trembling.

Godden came into the room. For a moment he hesitated, startled at seeing Sheila's resemblance to the president's mother. "They're saying it looks like cardiac arrest. Did she have a history of heart trouble?"

"She had severe asthma," Sheila told him. Tears were running down her face.

"I suppose that could have precipitated the attack."

"Godden, Sheila says Coulter was here. We need to contact the White House."

Godden hesitated. "I thought you wanted to keep this quiet, sir."

"Coulter had a gun."

Godden instantly reached for his cellular phone. "I'll have them get out the license number of Coulter's car and alert the Secret Service at the White House. I'd better get over there myself. They're rushing Mrs. Lange to the hospital. Miss Covell, I don't know at this point what the charge will be against you—or if there will be any—but we'll want you available for questioning." The next minute Godden was hurrying from the house, still speaking into his cellular phone.

"I'll get my things," Sheila told Ranta. She couldn't look at him. "I have to leave this house. I should never have come here, never usurped her place. I can't stay here another minute."

"Where will you go?" Ranta asked.

"Back to my apartment."

"You can't go back to your apartment. We're going to try to keep things quiet but if the story should hit the news, every reporter in Washington will be camped out on your doorstep." He hesitated, studying her face. "I have friends with a little place in Prince William County. It's not too far from here. They're in France for a month, and they gave me their key so I could get away from the city if I wanted to. It may be a while before I can see you again. These next few weeks are going to be rather busy times for me." He saw the questions in her eyes. "Whether we come to some kind of accommodation with the president or whether the story gets out and he is impeached, the result will be the same. God knows I never asked for it— I'm going to be the next president."

Sheila stared at him. The full implication of what he was saying suddenly dawned on her. If she had thought before that he was lost to her, now there could be no doubt. As President of the United States, T. Russell Ranta would certainly have nothing in common with Sheila Covell.

"If we can reach Coulter in time, this story will never get out. As far as we know, only a few people are aware of what has happened. Robert Lange and Coulter would go to any length to keep it quiet. I trust you to say nothing. I don't know much about the place where Mrs. Lange was held, but Godden will take care of the investigation and do what I tell him. He understands that if this gets out it would devastate the country: one more example of the corruption of our leaders."

In the emotion of the moment, all Sheila heard was that Toivo trusted her. Nothing seemed more important than that. "Could I go to the hospital and stay with Maida Lange until she's out of danger?"

"That won't be possible. The resemblance would immediately be noticed. Too many questions would be asked. It would place you in a difficult position. As to Maida exposing what her son has done, if in exchange for keeping everything quiet I can get him to scrap the Compassionate Care Bill, I know she won't give him away. Hard as it is to understand, I believe the woman still loves him."

XXIII

As he sped along the expressway from Alexandria to the capital, Ted Coulter frantically tried to think of what to do next. The day's events had turned into malevolently nimble imps that kept eluding him. The control he had felt earlier was gone. Sheila Covell and the president's mother were still alive, still a threat. He had accomplished nothing. "Bobby will be impeached," he told himself, "and it will be all my fault."

He could not stop thinking of Maida Lange's words, "He told me he kept you next to him not because he liked or needed you but... to punish you." Why should he care what was about to happen to Robert Lange? Because of Lange, Coulter was a kidnapper and nearly a murderer. He ought to despise Bobby for what Bobby had done to him. Though he could bear his own punishment, he could not bear to see Bobby stripped of his power and dignity before the whole world. And he refused to believe that Maida Lange was right about the way Bobby felt toward him.

The dog sat beside him on the front seat, alert, twisting his head to follow the cars that passed them on the expressway. From time to time Coulter reached over to pat the dog's head and was rewarded by the dog licking his hand. He knew he should release the dog, but he needed the friendly presence.

Desperately, he began to weave a daydream in which he would prevail on Robert Lange to escape with him. All Bobby would have to do would be to order up a helicopter and Air Force One. People did not ask questions of the president; they followed orders. Coulter tried to think of a country to which they could escape. Someplace where they would not be extradited. Their families could follow them later. This mad fantasy of their two families spending their days together, perhaps some place where the climate was attractive, became a pleasant idyll that occupied him from Virginia to the White House.

As he had done hundreds of times before, Coulter drove automatically past the sentry boxes and along the White House driveway, greeting the guards who were there to protect the life of the president. Preoccupied as he was, the irony of their smiles and waves of welcome were lost on him. The guards, seeing that it was Ted Coulter, merely called in to the next post to announce him with no concern other than, Coulter suspected, a mild curiosity as to what new crisis brought out the president's advisor so late in the evening. A minor revolt in the Congress? An international problem? If it were something serious, he knew they would be expecting someone from National Security and the armed services as well. Seeing him alone, they would dismiss his presence, knowing there was always something: that's what a president got paid for.

Two Secret Service agents were on duty immediately inside of the entrance. The agent manning the metal detector was a new recruit. He greeted Coulter uncertainly, motioning him toward the aperture of the detector. Coulter felt the weight of the gun in his coat pocket. He thought of handing the gun to the agent and apologizing for forgetting it. He could easily make up some story about recent threats on his life. But he knew even the greenest agent had been thoroughly trained not to let *anyone* near the president with a gun.

The second agent waved Coulter into the White House. "Sorry, sir. This guy didn't recognize you. Thinks he's going to turn up an assassin."

The new agent, his face burning, apologized profusely.

"No problem," said Coulter as he hurried inside.

Instead of waiting for the elevator, Ted Coulter climbed the two flights to the presidential living quarters and knocked on the door of Robert Lange's private study. Coulter's daydream of a blissful exile with Robert Lange disappeared instantly when the door opened and he saw the fury on the president's face.

"Where have you been, Coulter?" snapped Robert Lange. "I've been trying to get you for the last hour. Someone called the hospital and asked for my brother's medical files. Whoever it was must suspect something. Otherwise they wouldn't be fishing for information. You and Mother are the only ones who know. So how did someone else find out?"

Beneath Robert's anger, Coulter was touched to hear a plaintive note, if not a direct cry for help. Despite his misgivings, Coulter decided Maida was wrong about Bobby's feelings toward him. Even in this crisis, wasn't Bobby turning to him for help?

"The Bunges let your mother get away," Coulter said, emphasizing "the Bunges" so that no reproach should fall on him.

"Where is she?" demanded Lange.

"She headed straight for her house and that's where I found her. Bobby, we've got to leave Washington right now." Coulter rushed to get the words out. "We could board a helicopter and then a plane and go anywhere in the world. Paige and Elly and the children could come along later...."

As soon as he had spoken, Ted Coulter knew how foolish the idea was: the hiding places of the world had disappeared long ago. He found it an infinitely sad thought.

Lange stared at him in astonishment. "You must be insane! If I went away it certainly wouldn't be with you. I was crazy to confide in you. You're an incompetent fool. You've made a mess of things from the beginning. From the first time I met you, you were always underfoot. Like a fool I felt sorry for you. I must have been out of my head to let a parasite like you tag along all the way to the White House.

"Don't think for a minute I'm going to admit to having anything to do with kidnapping my own mother. I never said a word to the Bunges. That was all your idea, Ted. You were the one who thought this whole plan up. You made all the arrangements, and it was you who carried them out. I'll say I didn't know anything about the switch in birth certificates, that my mother told *you* about it and *you* took everything into your own hands....

"Everyone knows how you follow me around, feeding off of my power, growing fatter and fatter like some parasite burrowing its way into me. Only parasites are smarter than you. They don't destroy their host. You're a laughingstock around here, Ted. Do you know what they call you? Bootlicker."

Coulter's lower lip trembled. He clenched his fists to keep his hands from shaking. The weight of the gun pulled at his pocket. Bobby would not be going away with him. He would have willingly taken the blame for Robert if only Robert had asked him to. Instead, he must live the rest of his life knowing Bobby despised him. Coulter could not see how that would be possible.

The phone rang. Robert snatched it up and listened for a moment. He snapped, "I'll get back to you." He slammed down the receiver. "It's Sam Derker from our press office. Mother's been taken to the Alexandria hospital. It's a heart attack, brought on by her asthma. She may not live. He wants my reaction to Mother's illness."

Coulter watched as Robert Lange began to lose control. His chin trembled. His hands shook. He clenched his teeth, trying to will his face into its usual mask. Tears formed in his eyes. "You may not believe this, Coulter, but I love my mother. But when she looked at me, I always knew she was thinking, 'He is not Robert, he is Johann.' If she dies, the only person who knows who I really am will be gone. Nothing of my real identity will be left except this body I'm tired of hiding in."

The wail of sirens filled the room. It was not unusual to hear them in the capital streets but these seemed very close. A moment later they heard sounds of people racing up the stairway. Coulter pulled out his Beretta. Robert made no move to get away.

"I've been dead for years, Ted. You'll do me a favor." With a grimace that was meant as a smile, he said, "And I won't have to be here for the media circus."

The sound of the pistol firing was a deliverance. All the deceit dropped away. He was Johann again, just as his mother had always wished. As the pain and shadows closed in, the child of two, who had wanted nothing more of his brother's than his teddy bear, was running from his father to his mother for comfort. Johann's last thought was of the river in the forest where for the first time in his life he had felt peace. The blue heron was drifting down upon him its great wings, shutting off the light and shielding him.

"Cold steel," Ted Coulter thought as he stared intensely at the barrel of the pistol, "another lie." The barrel of the gun was still warm. If he had to account for what he had done, it would not be to Elly or the press. In that lingering second he made his choice. Hastily he pulled the trigger, determined not to leave Robert Lange alone, even in death.

XXIV

NATION MOURNS LEADER

FAMILY CONFIRMS LONGTIME MENTAL INSTABILITY OF CHIEF OF STAFF

By Ben Stokley and Jean Wright, Staff Writers

A shocked nation prepared to bury its fallen leader, Robert Lange. President Lange was killed last night by a single bullet, allegedly fired by his closest friend and most trusted advisor, Theodore Coulter, Jr. Coulter was said to have shot the president before turning the gun on himself. Both men were pronounced dead at 10:00 P.M. at the Georgetown Hospital.

Lange is the fifth president of the United States to be assassinated in office. A spokesman for Paige Lange, Robert Lange's widow, has announced that President Lange will lie in state in the Capitol Rotunda tomorrow from noon until five P.M. Leaders from around the world are expected to fly into Washington for Friday's funeral, which is to be held in the National Cathedral.

Close friends report that Mrs. Coulter had alluded to her husband's increasing signs of mental derangement numerous times over the past several months. Sources say Mrs. Coulter had repeatedly urged her husband to resign, but he had refused, citing his responsibility to his president. Coulter's widow, Eleanor Coulter, has been sequestered with her family.

Funeral plans for Coulter are incomplete.

Unofficial sources indicate that Secret Service agents stationed at the White House were only seconds too late to avert the tragedy. The secretary of treasury has reported that a thorough investigation is underway to determine whether or not all persons entering the White House should pass through a metal detector.

President T. Russell Ranta has announced that for the time being he has no plans to move into the White House. "I'm not thinking of that," he stated in a hastily called press conference. "My only responsibility now is to honor our gallant leader who has fallen in the line of duty." Barely able to conceal his emotion he recited the speech from Richard II: "All murdered: for within the hollow crown that rounds the mortal temples of a king keeps death his court."

Robert Lange's mother, Maida Lange, has not yet been informed of her son's death due to her medical condition. Mrs. Lange was rushed to the Alexandria Hospital last night after suffering a heart attack brought on by an acute asthmatic attack. Hospital sources state that she has been taken off the critical list and is expected to make a full recovery.

In a poignant reminder of Robert Lange's excellence, the chimes at the University of Virginia rang out upon the announcement of his death, revealing for the first time that Robert Lange had been a member of the Secret Seven Society. Each year seven seniors, unknown to the rest of the university, are selected for their outstanding leadership. Membership in the society is not revealed until the member's death, when the traditional chimes are rung in that person's honor.

In a related story, the FBI questioned and released a Virginia family who are said to be the owners of the dog found in Ted Coulter's car the night of the assassination. No explanation was given of the dog's presence so far from its home. Senator Jensen said Ted Coulter was the kind of man who would stop, even in the midst of his own turmoil, to pick up a lost dog.

The senator would not comment on the rumor that the new president will veto the Compassionate Care Bill. When pressed he said, "None of us are thinking about politics at a time like this. But we do have a new leader now and, in this most difficult of times, it is crucial that we give him our full support."

* * *

Randall Godden was admitted into the office of President T. Russell Ranta only after a thorough vetting by the Secret Service agents. Godden gritted his teeth, knowing the exhaustive check had less to do with security than the pleasure the Secret Service took in goading a member of the FBI. It would be a long time before the FBI were forgiven for being the ones to alert the Secret Service to an assassination attempt, an attempt they were too late to foil. Godden was amused by the change a week had wrought in Ranta. Instead of the chalk-striped suit and florid tie that was his hallmark, the new president was wearing a conservative dark blue suit and a rep tie.

He was more businesslike. The man who had once found time to swap stories seemed clearly anxious for Godden to come to the point. "I got here as soon as I could, Mr. President. I see you haven't moved into the Oval Office."

"Believe me, I'm in no hurry for that. In here I can pretend I'm still the vice president and no one is paying any attention to me. I've always been my own man, but I know when I walk into the Oval Office my freedom will disappear. I can almost hear the sound of the coffin lid being nailed down." He gave Godden a wry grin. "I suppose in the light of what happened that's an unfortunate simile. You've talked with Elly Coulter?

That woman and her children are the only innocent ones in this whole mess. I want to do all that I can for them."

"She was more than glad to go along with the mental derangement story," Godden assured him. "Oddly enough, the pretense that the man was crazy gives her something rational to tell people, especially her children."

Ranta shook his head. "She's a strong woman, obviously stronger than Ted Coulter ever was. I suppose, though, when all is said and done there is a certain irony to all this. It's a terrible thing to say, but when Coulter killed Robert Lange he saved the country not just from going through the mess of an impeachment but from the scandalous possibility of seeing the man who had been its president in jail for conspiracy to kidnap his own mother. The repercussions of that are unthinkable."

"What about the Secret Service?" Godden asked.

"They're still burning over not having been able to protect Lange, but they're willing to go along with what they think is the truth: that Coulter was seriously disturbed. Of course the attorney general's office is conducting an internal investigation, but they have no clue about the letter from Germany or the hospital files."

Ranta sighed, "Still, there's always someone who gets curious—some reporter with too many questions and too much time and the itch to be the next Bob Woodward. For now no one has made the connection. If it does happen we'll have a story prepared for them. Right now there's enough sensationalism in this fiasco to keep the media hopping; they're not looking for anything else. I only wish it were possible to do what they did to Roosevelt's medical records. Right after his death his chart vanished from the safe at the U.S. Naval Hospital in Bethesda. By the way, what did you do with the letter from Germany?"

"I tore it up," Godden lied. Instead, he had sat at his desk looking at the letter, trying to get up enough nerve to destroy it as Ranta had ordered him to. He told himself that was the safest course, but in the end he couldn't do it. He had in his hand a bit of history, a fateful piece of evidence, the primary clue. The investigator in him couldn't resist. He had slipped the letter into his pocket.

Godden was a fatalist. When the country needed the truth, somehow they would find it. Perhaps he would be the one to divulge it when the time came. He thought of the book he might write, not an exposé but something historical, a book where the talk-show host invited in academic heavyweights to be on a panel with you. Thinking about the possibility, Godden missed the first part of what Ranta was saying.

"... so I went to see Lange's mother yesterday. They're keeping her in the hospital for a few more days. That way she'll be out of the public eye and away from the media. She's still a little shaky but she'll be all right."

"She's going along with our version?" Godden asked.

"Absolutely, but she blames herself for his death. She's anxious to salvage as much of her son's reputation as she can. I assured her I'm going to veto the Compassionate Care Bill. That's cold comfort for all that she has had to suffer. What she wants now is to get back to her home and out of the limelight."

Godden smiled slyly and asked, "I don't suppose you ever thought you would be president—Robert Lange being so young and everything?"

Ranta looked closely at the man. "No, I never dreamed of being president," he said firmly and gave Godden a beguiling smile. "It was the farthest thing from my mind."

* * *

After Godden left, President Ranta considered Godden's question. It sounded suspiciously like the kind of question you heard from interviewers. He wondered why Godden was asking him that now. What did he have in mind? An article? A book? Ranta told himself he was becoming paranoid, a state of mind that went with the president's job. A president is shut away from ninety-nine percent of humanity; the only people he sees have their own agenda. Godden had deserved a polite answer to his question, but not necessarily an entirely truthful one. Ranta would save that for his own memoirs.

The truth was that up on the Minnesota Iron Range when his ninth grade civics teacher had told Ranta's class that anyone born in the United States could be president, T. Russell Ranta had believed her. One of the first things he had done after Robert Lange's inauguration three years ago was to go out and buy the presidential-looking suit he was now wearing. It had hung unused in his closet all these months, but once a year he'd sent it out to be cleaned. You never knew. He supposed even now the new vice president, Lillian Harris, was in Saks or Nieman Marcus shopping for a tailored navy blue suit.

He picked up his secure phone and put through a call to Prince William County. "Godden explained everything when he brought your things out to you? You're all right?"

"I don't see how I can ever be 'all right' but I'm managing. I keep going over and over what happened, trying to understand how I could have been such a fool."

"You've got to stop that kind of thinking. I wish I could come out and see you, but the Secret Service has doubled security. If I came it would be not only with motorcycles, squads of cars, and sharpshooters, but with a helicopter overhead and an ambulance. It's not possible. When are you going back to New York?"

"I'm going back tomorrow."

"I'll be in the city next month for an address to the United Nations. There will be a diplomatic reception afterward. If you receive an invitation, will you come?"

"Of course I'll come. Toivo, how can I thank you for everything you've done for me?"

"I'll tell you in New York."

XXV

During the hectic months following Robert Lange's death the White House curator, Elwood Brighton, had kept a discreet distance, but after President Ranta's marriage he had written a deferential note to the new Mrs. Ranta, asking if he could be of assistance in any redecoration projects she might have in mind. She had immediately replied that indeed he could and to bring a truck.

Now, trotting along at her side, he was full of gratitude and half in love with her. There had been plenty of gossip when President Ranta had married Sheila Covell. The media had discovered they had met at a diplomatic reception at the United Nations and had been drawn to each other by their interest in the theater. When in a press conference to announce the marriage a reporter had dared to point out how, apart from the color of her hair, his fiancée looked like Maida Lange, whom on one occasion he had taken out, the president had laughed and said, "Well, Mrs. Lange wouldn't have me, so I had to find someone as much like her as possible."

When the press repeated the story to Sheila Covell, the inference that she was "second best" had not bothered her in the least. "Looking like Mrs. Lange was the best thing that ever happened to me," she said.

As they walked along, Brighton remembered the article about her likeness to the president's mother. Brighton didn't see the resemblance. In her pictures Maida Lange appeared rather impassive and dour. This woman beside him was vibrant and full of excitement, taking pleasure in everything. "You have an eye for design," Brighton said. "That must come from your years in the theater."

"Perhaps, but you have to remember this is the first house I've been able to decorate. I feel like I've got my hand in the cookie jar." The two of them were like greedy children eagerly hunting through the White House storerooms for buried treasure, pouncing on things and giggling over their finds.

Brighton confided, "After what she's been through, I wouldn't want to utter one word of criticism about Paige Lange, but I'm afraid there were times when she was carried away by her generosity. It was kind of her to want to show the work of her fellow artists, but the White House is not quite the appropriate venue." Two assistants, who managed to be both obsequious and muscled, trailed behind them taking down the huge avant garde canvasses that adorned the walls. The four observers paused in front of the nude. "I don't suppose you'll miss this one," Brighton ventured while the assistants suppressed their snickers.

Sheila smiled slyly. "I won't, but it's one of President Ranta's favorites. By the way, what is Paige Lange doing these days?"

"I understand she's preparing an exhibit of portraits she did of foreign leaders. However, the State Department is very nervous about it. Most of the subjects detest what she's done to them." Hurriedly he added, "Of course the paintings are unique in their own way."

If there was one thing Brighton had learned over the years it was that you never knew for whom you would be working next. It was best to leave all the doors open.

A few minutes after Brighton left, Ranta strode into the family living room. Shutting the door on his retinue of Secret Service agents he put his arms around Sheila. "All I've got is five minutes, but I haven't seen you since breakfast."

"I told Elwood Brighton that the nude was your favorite."

"He probably believed you, too. I'm on my way over to the Capitol. I'm going to veto the Compassionate Care Bill in all the rococo elegance of the President's Room. That way they'll get the message that I'm not even giving them time to bring it to the Oval Office."

"Is there any chance of an override?"

"Not in a million years. The Bill is finished."

"Maida called to thank us for the iris bulbs we brought back for her from Japan. I tried to get her to have dinner with us here. I even told her if she's uncomfortable about coming to the White House, she could join us at Camp David. She said, no thanks. It's sad but I think she's happier left alone.

"Toivo, I've had a call from Robin Bader, the director who's putting together the benefit at the Kennedy Center for the Robert Lange Memorial Library. He wanted to know if I'd consider doing something."

"What did they have in mind?"

Sheila laughed, "You won't believe this, but they want me to do a scene from Shakespeare."

* * *

For days Maida lay in bed, asking God to end her life. It seemed impossible to live and bear the knowledge that what she had said to Ted Coulter might have led to the shooting of her son.

The day after she had returned from the hospital, she disobeyed the doctor's orders and left her bed. The nurse was busy in the kitchen. Gasping for breath Maida inched her way down the stairway and into the library. She saw her young son sitting at the library desk as he had night after night, walled in from the world by the books his father had forced on him.

She began to pull the books from the shelves, wrenching off their covers and tearing at their pages. She knew it wasn't the books but the way they had been used that enraged her. Still, she took her vengeance out on them. Alarmed at the noise, the nurse rushed into the library to find Maida in a crumpled heap on the floor, surrounded by the wounded books.

Two weeks later Maida ordered all the books destroyed. The nurse, with a strong sense of history and a need for a little extra cash, surreptitiously sold them to a rare book dealer, who in turn sold them at an enormous profit to the newly launched Robert Lange foundation. Funds were already being raised for a library to house the books.

It was nothing anyone said to her, nor the weeks slipping by, that began Maida's mending. The mending had begun the afternoon she caught sight from her window of a patch of ferns in the garden dying from lack of water. When she asked the nurse to turn the sprinkler on, the nurse replied haughtily that she didn't do "yard work."

Maida watched the ferns droop and crisp in the hot winds of the afternoon. While the nurse took her usual after-lunch nap, Maida, in her nightgown, walked barefoot into the garden. She tugged at the heavy hose, panting at the effort of fastening the sprinkler, and turned on the water.

She was not quick enough to move out of the way. The water drenched her. She found the sensation pleasant. It was a sweltering day and she stood there eagerly awaiting the spray of cool water that reached her with each revolution of the sprinkler. For weeks she had tried to recall something of great importance. Now, standing in the water's cleansing spray, she remembered what it was. God was inexhaustible. He would forgive her, and He would forgive Robert as she had forgiven Robert.

The nurse came running out, screaming at her. Maida promptly fired her. It was time to begin to take care of herself; God was not finished with Maida.

On this warm spring afternoon with the sun shining through the kitchen window as warm and light on her shoulders as a gossamer shawl, she leafed through a throwaway magazine that had come in the mail. It was put out by the Northeast Virginia Chamber of Commerce. As she sipped her Formosa oolong tea, she came upon the bed-and-breakfast section.

> Brand-new in Singleton this year is Bunges' B & B. This gracious old home has been transformed into a Victorian mansion with authentic antiques of the period. The many extra touches in the decor are

the doing of the proprietress, Elizabeth Bunge, while the proprietor, Tom Bunge, is responsible for the smooth running of this fine establishment. There are seven rooms as well as a private suite with sitting room and bath. Breakfasts here are a specialty, and the fortunate guests feast upon Elizabeth's homemade muffins and scones. A unique feature is the lovely garden with fountain and flowers where tea may be taken in the afternoons.

Maida wondered where the Bunges' money had come from. From Coulter? From some secret source in the government? What did it matter? She did not hate the Bunges. She only wondered what had become of the elderly residents. She had seen them just once, on the day she walked out of the house to her own freedom, leaving them behind.

Maida wandered out into her garden as though even her own house were a kind of captivity. In her Alexandria garden closed in by its brick walls and shrubbery, she walked expectantly among the imminent, hatching flowers. It was the time of year that Maida loved best; a day or so before her irises bloomed. She had five new hybrids this year. Soon there would be the excitement of seeing what she had accomplished. Whatever master species she created would never say a word to harm anyone, only give pleasure with their silent beauty and perfection.

* * *

When a messenger from the White House brought the Goddens two tickets for the Robert Lange Library benefit to be held at the Kennedy Center, Randall Godden's wife, Emily, had insisted he rent a dinner jacket. Now, enthroned in the third row center and resplendent in a plaid cummerbund with matching tie and handkerchief, Godden consulted the program of "An Evening with the Bard." Sheila Ranta's scene from *Richard III* was sandwiched between the Mel Gibson and Julia Roberts *Anthony and Cleopatra* that they had just seen, and Lynn and Vanessa Redgrave doing *The Merry Wives of Windsor*.

"I can't believe Sheila Ranta would let herself in for something like this," Godden whispered. "With actors like this she'll be destroyed. To tell you the truth, I think that's why the president isn't here tonight. It has nothing to do with a Middle East crisis and everything to do with being embarrassed by his wife up there making a fool of herself."

Emily slipped off her shoes, which she hadn't worn since her sister's wedding eight years before. "How could any actress pass up a chance to play Shakespeare to a full house at the Kennedy Center? Anyhow, the audience will give her the benefit of the doubt."

"I suppose half of this sell-out crowd is here hoping she'll wow them, and the other half that she'll fall on her face. What's the story on *Richard III?*" It was understood in the Godden family that Emily had the time for culture.

"I read the scene this afternoon. This creepy Duke of Gloucester, who eventually becomes Richard III, has just killed his brother so he can ascend to the throne. They're in the middle of the funeral when Gloucester stops his brother's widow and proposes marriage to her."

"Bad timing."

"Actually he's successful."

Godden studied the program. "It doesn't say who's playing Richard III."

"I read in *The Post* that the only way Sheila Lange would agree to do it was if she could not only choose who played opposite her but keep his name a secret. There's a rumor that it's going to be Dustin Hoffman."

Godden had expected that with the president's wife on the program, the Secret Service would be stationed around the theater. He wasn't prepared for the brace of agents who mounted the stairway to the proscenium and then were nearly swept away as the curtain opened. "Overkill," Godden thought. Four bearers walked onto the stage carrying a coffin. Godden spotted holsters bulging under their capes. More agents. Following them, dramatic in a flowing black gown, came Sheila Ranta.

From the wings a swaggering Gloucester appeared, crying out, "Stay, you that bear the corpse, and set it down." The voice was juicy and rotund, full of villainous threat and lecherous intent.

"I don't believe it!" Godden said aloud. "It's Ranta. It's the president!"

The theater rocked with thunderous applause. The Rantas stood immobile, waiting out the bedlam. At last the audience quieted expectantly, like children who have just received the Christmas present of their lives and are waiting to see if more is to come.

* * *

Sheila began her line, "What black magician conjures up this fiend..."

Back and forth the lines snapped, climaxing in Gloucester's "Why dost thou spit at me?" and Anne's hissed response, "Would it were mortal poison for thy sake!" Anne's succumbing to her suitor's evil charm had an arch tinge, while Gloucester's advances were full of passionate inducement. As the scene ended the auditorium exploded with cheers of "Bravo!" The president and his wife returned again and again from the wings, hand in hand, to take their bows, the president bending slightly, his right arm sweeping across his chest, Sheila dipping gracefully in a deep curtsey, her head modestly down. They were fighting their grins, trying to keep in character as the entire audience rose in a standing ovation.

"That was awful, wasn't it?" Godden asked his wife, all the while applauding as loudly as the rest of the theater.

"Yes, but in a sort of marvelous way."

"Well, why shouldn't he be up there on the stage? Politicians are all performers now." Godden smiled to himself, thinking, "The old ham. I suppose if I ever wrote the story of what really happened to Robert Lange, Ranta would insist on playing himself in the movie."

* * *

As he held tightly to Sheila's hand, T. Russell Ranta bowed to the audience. The breeches the costumers had given him were at least a size too small, so his bow was not a deep one. Looking out into the audience he saw congressmen and women and members of the Supreme Court. Even the head of the Joint Chiefs-of-Staff was there. He had met with him earlier in the day and found to his relief that in Russia, Obronsky was backing down. For now...

From the third row Godden and his wife grinned up at him. Ranta supposed he had made a fool of himself, but it wasn't the first time and it wouldn't be the last. It was built into the job. As they bowed once more the vice president recited to himself the last lines of *Richard III*:

> Now civil wounds are stopp'd,
> Peace lives again;
> That she may long live here,
> God say Amen!